It was a top secret government project, its funds coming quietly from the Bureau of Standards, its orders directly from the President. The project's goal was to survey the future.

The survey would be made in person, by use of the newly-developed Time Displacement Vehicle. Three specially trained men would be sent to the year 2000, and they would return with invaluable data about the problems to be faced by the government in decades to come.

It seemed almost routine at first. But when the survey team reached their target they found a savage land . . . an awesome world they *may* have made, and they had to wonder if any would return to tell about it.

ARTHUR WILSON TUCKER has been a highly successful writer of both mystery novels and science fiction for over two decades. *The New York Times* says he is "an author whose name is deservedly acclaimed in science fiction," and Damon Knight, in his critical book IN SEARCH OF WONDER, proclaimed him "one of the most brilliant writers in the business."

His science fiction novels include THE LONG LOUD SILENCE, WILD TALENT and THE LINCOLN HUNTERS, a previous Ace Science Fiction Special. THE YEAR OF THE QUIET SUN is a new novel for the SF Specials series, never before published anywhere.

THE YEAR OF THE QUIET SUN

by WILSON TUCKER

AN ACE BOOK

Ace Publishing Corporation
1120 Avenue of the Americas
New York, N.Y. 10036

THE YEAR OF THE QUIET SUN

DEDICATION:

For the Fifteen and their mates,

who are looser because they grok a lot.

Printed in U.S.A.

Indian Rocks Beach, Florida
7 June 1978

The kind of prophet these people want
is a windbag and a liar,
Prophesying a future of wine and spirits.

— The Book of Micah

ONE

THE LEGGY GIRL was both alpha and omega: the two embodied in the same compact bundle. The operation began when she confronted him on a Florida beach, breaking his euphoria; it ended when he found her sign on a grave marker, hard by a Nabataean cistern. The leap between those two points was enormous.

Brian Chaney was aware of only a third symbol when he discovered her: she was wearing a hip-length summer blouse over delta pants. No more than that—and a faint expression of disapproval—was evident.

Chaney intended to make short work of her.

When he realized the girl was coming at him, coming for him, he felt dismay and wished he'd had time to run for it. When he saw the object she carried—and its bright red dustjacket couldn't be missed—he was tempted to jump from the beach chair and run anyway. She was another tormentor. The furies had been hounding him since he left Tel Aviv—since the book was published—hounding him and crying heresy in voices hoarse with indignation. String up the traitor! they cried. Burn the infidel!

He watched the approach, already resenting her.

He had been idling in the sun, half dozing and half watching a mail Jeep make box deliveries along the beach road when she suddenly appeared in his line of sight. The beach had been deserted except for himself, the Jeep, and the hungry gulls; the inland tourists with their loud transistor radios wouldn't be along for another several weeks. The girl walked purposefully along the shoulder of the road until she was nearly opposite him, then quickly wheeled and stepped across a narrow band of weedy grass onto the sand. She paused only long enough to pull off her shoes, then came across the beach at him.

When she was near, he threw away his earlier supposition: she was a leggy, disapproving woman, not a girl. He guessed her age at twenty-five because she looked twenty; she wasn't very tall nor very solid—no more than a hundred pounds. A troublesome woman.

Chaney deliberately turned in his chair to watch the raging surf, hoping the woman would about-face. She carried the red-jacketed book clutched in hand as though it were a purse, and tried unsuccessfully to hide her disapprobation. She might be a scout from one of those damned TV shows.

He liked the sea. The tide was coming in and there had been a storm on the water the night before; now the whitecaps boomed in to break on the beach only a dozen feet away, hurling spray into his face. He liked that; he liked the feel of stinging spray on his skin. He liked being outdoors under a hot sun, after too many months at desk and bench. Israel had a lovely climate but it did nothing for a man working indoors. If these intruders would only let him alone, if they would allow him another week or two on the beach, he'd be willing to end his holiday and go back to work in the tank—the dusty, fusty tank with its quota of dusty, fusty wizards making jokes about sunburns and back tans.

The leggy woman halted beside him.

"Mr. Brian Chaney."

He said: "No. Now run along."

"Mr. Chaney, my name is Kathryn van Hise. Forgive the intrusion. I am with the Bureau of Standards."

Chaney blinked his surprise at the novelty and turned away from the whitecaps. He stared at her legs, at the form-fitting delta pants, at the tease-transparent blouse wriggling in an off-shore breeze, and looked up finally at her face against the sunshine-hot Florida sky. Her nearness revealed more. She was small in stature—size eight, at a guess—and light of weight, giving the impression of being both quick and alert. Her skin was well tanned, telling her good use of the early summer sun, and it nicely complimented her eyes and hair. The eyes were one attractive shade of brown and the hair was another. Her face bore only a hint of cosmetics. There were no rings on her fingers.

He said skeptically: "*That's* a novel approach."

"I beg your pardon?"

"Usually, you're from the Chicago *Daily News*, or the Denver *Post*, or the Bloomington *Bulletin*. Sometimes you're from a TV talk show. You want a statement, or a denial, or an apology. I like your imagination, but you don't get one."

"I am not a newspaper person, Mr. Chaney. I *am* a research supervisor with the Bureau of Standards, and I am here for a definite purpose. A serious purpose."

"No statement, no denial, and certainly not an apology. What purpose?"

"To offer you a position in a new program."

"I have a job. New programs every day. Sometimes we have new programs running out of our ears."

"The Bureau is quite serious, Mr. Chaney."

"The Bureau of Standards," he mused. "The *government* Bureau of Standards, of course—the one in Washington, cluttered with top-heavy bureaucrats speaking strange dialects. That would be a fate worse than death. I worked for them once and I don't want to again, ever." But the wind-whipped blouse was an eye-puller.

She said: "You completed a study for the Bureau three years ago, before taking leave to write."

"Does the Bureau have a complaint about my book? Short weight? Pages missing? Too much fat in the text? Have I defrauded the consumers? Are they going to sue? Now *that* would cap everything."

"Please be serious, Mr. Chaney."

"No—not today, not tomorrow, not this week and maybe not the next. I've been run through the mill but now I'm on vacation. I earned it. Go away, please."

The woman stubbornly held ground.

After a while, Chaney's attention drifted back from a prolonged study of the racing whitecaps and settled on the bare feet firmly embedded in the sand near his chair. A fragrant perfume was worn somewhere beneath the blouse. He searched for the precise source, for the spot where it had kissed her skin. It was difficult to ignore his visitor when she stood so close. Her legs and the delta pants earned one more inspection. She certainly wore her skin and that tantalizing clothing well.

Chaney squinted up at her face against the sky. The brown eyes were direct, penetrating, attractive.

"Dress like yours is prohibited in Israel—did you know that? Most of the women are in uniform and the high command worries about male morale. Delta lost." Chaney conveyed his regret with a gesture. "Are you serious?"

"Yes, sir."

"The Bureau wants a biblical translator?"

"No, sir. The Bureau wants a demographer, one who is experienced in both lab and field work." She paused. "And certain other prerequisites, of course."

"A demographer!"

"Yes, sir. *You.*"

"But the woods are full of demographers."

"Not quite, Mr. Chaney. You were selected."

"Why? Why me? What other prerequisites?"

"You have a background of stability, of constancy and resolution; you have demonstrated your ability to withstand pressures. You are well adjusted mentally and your physical stamina is beyond question. Other than your biblical research, you have specialized in socio-political studies and have earned a reputation as an extrapolative statistician. You *are* the definition of the term, futurist. You authored that lengthy study for the Bureau. You have a security clearance. You were selected."

Chaney turned with astonishment and stared. "Does the Bureau know I also chase women? Of all colors?"

"Yes, sir. That fact was noted in your dossier, but it wasn't considered a detriment."

"Please thank the good gray Bureau for me. I *do* appreciate the paternal indulgence."

"There is no need to be sarcastic, Mr. Chaney. You have a well-balanced computer profile. Mr. Seabrooke has described you as an ideal futurist."

"I'm *ever* so grateful. Who is Seabrooke?"

"Gilbert Seabrooke is our Director of Operations. He personally selected you from a narrow field of candidates."

"I'm not a candidate; I volunteered for nothing."

"This is a top secret project of some importance, sir. The candidates were not consulted in advance."

"That's why we're all so happy about it." Chaney indicated the book in her hand. "You're *not* interested in my hobby? In that? The Bureau doesn't expect me to deny my translation of the Revelations scroll?"

The faint expression of disapproval again crossed her face but was thrust aside. "No, sir. The Bureau *is* unhappy with your work, with the resultant notoriety, and Mr. Seabrooke wishes you *hadn't* published it—but he believes the public will have forgotten by the time you have surfaced again."

Emphatically: "*I'm* not going undergound."

"Sir?"

"Tell Mr. Seabrooke I'm not interested. I do very well without him and his Bureau. I have a job."

"Yes, sir. With the new project."

"No, sir, with the Indiana Corporation. It's called Indic, for short, and it's a think-tank. I'm a genius—does your computer know that, Miss van Hise? Indic has a hundred or so captive geniuses like me sitting around solving problems for know-nothings. It's a living."

"I am familiar with the Indiana Corporation."

"You should be. We did that job for your people three years ago and scared the hell out of them—and then we submitted a bill which unbalanced their budget. We've done work for State, for Agriculture, for the Pentagon. I *hate* Pentagon work. Those people are in a hell of a rut. I wish they'd climb off the Chinese back and find some other enemy to study and outwit." He dropped back into the beach chair and returned his attention to the surf. "I have a job waiting; I rather like it. I'm going back to it when I get tired of sitting here doing nothing —tired of loafing. Find yourself another demographer."

"No, sir. Indic has assigned you to the Bureau."

Chaney came out of the chair like a rocket. He towered over the diminutive woman.

"They have not!"

"They have, Mr. Chaney."

"They wouldn't do that without my consent."

"I'm sorry, but they have."

Insistently: "They *can't*. I have a contract."

"The Bureau has purchased your contract, sir."

Chaney was dumbfounded. He gaped at the woman.

She removed a folded letter from the pages of the book and handed it to him to read. The letter was couched in stiff corporate language, it was signed, and it bore the great seal of the Indiana Corporation. It transferred the balance of term of employment of Brian Chaney from the private corporation to the public agency, then generously arranged to share with him on an equal basis the financial consideration paid for the transfer. It wished him well. It politely mentioned his book. It was very final.

The waiting woman did not understand the single Aramaic word hurled down the Florida beach.

The waves were crashing around his knees, spraying his chest and face. Brian Chaney turned in the surf and looked back at the woman standing on the beach.

He said: "There are only two buses a day. You'll miss the last one if you don't hurry."

"I have not completed my instructions, Mr. Chaney."

"I'd be pleased to give you certain instructions."

Kathryn van Hise stood her ground without answer. The gulls came swooping back, only to take flight again.

Chaney shouted his frustration. "*Why?*"

"The special project needs your special skills."

"*Why?*"

"To survey and map the future; you are a futurist."

"I'm not a surveyor—I'm not a cartographer."

"Those were figures of speech, sir."

"I don't *have* to honor that contract. I can break it, I can turn black-leg and go to work for the Chinese. What will the Pentagon do *then,* Miss van Hise?"

"Your computer profile indicated that you would honor it, sir. It also indicated your present annoyance. The Pentagon knows nothing of this project."

"Annoyance! I can also give that computer explicit instructions, but they would be as hard to obey as yours. Why don't you go home? Tell them I refused. Rebelled."

"When I have finished, sir."

"Then finish up, damn it, and get along!"

"Yes, sir." She moved closer to him to avoid raising her voice and permitting the gulls to overhear top secret information. "The first phase of the operation began shortly after Indic submitted its report three years ago, and continued all the while you were studying in Israel. As the author of that report, you were considered one of the most likely persons to participate in the next phase, the field implementations. Expertise. The Bureau is now ready to move into the field, and has recruited a select team to conduct field operations. You will be a member of that team, and then participate in the final report. Mr. Seabrooke expects to submit it to the White House; he is counting on your enthusiastic support."

"Bully for Seabrooke; he shanghais me and then expects my enthusiastic support. What implementations?"

"A survey of the future."

"We've already done that. Read the Indic report."

"A physical survey of the future."

Brian Chaney looked at her for a long moment with unconcealed amusement and then turned back to the sea. A red and white sail was beating across the Gulf in the middle distance and the tacking fascinated him.

He said: "I suppose some nutty genius somewhere has really invented a tachyon generator, eh? A generator and deflector and optical train that works? The genius can peer through a little telescope and observe the future?"

The woman spoke quietly. "The engineers at Westinghouse have built a TDV, sir. It is undergoing tests at the present time."

"Never heard of it." Chaney shaded his eyes against the sun the better to watch the bright sail. "*V* is for vehicle, I suppose? Well—that's better than a little telescope. What is the *TD*?"

"Time Displacement. An engineering term." There was a peculiar note of satisfaction in her voice.

Brian Chaney dropped his hand and turned all the way around in the water to stare down at the woman. He felt as if he'd been hit.

"*Time* Displacement Vehicle?"

"Yes, sir." The satisfaction became triumph.

"It can't work!"

"The vehicle is in test operation."

"I don't believe it."

"You may see it for yourself, sir."

"It's *there?* It's sitting there in your lab?"

"Yes, sir."

"Operating?"

"Yes, sir."

"I'll be damned. What are you going to do with it?"

"Implement our new program, Mr. Chaney. The Indic report has become an integral part of the program in that it offered several hard guidelines for a survey of the future. We are now ready to initiate the second phase, the field explorations. Do you see the possibilities, sir?"

"You're going to get *in* that thing, that vehicle, and go somewhere? Go into the future?"

"No, sir. *You* are; the team will."

Chaney was shocked. "Don't be an idiot! The team can do what they damned please, but I'm not going anywhere. I didn't volunteer for your program; I wasn't a willing candidate; I oppose peonage on humanitarian grounds."

He quit the surf and stalked back to the beach chair, not caring if the woman followed him. Gulls shrieked their annoyance at his passage. Chaney dropped into the chair with another muttered imprecation of stiff-necked bureaucrats, a scurrilous declaration couched in Hebraic terms the woman wouldn't understand. It commented on her employer's relations with jackasses and Philistines.

TDV. A furious stimulant to the imagination.

The gulls, the tide, the salt spray, the descending sun were all ignored while his racing imagination toyed with the information she had given him. He saw the possibilities—some of them—and began to appreciate the interest his Indic report had aroused in those people possessing the vehicle. A man could peer forward—no, leap forward into the future and check out his theories, his projections of events to come. A man could see for himself the validity of a forewarning, the eventual result of a prefiguration, the final course of a trend. Would sixteen-year-olds marry and vote? Would city and county governments be abolished, relinquishing authority to local state districts? Would the Eastern seaboard complex break down and fail to support life?

TDV. A vehicle to determine answers.

Chaney said aloud: "I'm not interested. Find another demographer, Miss van Hise. I object to being ambushed and sold across the river."

A man could inspect—personally inspect—the Great Lakes to determine if they had been saved or if the Lake Reconstruction program had come too late. A man could study the census figures for a hundred years to come and then compare them to the present tables and projections to find the honesty of those projections. A man could discover if the recently inaugurated trial-marriage program was a success or failure—and learn first-hand what effect it was having on the birth rate, if any. It would be good to know the validity of earlier predictions concerning the population shifts and the expected concentration of human mass along the central waterways. A man could—

Chaney said aloud: "Give the team my regards, Miss

van Hise. And tell them to watch out for traffic cops. I'll read about their adventures in the newspapers."

Kathryn van Hise had left him.

He saw her tracks in the sand, glanced up and saw her putting on the shoes near the weedy border of the beach. The delta pants stretched with her as she bent over. The mail Jeep was again visible in the distance, now coming toward him and servicing the boxes on the other side of the beach road. The interview had been completed in less than an hour.

Chaney felt the weight of the book in his lap. He hadn't been aware of the woman placing it there.

The legend on the red dustjacket was as familiar as the back of his hand. *From the Qumran Caves: Past, Present, and Future.* The line of type next below omitted the word *by* and read only: *Dr. Brian Chaney.* The bright jacket was an abomination created by the sales department over the inert body of a conservative editor; it was designed to appeal to the lunatic fringe. He detested it. Despite his careful explanations, despite his scholarly translation of a suspect scroll, the book had stirred up twice the storm he'd expected and aroused the ire of righteous citizens everywhere. String up the blasphemer!

A small card protruded from the middle pages.

Chaney opened the volume with curiosity and found a calling card with her name imprinted on one side, and the address of a government laboratory in Illinois written on the other. He supposed that the ten fifty-dollar bills tucked between the pages represented travel money. Or a shameless bribe added to the blouse, the pants, and the perfume worn on her breast.

"I'm not going!" he shouted after the woman. "The

computer lied—I'm a charlatan. The Bureau can go play with its weights!"

She didn't turn around, didn't look back.

"That woman is too damned sure of herself."

Elwood National Research Station
Joliet, Illinois
12 June 1978

A hair perhaps divides the false and true;
Yes, and a single Alif were the clue
(could you but find it) to the treasure-house,
And peradventure to the Master too.
— Omar Khayyam

TWO

Two STEPS AHEAD, the military policeman who had escorted him from the front gate opened a door and said: "This is your briefing room, sir."

Brian Chaney thanked him and went through the door. He found the young woman critically eyeing him, assessing him, expecting him. Two men in the room were playing cards. An oversized steel table—the standard government issue—was positioned in the center of the room under bright lights. Three bulky brown envelopes were stacked on the table near the woman, while the men and their time-killing game occupied the far end of it. Kathryn van Hise had been watching the door as it opened, anticipating him, but only now did the players glance up from their game to look at the newcomer.

He nodded to the men and said: "My name is Chaney. I've been—"

The hurtful sound stopped him, cut off his words.

The sound was something like a massive rubber band snapped against his eardrums, something like a hammer or a mallet smashing into a block of compressed air. It made a noise of impact, followed by a reluctant sigh as if the hammer was rebounding in slow motion through an oily fluid. The sound hurt. The lights dimmed.

The three people in the briefing room were staring at something behind him, above him.

Chaney spun around but found nothing more than a wall clock above the door. They were watching the red sweep hand. He turned back to the trio with a question on his lips, but the woman made a little motion to silence him. She and her male companions continued to watch the clock with a fixed intensity.

The newcomer waited them out.

He saw nothing in the room to cause the sound, nothing to explain their concentrated interest; there was only the usual furniture of a government-appointed briefing room and the four people who now occupied it. The walls were bare of maps, and that was a bit unusual; there were three telephones of different colors on a stand near the door, and that was a bit unusual; but otherwise it was no more than a windowless, guarded briefing room located on an equally well-guarded military reservation forty-five minutes by armored train from Chicago.

He had entered through the customary guarded gate of a restricted installation encompassing about five square miles, had been examined and identified with the customary thoroughness of military personnel, and had been escorted to the room with no explanation and little delay. Massive outer doors on a structure that appeared earthquake-proof stirred his wonder. There were several widely scattered buildings on the tract—but none as substantial as *this* one—which led him to believe it had once been a munitions factory. Now, the presence of a number of people of both sexes moving about the grounds suggested a less hazardous installation. No outward hint or sign indicated the present activity, and Chaney wondered if knowledge of the vehicle was shared with station personnel.

He held his silence, again studying the woman. She was sitting down, and he mentally speculated on the length of the skirt she was wearing today, as compared to the delta pants of the beach.

The younger of the two men suddenly pointed to the clock. "Hold onto your hat, mister!"

Chaney glanced at the clock then back to the speaker. He judged the fellow at about thirty, only a few years younger than himself, but having the same lanky height. He was sandy haired, muscular, and something about the set of his eyes suggested a seafarer; the skin was deeply bronzed, as opposed to the girl's new tan, and now his open mouth revealed a silver filling in a front tooth. Like his companions, he was dressed in casual summer clothing, his sportshirt half unbuttoned down the front. His finger pointed at the clock dropped, as if in signal.

The reluctant sigh of the hammer or the mallet plowing sluggishly through a fluid filled the room, and Chaney wanted to cover his ears. Again the unseen hammer smashed into compressed air, the rubber band struck his eardrums, and there was a final, anticlimactic pop.

"There you are," the younger man said. "The same old sixty-one." He glanced at Chaney and added what appeared to be an explanation. "Sixty-one seconds, mister."

"Is that good?"

"That's the best we'll ever have."

"Bully. What's going on?"

"Testing. Testing, testing, testing, over and over again. Even the monkeys are getting tired of it." He shot a quick glance at Kathryn van Hise, as if to ask: *Does he know?*

The other card player studied Chaney with some reserve, wanting to fit him into some convenient slot. He was an older man. "Your name is Chaney," he repeated dourly. "And you've been—what?"

"Drafted," Chaney replied, and saw the man wince.

The young woman said quickly: "Mr. Chaney?"

He turned and found her standing. "Miss van Hise."

"We expected you earlier, Mr. Chaney."

"You expected too much. I had to wait for a few days for sleeper reservations, and I laid over in Chicago to visit old friends. I wasn't eager to leave the beach, Miss van Hise."

"Sleeper?" the older man demanded. "The *railroad?* Why didn't you fly in?"

Chaney felt embarrassed. "I'm afraid of planes."

The sandy-haired man exploded in howling laughter and pointed an explanatory finger at his dour companion. "Air Force," he said to Chaney. "Born in the air and flies by the seat of his pants." He slapped the table and the cards jumped, but no one shared his high humor. "You're off to a fine start, mister!"

"Must I hold a candle to my shame?" Chaney asked.

The woman said again: "Mr. Chaney, please."

He gave her his attention, and she introduced him to the card players.

Major William Theodore Moresby was the disapproving Air Force career man, now in his middle forties, whose receding hairline accented his rather large and penetrating gray-green eyes. The ridge of his nose was sharp, bony, and had once been broken. There was the suspicion of a double chin, and another suspicion of a building paunch beneath the summer shirt he wore outside his trousers. Major Moresby had no humor, and he shook hands with the tardy newcomer with the air of a man shaking hands with a draft dodger newly returned from Canada.

The younger man with the bronzed muscular frame and the prominent dental work was Lieutenant Commander Arthur Saltus. He congratulated Chaney on having the good sense of being reluctant to leave the sea, and said he'd been Navy since he was fifteen years old. Lied about his age, and furnished forged papers to underscore the lie. Even in the windowless room his eyes were set against the bright sunlight on the water. He was likable.

"A civilian?" Major Moresby asked gravely.

"Someone has to stay home and pay the taxes," Chaney responded in the same tone.

The young woman broke in quickly, diplomatically. "Official policy, Major. Our directive was to establish a balanced team." She glanced apologetically at Chaney. "Some people in the Senate were unhappy with the early NASA policy of selecting only military personnel for the orbital missions, and so *we* were directed to recruit a more balanced crew to—to avert a possible future inquiry. The Bureau is mindful of Congressional judgments."

Saltus: "Translation: we've got to keep those funds rolling in."

Moresby: "Damn it! Is politics into this thing?"

"Yes, sir, I'm afraid so. The Senate subcommittee overseeing our project has posted an agent here to maintain liaison. It is to be regretted, sir, but some few of them profess to see a parallel to the old Manhattan project, and so they insisted on continuous liaison."

"You mean surveillance," Moresby groused.

"Oh, cheer up, William." Arthur Saltus had picked up the scattered cards and was noisily shuffling the deck. "This one civilian won't hurt us; we outnumber him two to one, and look at the rank he *hasn't* got. Tail-end of the team, last man in the bucket, and we'll make him do the writing." He turned back to the civilian. "What do you do, Chaney? Astronomer? Cartographer? Something?"

"Something," Chaney answered easily. "Researcher, translator, statistician, a little of this and that."

Kathryn van Hise said: "Mr. Chaney authored the Indic report."

"Ah," Saltus nodded. "*That* Chaney."

"Mr. Chaney authored a book on the Qumran scrolls."

Major Moresby reacted. "*That* Chaney?"

Brian Chaney said: "Mr. Chaney will walk out of here in high pique and blow up the building. He objects to being the bug under the microscope."

Arthur Saltus stared at him with round eyes. "I've heard about you, mister! William has your book. They want to hang you up by your thumbs."

Chaney said amiably: "That happens every now and then. St. Jerome upset the Church with *his* radical translation in the fifth century, and they were intent on stretching more than his thumbs before somebody quieted them down. He produced a new Latin translation of the Old Testament, but his critics didn't exactly cheer him. No matter—his work outlived them. Their names are forgotten."

"Good for him. Was it successful?"

"It was. You may know the Vulgate."

Saltus seemed vaguely familiar with the name, but the Major was reddened and fuming.

"Chaney! You aren't comparing this poppycock of yours to the Vulgate?"

"No, sir," Chaney said softly to placate the man. He now knew the Major's religion, and knew the man had read his book with loose attention. "I'm pointing out that after fifteen centuries the radical is accepted as the norm. My translation of the Revelations only seems radical now. I may have the same luck, but I don't expect to be canonized."

Kathryn van Hise said insistently: "*Gentlemen.*"

Three heads turned to look at her.

"Please sit down, gentlemen. We really should get started on this work."

"Now?" Saltus asked. "Today?"

"We have already lost too much time. Sit down."

When they were seated, the irrepressible Arthur Saltus turned in his chair. "She's a hard taskmaster, mister. A martinet, a despot—but she's trim for all of that. A really shipshape civilian, not an ordinary government girl. We call her Katrina—she's Dutch, you know."

"Agreed," Chaney said. He remembered the transparent blouse and the delta pants, and nodded to her in a manner that might be the beginning of a bow. "I treasure a daily beauty in my life." The young woman colored.

"To the point!" Saltus declared. "I'm beginning to have ideas about you, civilian researcher. I thought I recognized that first one you pulled, that candle thing."

"Bartlett is a good man to know."

"Look, now, about your book, about those scrolls you translated. How did you ever get them declassified?"

"They were never classified."

Saltus showed his disbelief. "Oh, they had to be! The government over there wouldn't want them out."

"Not so. There was no secrecy involved; the documents were there to read. The Israeli government kept ownership of them, of course, and now the scrolls have been sent to another place for safekeeping for the duration of the war, but that's the extent of it." He glanced covertly at the Major. The man was listening in sullen silence. "It would be a tragedy if they were destroyed by the shelling."

"I'll bet you know where they are."

"Yes, but that's the only secret concerning them.

When the war is over they'll be brought out and put on display again."

"Hey—do you think the Arabs will crack Israel?"

"No, not now. Ten, twenty years ago, they may have, but not now. I've seen their munitions plants."

Saltus leaned forward. "*Have* they got the H-bomb?"

"Yes."

Saltus whistled. Moresby muttered: "Armageddon."

"Gentlemen! May I have your attention *now*?"

Kathryn van Hise was sitting straight in her chair, her hands resting on the brown envelopes. Her fingers were interlaced and the thumbs rose to make a pointed steeple.

Saltus laughed. "You always have it, Katrina."

Her responding frown was a quick and fleeting thing. "I am your briefing officer. My task is to prepare you for a mission which has no precedent in history, but one that is very near culmination. It is desirable that the project now go forward with all reasonable speed. I must insist that we begin preparations at once."

Chaney asked: "Are *we* working for NASA?"

"No, sir. You are directly employed by the Bureau of Standards and will not be identified with any other agency or department. The nature of the work will not be made public, of course. The White House insists on that."

He knew a measure of relief when she answered the next question, but it was of short duration. "You're not going to put us into orbit? We won't have to do this work on the moon, or somewhere?"

"No, sir."

"That's a relief. I won't have to fly?"

She said carefully: "I cannot reassure you on that

point, sir. If we fail to attain our primary objective, the secondary targets may involve flying."

"That's bad. There *are* alternatives?"

"Yes, sir. Two alternatives have been planned, if for any reason we cannot accomplish the first objective."

Major Moresby chuckled at his discomfiture.

Chaney asked: "Do we just sit here and wait for something to happen—wait for that vehicle to work?"

"No, sir. I will help you to prepare yourself, on the assurance that something *will* happen. The testing is nearly completed and we expect the conclusion at any time. When it *is* completed, all of you will then acquaint yourselves with vehicle operation; and when *that* is done a field trial will be arranged. Following a successful field trial, the actual survey will get underway. We are most optimistic that each phase of the operation will be concluded in good order and in the shortest possible time." She paused to lend emphasis to her next statement. "The first objective will be a broad political and demographic survey of the near future; we wish to learn the political stability of that future and the well-being of the general populace. We may be able to contribute to both by having advance knowledge of their problems. Toward that end you will study and map the central United States at the turn of the century, at about the year 2000."

Saltus: "Hot damn!"

Chaney felt a recurrence of the initial shock he'd known on the beach; this wasn't to be an academic study.

"We're going up there? That far?"

"I thought I had made that clear, Mr. Chaney."

"Not *that* clear," he said with some embarrassment and confusion. "The wind was blowing on the beach—my mind was on other things." Hasty side glances at Saltus and the Major offered little comfort: one was grinning at him and the other was contemptuous. "I had supposed my role was to be a passive one: laying out the guidelines, preparing the surveys and the like. I had supposed you were using instruments for the actual probe—" But he realized how lame that sounded.

"No, sir. Each of you will go forward to conduct the survey. You *will* employ certain instruments in the field, but the human element is necessary."

Moresby may have thought to needle him. "Seniority will apply, after all. We will move up in the proper order. Myself first, then Art, and then you."

"We expect to launch the survey within three weeks, given the completion of the testing schedule." Her voice may have held a trace of amusement at his expense. "It may be sooner if your training program can be completed sooner. A physical examination is scheduled for later this afternoon, Mr. Chaney; the others have already had theirs. The examinations will continue at the rate of two per week until the survey vehicle is actually launched."

"Why?"

"For your protection and ours, sir. If a serious defect exists we must know it now."

He said weakly: "I have the heart of a chicken."

"But I understood you were under fire in Israel?"

"That's different. I couldn't stop the shelling and the work had to be done."

"You could have quit the country."

"No, I couldn't do that—not until the work was done, not until the translation was finished and the book ready."

Kathryn van Hise tapped her fingers together and only looked at him. She thought that was answer enough.

Chaney recalled something she had said on the beach, something she had quoted or inferred from his dossier. Or perhaps it was that damned computer profile rattling off his supposed resolution and stability. He had a quick suspicion.

"Did you read my dossier? All of it?"

"Yes, sir."

"*Ouch.* Did it contain information—ah, gossip about an incident on the far side of the New Allenby Bridge?"

"I believe the Jordanian government contributed a certain amount of information on the incident, sir. It was obtained through the Swiss Legation in Amman, of course. I understand you suffered a rather severe beating."

Saltus eagerly: "Hey—what's this?"

Chaney said: "Don't believe everything you read. I was damned near shot for a spy in Jordan, but that Moslem woman wasn't wearing a veil. Mark that—no veil. It's supposed to make all the difference in the world."

Saltus: "But what has the woman to do with a spy?"

"They thought I was a Zionist spy," Chaney explained. "The woman without a veil was only a pleasant interlude—well, she was supposed to be a pleasant interlude. But it didn't turn out that way."

"And they nabbed you? Almost shot you?"

"And beat the hell out of me. Arabs don't play by the same rules we do. They use garrotes and daggers."

Saltus: "But what happened to the woman?"

"Nothing. No time. She got away."

"Too *bad,*" Saltus exclaimed.

Kathryn van Hise asked: "May we continue, please?"

Chaney thought he detected a touch of color in her cheeks. "We're going up," he said with finality.

"Yes, sir."

He wished he were back on the beach. "Is it safe?"

Arthur Saltus broke in again before the woman could respond. "The monkeys haven't complained—you shouldn't."

"Monkeys?"

"The test monkeys, civilian. The critters have been riding that damned machine for weeks, up, back, sideways. But they haven't filed any complaints—not in writing."

"But supposing they did?"

Airily: "Oh, in that event, William and I would wave our seniority rights to you. *You* could go riding off somewhere to investigate their complaints, find out the trouble. The taxpayers deserve *some* breaks."

Kathryn van Hise said: "Once again, *please.*"

"Sure, Katrina," Saltus said easily. "But I think you should tell this civilian what he's in for."

Moresby caught his meaning and laughed.

Chaney was wary. "What am I in for?"

"You're going up naked." Saltus lifted his shirt to slap a bare chest. "We're all going up naked."

Chaney stared at him, searching for the point of the joke, and belatedly realized it was no joke. He turned on the woman and found the flush had returned to her face.

She said: "It's a matter of weight, Mr. Chaney. The machine must propel itself and you into the future, which is an operation requiring a tremendous amount of electrical energy. The engineers have advised us that total weight is a critical matter, that nothing but the passenger must be put forward or returned. They insist upon minimum weight."

"Naked? All the way naked?"

Saltus: "Naked as a jaybird, civilian. We'll save ten, fifteen, twenty pounds of excess weight. They demand it. You wouldn't want to upset those engineers, would you? Not with your life riding in their hands? They're sensitive chaps, you know—we have to humor them."

Chaney struggled to retain his sense of humor. "What happens when we reach the future, when we reach 2000?"

Again the woman attempted a reply but again Saltus cut her off. "Oh, Katrina has thought of everything. Your old Indic report said future people will wear less clothing, so Katrina will supply us with the proper papers. We're going up there as licensed nudists."

THREE

BRIAN CHANEY SAID: "I wish I knew what was going on here." His voice carried an undertone of complaint.

"I have been trying to tell you for the past hour, Mr. Chaney."

"Try once more," he begged.

Kathryn van Hise studied him. "I said on the beach that Westinghouse engineers have built a TDV. The vehicle was built here, in this building, under a research contract with the Bureau of Standards. The work has gone forward in utmost secrecy, of course, with a Congressional group—a Subcommittee—supplying direct funds and maintaining a close supervision over the project. We operate with the full knowledge of, and responsibility to the White House. The President will make the final choice of objectives."

"*Him?* A committee will have to make up his mind for him."

Her expression was one of pronounced disapproval and he guessed that he'd touched a sore spot—guessed that her loyalty to the man was motivated by political choice as much as by present occupation.

"The President is *always* kept informed of our daily progress, Mr. Chaney. As was his predecessor." The woman seemed belligerent. "His predecessor created this project by an Executive order three years ago, and we continue to operate today only with the consent and approval of the new President. I am sure you are aware of the political facts of life."

Ruefully: "Oh, I'm aware. The Indic report failed to anticipate a weak President. It was written and submitted during the administration of a strong one, and was based on the assumption that man would continue in office for two full terms. Our mistake; we didn't anticipate his death. But this new man has to be nudged off the dime—every dime, every day. He lacks initiative, lacks drive." A side glance told Chaney that the Major had agreed with him on one point. Moresby was absently nodding concurrence.

Kathryn van Hise cleared her throat.

"To proceed. An experimental laboratory is located in another part of this building, beneath us, and the testing of the vehicle has been underway for some time. When the testing had reached a stage which indicated eventual success, the survey field team was recruited. Major Moresby, Commander Saltus, and you were each the first choices in your respective fields, and the only ones contacted. As yet there is no back-up team."

Chaney said: "That's uncharacteristic of them. The military always buys two of everything, just in case."

"This is *not* a military operation, and their superiors were *not* informed why Major Moresby and Commander Saltus were transferred to this station. But I would think a back-up team will be recruited in time, and perhaps the military establishment will be informed of our operations." She folded her hands, regaining composure. "The engineers will explain the vehicle and its operation to you; I am not well enough informed to offer a lucid explanation. I understand only that an intense vacuum is created when the vehicle is operated, and the sound you heard was the result of an implosion of air into that vacuum."

"They're making sixty-one second tests?"

"No, sir. The tests may be of any duration; the longest to date has probed twelve months into the past, and the shortest only one day. Those sixty-one seconds represent a necessary margin of safety for the passenger; the passenger may not return to his exact moment of departure, but will instead return sixty-one seconds after his departure regardless of the amount of elapsed time spent in the field." But she seemed troubled by something not put into words.

Brian Chaney was certain she held something back.

She said: "At the present time, the laboratory is employing monkeys and mice as test passengers. When that phase is completed, each of you will embark on a test to familiarize yourself with the vehicle. You will depart singly, of course, because of the smallness of the vehicle. The engineers will explain the problems of mass and volume being propelled by means of a vacuum."

Chaney said: "I see the point. I wouldn't like it very well if I came back from a survey and landed on top of myself. But why sixty-one?"

"That figure is something of a laboratory fluke. The engineers were intent on a minimum of sixty seconds, but when the vehicle returned at sixty-one on two successive tests they locked it down there, so to speak."

"All the tests were successful?"

She hesitated, then said: "Yes, sir."

"You haven't lost a monkey? Not one?"

"No, sir."

But his suspicions were not quieted. "What would happen if the tests weren't successful? What if one should still fail, after all this?"

"In that event, the project would be cancelled and each of you will be returned to your stations. *You* would be free to return to Indiana, if you chose."

"I'll be fired!" Arthur Saltus declared. "Back to that bucket in the South China Sea: diesel oil and brine."

"Back to the Florida beach," Chaney told him. "And beauteous maidens in delicious undress."

"You're a cad, civilian. You ripped off that veil."

"But the maidens make that unnecessary."

"Gentlemen, *please*."

Saltus wouldn't be stopped. "And think of our poor Katrina—back to a bureaucrat's desk. Congress will cut off our slush funds: *chop*. You know how they are."

"Tightfisted, except for their pet rivers and harbors.

So I suppose we must carry on for her sake, naked and shivering, up to the brink of 2000." Chaney was bemused. "What will the coming generation think of us?"

"Please!"

Chaney folded his arms and looked at her. "I still think someone has made a mistake, Miss van Hise. I have no military skills and I'm seldom able to distinguish a nut from a bolt; I can't imagine why you would want me for a field survey—despite what you say—but you'll find me a fairly complacent draftee if you promise no more jolts. Are you holding back anything else?"

Her brown eyes locked with his, showing a first hint of anger. Chaney grinned, hoping to erase that. Her glance abruptly dropped away, and she slid the bulky envelopes across the table to the three men.

"Now?" Saltus asked.

"You may open them now. This is our primary target area, together with all necessary data to enter the field."

Brian Chaney undid the clasp and pulled out a thick sheaf of mimeographed papers and several folded maps. His glance went back to the face of the envelope. A code name was typed there, under the ubiquitous *Top Secret* rubber stamp. He read it a second time and looked up.

"Project Donaghadee?"

"Yes, sir. Mr. Donaghadee is the Director of the Bureau of Standards."

"Of course. The monument is the man."

Chaney opened the map on the top of the pile and turned it about so that north was at the top, to read the name of the first city to catch his eye: Joliet. It was a map of the north central section of the United States with Chicago placed precisely in the center, and showing great chunks of those states surrounding the metropolitan area: Illinois, Indiana, Michigan, Wisconsin, and the eastern tip of Iowa. Elwood Station was indicated by a red box just south of Joliet. He noted that the map had been prepared by Army cartographers and was stamped Top Secret. Except for the red box it was identical to gasoline station maps.

The second map was a large one of Illinois alone and now the extra size revealed Elwood Station to be about eight miles south of Joliet, adjacent to an old route marked Alternate 66. The third map was equally large: a detailed plan of Will County with Joliet located nearly in the center of it. On this map, Elwood Station was a great red box of about five square miles, with several individual houses and buildings identified by a numbered key. The station had two private service roads opening onto the highway. The main line of the Chicago & Mobile Southern Railroad passed within hailing distance of the military reservation, and a spur of that railroad branched off to enter the enclosure.

The Major looked up from his scrutiny of the maps. "Katrina. The field trials will be here on station?"

"Only in part, sir. If you find the station normal when you surface, you will proceed to Joliet in transportation which will be provided. Always keep your safety in mind."

Moresby seemed disappointed. "Joliet."

"That city will be the limit of the trials, sir. The risk must not be underestimated. However, the actual survey will be conducted in Chicago and its suburbs if the field trials prove satisfactory. Please study the maps carefully and memorize at least two escape routes; you may be forced to walk in the event of a motor breakdown."

Saltus: "Walk? With cars everywhere?"

The woman frowned. "Do *not* attempt to steal an automobile. It may be difficult, perhaps impossible, to free you from jail. It simply wouldn't do, Commander."

"Naked and forlorn in a Joliet jail," Chaney mumbled. "I believe there is a state penitentiary there."

She eyed him narrowly. "I think that little joke has gone far enough, Mr. Chaney. You will be clothed in the field, of course; you will dress for the field trial and later for the full survey, but each time you must disrobe before returning in the vehicle. You will find an adequate supply of clothing, tools, and instruments awaiting you at each point of arrival. And the laboratory will be continuously manned, of course; engineers will always be expecting your arrival and will assist in the transits."

"I thought he was pulling my leg," Chaney admitted. "But how will you manage the clothing and the engineers—how will you have it and them up there waiting for us?"

"That has already been arranged, sir. A fallout shelter and storage depot is located below us, adjacent to the laboratory. It is stocked with everything you may possibly need for any season of the year, together with weapons and provisions. Our program requires that the laboratory and the vehicle be continuously manned for an indefinite period; a hundred or more years, if necessary. All times of arrival in the future will be known to those future engineers, of course. It has been arranged."

"Unless they've walked out on strike."

"Sir?"

"Your long-range planning is subject to the same uncertainties as my projections—one fluke, one chance event may knock everything askew. The Indic report failed to allow for a weak Administration replacing a strong one, and if that report was placed before me today I wouldn't sign it; the variable casts doubt on the validity of the whole. We can only hope the engineers will still be on the job tomorrow, and will still be using standard time."

"Mr. Chaney, the Bureau's long-range planning is more thorough than that. It is solidly grounded and has been designed for permanency. I would remind you that the primary target area is only twenty-two years distant."

"I have this feeling that I'll come out—come to the surface—a thousand years older."

"I am sure you will make do, sir. Our team is notable for individual self-reliance."

"Which properly puts me in my place, Miss van Hise."

Moresby interrupted. "What about those stores?"

"Yes, sir. The shelter is stocked with necessities: motion picture cameras, tape recorders, radios, weapons and weapons detectors, hand radar, and so forth. There is money and gems and medical supplies. Materials such as film, tape, ammunition and clothing will be restocked at intervals to insure fresh or modern supplies."

Major Moresby said: "I'll be damned!" and fell silent for a moment of admiration. "It makes good sense, after all. We'll draw what we need from the stores to cover the target, and replace the remainder before coming back."

"Yes, sir. No part of the supplies may be carried back with you, except tapes and film exposed in the field. The engineers will instruct you on how to compensate for that small extra weight. Do not bring back the recorders and cameras, and you are expressly forbidden to bring back any personal souvenir such as coins or currency. But you may photograph the money if you wish."

"Those engineers have an answer for everything," Chaney observed. "They must work around the clock."

"Our project has been working around the clock for the past three years, sir."

"Who pays the electric bill?"

"A nuclear power station is located on the post."

He was quickly interested. "Their own reactor? How much power does it generate?"

"I don't know, sir."

"I know," Saltus said. "Commonwealth-Edison has a new one up near Chicago putting out eight hundred thousand kilowatts. Big thing—I've seen it, and I've seen ours. They look like steel light bulbs turned upside down."

Chaney was still curious. "Does the TDV *need* that much power?"

"I couldn't say, sir." She changed the subject by calling attention to the sheaf of mimeographed papers taken from the envelopes. "We have time this afternoon to begin on these reports."

The first sheet bore the stylized imprint of the Indiana Corporation, and Chaney quickly recognized his own work. He gave the woman an amused glance but she avoided his eyes; another glance down the table revealed his companions staring at the massive report with anticipated boredom.

The next page plunged immediately into the subject

matter by offering long columns of statistics underscored by footnotes: the first few columns were solidly rooted in the census figures of 1970, while the following columns on the following pages were his projections going forward to 2050. Chaney recalled the fun and the sweat that had gone into the work—and the very shaky limb on which he perched as he worked toward the farthest date.

Births: legitimate and otherwise, predicted annually by race and by geographical area (down sharply along the Atlantic seaboard below Boston, and the southern states except Florida; figures did not include unpredictable number of laboratory-hospital births by artificial means; figures did not include unpredictable number of abnormal births in Nevada and Utah due to accumulation of radioactive fallout).

Deaths: with separate figures for murders and known suicides, projected annually by age groups (suicides increasing at predictable rate below age thirty; females outliving males by twelve point three years by year 2000; anticipated life-expectancy increased one point nine years by year 2050; figures did not include infant mortalities in Nevada-Utah fallout area; figures did not include infant mortalities in laboratory-hospital artificial births).

Marriages and trial marriages: with subsequent divorces and annulments forecast on an annual basis after 1980, first full year of trial marriage decree (trial marriages not appreciably contributing to the birth rate except in Alabama and Mississippi, but tending to increase the murder and suicide rate, and contributing to the slow decline of long-term marriages). *Footnote*: renewable term trial marriage recommended; i.e., a second year of trial be granted upon application by both parties.

Incidence of crime: detailed projections in twenty categories, separated by states having and not having the death penalty (murder and robbery up sharply, but rape down by a significant percentage due to trial marriages and lowered legal age of all marriages).

Probable voter registrations and profiles: gradual emergence of enduring three-party system after 1980 (with registrations divided unevenly among three major and one minor party; black voters concentrated in one major and the minor party; pronounced swing to the conservative right in two white major parties during the next decade, with conservative Administrations probable until year 2000, plus or minus four years).

Total population by the turn of the century: based upon the foregoing, three hundred and forty million people in the forty-eight contiguous states and an additional ten million in the three remaining states (the northern tier of plains states projected as consistent annual losers but with Alaska up significantly; Manhattan Island reaching point of saturation within two years, California by 1990, Florida by 2010). *Footnote*: recommended that immigration to Manhattan Island, California, and Florida be forbidden by law, and that monetary inducements be offered to relocate in middle states having low densities of population.

Brian Chaney felt a certain unease about some of his conclusions.

Trial marriages could be expected to increase at a phenomenal rate once their popularity caught on, but with the trial term limited to one year he fully expected both the murder and suicide rates to climb; the murders were apt to be crimes of passion committed by the female because of the probability of losing her short-term husband to another short-term wife, while the suicides were predicted for the same reason. The recommended two-year renewable term would tend to dampen the possibility of either violent act.

A certain amount of joy-riding was to be expected in trial marriages, but he was gambling they would contribute almost nothing to the birth rate. Nor did he believe that another pill—the new pill—would affect his projections. Chaney held a low opinion of the recently introduced KH3-B pill, and refused to believe it had any restorative powers; he clung to the belief that man was alloted a normal three score and fifteen, and the projected increase of one point nine years by 2050 would be attributed to the eradication of diseases—not to pills and nostrums purportedly having the power to restore mental and physical vigor to the aged. The patients *might* live six months longer than their normal spans because they were buoyed by euphoria, but six months would not affect a mass of statistics.

Great population shifts had been earlier predicted and borne out, with the emphasis of change along the natural waterways. The greater densities of population —by 2050—would lie along five clearly defined areas: the Atlantic seaboard, the Pacific seaboard, the Gulf Coast from Tampa to Brownsville, the southern shores of all the Great Lakes, and the full lengths of the Ohio and Mississippi rivers. But he knew serious misgivings about those Lakes belts. The water levels in the Lakes had been rising steadily since the beginning of the twentieth century, and the coming flooding and erosion—combined with heavier populations—would create problems of catastrophic proportions in those areas.

Major Moresby broke the silence. "We will be expected to confirm all this, after all."

"Yes, sir. Careful observations are desired for each of the three target dates, but the greater amount of work will fall upon Mr. Chaney. His projections will need to be verified or modified."

Chaney, with surprise: "Three? Aren't we going up together? Going to the same target?"

"No, sir, that would be wasteful. The schedule calls for three individual surveys on carefully separated dates, each at least a year apart to obtain a better overall view. You will each travel separately to your predetermined date."

"The people up there will sneer at our clothes."

"The people up there should be too preoccupied to notice you, unless you call attention to yourself."

"Oh? What will preoccupy them?"

"They will be preoccupied with themselves and their problems. You haven't spent much time in American cities of late, have you, Mr. Chaney? Didn't you notice that the trains you rode into and out of Chicago were armored trains?"

"Yes, I noticed that. The Israeli newspapers did publish *some* American news. I read about the curfews. The people of the future won't notice our cameras and recorders?"

"We sincerely hope not. All would be undone if the present demand for privacy is projected into the turn of the century, if that present demand is intensified."

Chaney said: "I'm on their side; I enjoy privacy."

The woman continued. "And of course, we don't

know what status your instruments may have at that future date, we don't know if cameras and recorders will be permissible in public, nor can we guess at the efficiency of the police. You may be handicapped." She glanced at Saltus. "The Commander will teach you to work surreptitiously."

Saltus: "I will?"

"Yes, sir. You must devise a technique for completing that part of the assignment without discovery. The cameras are very small, but you must find a way to conceal them and still operate them properly."

"Katrina, do you really think it'll be illegal to take a picture of a pretty girl on a street corner?"

"We do not know the future, Commander; the survey will inform us what is and is not legal. But whatever the technique, you must photograph a number of objects and persons for a period of time without others being aware of what you are doing."

"For how long a period of time?"

"For as long as possible; for as long as you are in the field and your supply of film lasts. The emphasis is on depth, Commander. A survey in depth, to determine the accuracy of the Indic projections. Ideally, you would be in the field several days and expose every roll of film and every reel of tape you are carrying; you would record every object of major interest you might see, and as many lesser objects as time allowed. You would penetrate the field safely, accomplish all objectives, and withdraw without haste at a time of your choosing." A shadow of a smile. "But more realistically, the ideal is seldom attained. Therefore you will go in, record all you are able, and retreat when it becomes necessary. We will hope for the maximum and have to be content with the minimum."

Chaney turned in the chair. "You make this sound like a dangerous thing."

"It could be dangerous, Mr. Chaney. What you will be doing has never before been done. We can offer you no firm guidelines for procedure, field technique, or your own safety. We will equip you as best we can, brief you to the fullest extent of our present knowledge, and send you in on your own."

"We're to report *everything* we find up there?"

"Yes, sir."

"I only hope Seabrooke has anticipated public reaction. He's headed for a rift within the lute."

"Sir?"

"I suspect he's headed for trouble. A large part of the public will raise unholy hell when they find out about the TDV—when they find out what lies twenty years ahead of them. There's something in that Indic report to scare everybody."

Kathryn van Hise shook her head. "The public will *not* be informed, Mr. Chaney. This project and our future programs are and will remain secret; the tapes and films will be restricted and the missions will not be publicized. Please remember that all of you have security clearances and are under oath and penalty. Keep silent. President Meeks has ruled that knowledge of this operation is not in the public interest."

Chaney said: "Secret, and self-contained, and solitary as an oyster."

Saltus opened his mouth to laugh when the engineers pushed their rig into a vacuum. The lights dimmed.

The massive rubber band snapped painfully against

their eardrums; or it may have been a mallet, or a hammer, driven under cruel pressure into a block of compressed air. The thing made a noise of impact, then sighed as if it rebounded in slow motion through thick liquid. The sound hurt. Three faces turned together to watch the clock.

Chaney contented himself with watching their faces rather than the clock. He guessed another monkey was riding the vehicle into somewhere, somewhen. Perhaps the animal bore a label: *Restricted* and was under orders not to talk. The President had ruled his trip was not in the public interest.

FOUR

Brian Chaney awoke with the guilty feeling that he was tardy again. The Major would never forgive him.

He sat on the side of the bed and listened carefully for tell-tale sounds within the building, but none were audible. The station seemed unusually quiet. His room was a small one, a single unit sparsely furnished, in a double row of identical rooms fitted into a former army barracks. The partitions were thin and appeared to have been cheaply and hastily erected; the ceiling was less than three feet above his head—and he was a tall man. Larger common rooms at either end of the only corridor contained the showers and toilets. The place bore an unmistakable military stamp, as though troops had moved out the day before he moved in.

Perhaps they had done just that; perhaps troops were now riding those armored trains serving Chicago and Saint Louis. Without armored siding, a passenger train seldom could traverse Chicago's south side without every window in every car being broken by stones or gunfire.

Chaney opened his door and peered into the corridor. It was empty, but recognizable sounds from the two rooms opposite his brought a measure of relief. In one of the rooms someone was opening and closing bureau drawers in frustrated search of something; in the other room the occupant was snoring. Chaney picked up a towel and his shaving kit and went to the showers. The snoring was audible all the way down the corridor.

The cold water was *cold* but the hot water was only a few degrees warmer—barely enough to feel a difference. Chaney came out of the shower, wrapped a towel about his middle and began rubbing lather on his face.

"Stop!" Arthur Saltus was in the doorway, pointing an accusatory finger. "Put down the razor, civilian."

Startled, Chaney dropped the razor into the bowl of tepid water. "Good morning, Commander." He recovered his wits and the razor to begin the shave. "Why?"

"Secret orders came in the middle of the night," Saltus declared. "All the people of the future wear long beards, like old Abe Lincoln. We must be in character."

"Nudists with bushy beards," Chaney commented. "That must be quite a sight." He kept on shaving.

"Well, you bit hard yesterday, civilian." Saltus put an exploratory hand under the shower and turned on the water. He had anticipated the result. "This hasn't changed since boot camp," he told Chaney. "Every barracks is allotted ten gallons of hot water. The first man in uses it all."

"I *thought* this was a barracks."

"This building? It must have been at one time or another, but the station wasn't always a military post. I spotted that coming in. Katrina said it was built as an ordnance plant in 1941—you know, during *that* war." He stepped under the shower. "That was—what? Thirty-seven years ago? Time flies and the mice have been at work."

"That other building is new."

"The lab building is brand new. Katrina said it was built to house that noisy machine—built to last forever. Reinforced concrete all the way down; a basement, and a sub-basement, and other things. The vehicle is down there somewhere hauling monkeys back and forth."

"I'd like to *see* that damned thing."

"You and me together, civilian. You and me and the Major." His head popped out of the shower and his voice dropped to a stage whisper. "But I've got it figured."

"You have? What?"

"Promise you won't tell Katrina? You won't tell the man in the White House I broke security?"

"Cross my heart, spit at the moon and everything."

"All right: all this is a plot, a trick to be ahead of everybody else. Katrina has been misleading us. We're not going up to the turn of the century—we're going back down, back into history!"

"Back? Why?"

"We're going back two thousand years, civilian. To grab those old scrolls of yours, pirate them, as if they *were* classified or something. We're going to sneak in there some dark night, find a batch of them in some cave or other and copy them. Photograph them. *That's* why we're using cameras. And meanwhile, you'll be using a recorder, making tapes of the location and the like. Maybe you could unroll a parchment or two and read off the titles, so we'll know if we have anything important."

"But they seldom have titles."

Saltus was stopped. "Why not?"

"Titles just weren't important at the time."

"Well—no matter; we'll make do, we'll just copy everything we can find and sort them out later. And when we're finished we'll put everything back the way we found it and make our escape." Saltus snapped his fingers to indicate a job well done and went back into the shower.

"Is that all?"

"That's enough for us—we've scooped the world! And a long time afterward—you know, whatever year it was—some shepherd will stumble into the cave and find them in the usual way. Nobody but us will be the wiser."

Chaney wiped his face dry. "How do we get into the Palestine of two thousand years ago? Cross the Atlantic in a canoe?"

"No, no, we don't ride backwards *first*, civilian—not here, not in Illinois. If we did that we'd have to fight our way though Indians! Look, now: the Bureau of Standards will ship the vehicle over there in a couple of weeks, after we've had our field trials. They'll pack it in a box marked *Agricultural Machinery*, or some such thing, and smuggle it in like everybody else does. How do you think the Egyptians got that baby bomb into Israel? By sending it parcel post?"

Chaney said: "Fantastic."

A face emerged from the shower. "Are you being disagreeable, civilian?"

"I'm being skeptical, sailor."

"Spoil-sport!"

"Why would we want to copy the scrolls?"

"To be first."

"Why that?"

Saltus stepped all the way out of the shower.

"Well—to be *first*, that's all. We like to be first in everything. Where's your patriotism, civilian?"

"I carry it in my pocket. How do we copy the scrolls in the dark, in a cave?"

"Now that's my department! Infra-red equipment, of course. Don't fret about the technical end, mister. I'm an old cameraman, you know."

"I didn't know."

"Well, I *was* a cameraman, a working cameraman, when I was an EM. Do you remember the Gemini flights about thirteen or fourteen years ago?"

"I remember."

"I was right there on deck, mister. Photographer's apprentice, stationed on the *Wasp* when the flights began; I manned the deck cameras on some of those early flights in 1964, but when the last one splashed down in 1966, I was riding the choppers out to meet them." A disparaging wave of the hand. "Now, would you believe it, I'm riding a desk. Operations officer." His face mirrored his dissatisfaction. "I'd rather be behind the camera; the enlisted men have the fun with that job."

Chaney said: "I've learned something new."

"What's that?"

"Why you and I were brought in here. I map and structure the future; you will film it. What's the Major's specialty?"

"Air Intelligence. I thought you knew."

"I didn't. Espionage?"

"No, no—he's another desk man, and he hates it as much as I do. Old William is a brain: interrogation and interpretation. He briefs the pilots before they fly out, tells them where to find the targets, what is concealing them, and what is defending them; and then he quizzes the hell out of them when they come back to learn what they saw, where they saw it, how it behaved, how it smelled, and what was new firing at them."

"Air Intelligence," Chaney mused. "A sharpie?"

"You can bet your last tax dollar, civilian. Do you remember those maps Katrina gave us yesterday?"

"I'm not likely to forget them. Top secret."

"Read that literally for the Major: he memorized them. Mister, if you could show him another map today with one small Illinois town shifted a quarter of an inch away from yesterday's location, old William would put his long finger on the spot and say, 'This town has moved.' He's *good.*" Saltus was grinning with high humor. "The enemy can't hide a water tank or a missile launcher or an ammo bunker from him—not from *him.*"

Chaney nodded his wonder. "Do you see what kind of team Katrina is putting together? What kind the mystery man Seabrooke has recruited? I wish I knew what they really expect us to find up there."

Arthur Saltus left his room and crossed the corridor to stand at Chaney's door, dressed for a summer day.

"Hey—how do you like our Katrina?"

Chaney said: "Let us consider beauty a sufficient end."

"Mister, did you swallow a copy of Bartlett?"

A grin. "I like to prowl through old cultures, old times. Bartlett and Haakon are my favorites; each in his way offers a rich storehouse, a treasury."

"Haakon? Who is Haakon?"

"A latter-day Viking; he was born too late. Haakon wrote *Pax Abrahamitica*, a history of the desert tribes. I would say it was more of a treasury than a history: maps, photographs, and text telling one everything he would want to know about the tribes five to seven thousand years ago."

"Photographs five thousand years ago?"

"No; photographs of the remains of tribal life five thousand years ago: Byzantine dams, Nabataean wells, old Negev water courses still holding water, still serving the people who live there today. The Nabataeans built things to *last*. Their wells are water-tight today; they're still used by the Bedouin. Several good photographs of them."

"I'd like to see that. May I borrow the book?"

Chaney nodded. "I have it with me." He stared at a closed door and listened to the snores. "Wake him up?"

"No! Not if we have to live in the same room with him all day. He's a bear when he's routed out of his cave before he's ready—and he doesn't eat breakfast. He says he thinks and fights well on an empty stomach."

Chaney said: "The company is Spartan; see all their wounds on the front."

"I give up! Let's go to breakfast."

They quit the converted barracks and struck off along the narrow concrete sidewalk, walking north toward the commissary. A jeep and a staff car moved along the street, while in the middle distance a cluster of civilian cars were parked about a large building housing the commissary. They were the only ones who walked.

Chaney asked: "This is swimming weather. Is there a pool here?"

"There has to be—Katrina didn't get that beautiful tan under a sun lamp. I think it's over that way—over on E Street, near the Officers' Club. Want to try it this afternoon?"

"If she will permit it. We may have to study."

"I'm already tired of that! I don't *care* how many million voters with plastic stomachs affiliated with Party *A* will be living in Chicago twenty years from now. Mister, how can you spend years playing with numbers?"

"I'm fascinated by them—numbers and people. The relief of a plastic stomach may cause a citizen to switch from the activist *A* to the more conservative *B;* his vote may alter the outcome of an election, and a conservative administration—local, state, or national—may stall or do nothing about a problem that needed solving yesterday. The Great Lakes problem *is* a problem because of just that."

Saltus said: "Excuse me. What problem?"

"You've been away. The Lakes are at their highest levels in history; they're flooding out ten thousand miles of shoreline. The average annual precipitation in the Lakes watersheds has been steadily increasing for the past eighty years and the high water is causing damage. Those summer houses have been toppling into the Lakes for years as the water eroded the bluffs; in a very short while more than summer houses will topple in. Beaches are gone, private docks are going, low land is becoming marshes. Sad thing, Commander."

"Hey—when we go into Chicago on the survey, maybe we should look to see if Michigan Avenue is underwater."

"That's no joke. It may be."

"Oh, doom, doom, doom!" Saltus declared. "Your books and tables are always crying doom."

"I've published only one book. There was no doom."

"William said it was poppycock. I haven't read it, I'm not much of a reader, mister, but he looked down his nose. And Katrina said the newspapers gave you hell."

"You've been talking about me. Idle gossiping!"

"Hey—you were two or three days late coming in, remember? We had to talk about something, so we talked about you, mostly—curiosity about one tame civilian on a military team. Katrina knew all about you; I guess she read your dossier forward and backward. She said you were in trouble—trouble with your company, with reviewers and scholars and churches and—oh, everybody." Saltus gave his walking companion a slanted glance. "Old William said you were bent on destroying the foundations of Christianity. You must have done *something*, mister. Did you chip away at the foundation?"

Chaney answered with a single word.

Saltus was interested. "I don't know that."

"It's Aramaic. You know it in English."

"Say it again—slowly—and tell me what it is."

Chaney repeated it, and Saltus turned it on his tongue,

delighted with the sound and the fresh delivery of an old transitive verb. "Hey—I like that!" He walked on, repeating the word just above his breath.

After a space: "What about those foundations?"

"I translated two scrolls into English and caused them to be published," Chaney said with resignation. "I could have saved my time, or spent my holiday digging up buried cities. One man in ten read the book slowly and carefully and understood what I had done—the other nine began yapping before they finished the first half."

His companion was ready with a quick grin. "William yapped, and Katrina seemed scandalized, but I guess Gilbert Seabrooke read it slowly: Katrina said the Bureau was embarrassed, but Seabrooke stood up for you. Now *me*, I haven't read it and I probably won't, so where does that put me?"

"An honest neutral, subject to intimidation."

"All right, mister: intimidate this honest neutral."

Chaney looked down at the commissary, guessing at the remaining distance. He intended to be short; the subject was painful since a university press had published the book and a misunderstanding public had taken it up.

"I don't want you yapping at me, Commander, so you need first to understand one word: *midrash.*"

"*Midrash.* Is that another Aramaic word?"

"No—it's Hebraic, and it means fiction, religious fiction. Compare it to whatever modern parallel you like: historical fiction, soap opera, detective stories, fantasy; the ancient Hebrews liked their *midrash.* It was their favorite kind of fantasy; they liked to use biblical events and personages in their fiction—call it bible-opera if you like. Scholars have long been aware of that; they know *midrash* when they find it, but the general public hardly seems to know it exists. The public tends to believe that everything written two thousand years ago was sacred, the work of one saint or another."

"I guess nobody told them," Saltus said. "All right, I'll go along with that."

"Thank you. The public should be as generous."

"Didn't you tell them about *midrash*?"

"Certainly. I spent twelve pages of the introduction explaining the term and its general background; I pointed out that it was a commonplace thing, that the old Hebrews frequently employed religious or heroic fiction as a means of putting across the message. Times were hard, the land was almost always under the heel of an oppressor, and they desperately wanted freedom—they wanted the messiah that had been promised for the past several hundred years."

"Ah—there's your mistake, civilian! Who wants to waste twelve pages gnawing on the bone to get at the marrow?" He glanced around at Chaney and saw his pained expression. "Excuse me, mister. I'm not much of a reader—and I guess they weren't either."

Chaney said: "Both my scrolls were *midrash*, and both used variations of that same theme: some heroic figure was coming to rid the land of the oppressor, to free the people from their ills and starvations, to show them the door to a brand new life and happy times forever after. The first scroll was the longer of the two with greater detail and more explicit promises; it foretold wars and pestilence, of signs in the heavens, of invaders from foreign lands, of widespread death, and finally of the coming of the messiah who would bring eternal peace to the world. I thought it was a great work."

Saltus was puzzled. "Well—what's the trouble?"

"Haven't you read the Bible?"

"No."

"Nor the Book of Revelations?"

"I'm not much of a reader, civilian."

"The first scroll was an orginal copy of the Book of Revelations—original, in that it was written at least a hundred years earlier than the book included in the Bible. And it was presented as fiction. That's why Major Moresby is angry with me. Moresby—and people like him —don't *want* the book to be a hundred years older than believed; they don't *want* it to be revealed as fiction. They can't accept the idea that the story was first written by some Qumran priest or scribe, and circulated around the country to entertain or inspire the populace. Major Moresby doesn't *want* the book to be *midrash.*"

Saltus whistled. "I should think not! He takes all that seriously, mister. He believes in prophecies."

"I don't," Chaney said. "I'm skeptical, but I'm quite willing to let others believe if they so choose. I said nothing in the book to undermine their beliefs; I offered no opinions of my own. But I *did* show that the first Revelations scroll was written at the Qumran school, and that it was buried in a cave a hundred years or more before the present book was written—or copied—and included in the Bible. I offered indisputable proof that the book in the Christian Bible was not only a later copy, but that it had been altered from the original. The two versions didn't match; the seams showed. Whoever wrote the second version deleted several passages from the first and inserted new chapters more in keeping with *his* times. In short, he modernized it and made it more acceptable to his priest, his king, his people. His only failing was that he was a poor editor—or a poor seamstress—and his seams were visible. He did a poor job of rewriting."

Saltus said: "And old William went up in smoke. He blamed you for everything."

"Almost everyone did. A newspaper reviewer in Saint Louis questioned my patriotism; another in Minneapolis hinted that I was the anti-Christ, and a communist tool to boot. A newspaper in Rome skewered me with the unkindest cut of all: it printed the phrase *Traduttore Traditore* over the review—the Translator is a Traitor." Despite himself a trace of bitterness was evident. "On my *next* holiday I'll confine myself to something safe. I'll dig up a ten-thousand-year-old city in the Negev, or go out and rediscover Atlantis."

They walked in silence for a space. A car sped by them toward the busy commissary.

Chaney asked: "A personal question, Commander?"

"Fire away, mister."

"How did you manage your rank so young?"

Saltus laughed. "You haven't been in service?"

"No."

"Blame it on *our* damned war—the wits are calling it our Thirty Years War. Promotions come faster in wartime because men and ships are lost at an accelerated rate—and they come faster to men in the line than to men on the beach. I've always been in the line. When the Viet Nam war passed the first five years, I started moving up; when it passed ten years without softening, I moved up faster. And when it passed fifteen years—

after that phony peace, that truce—I went up like a skyrocket." He looked at Chaney with sober expression. "We lost a lot of men and a lot of ships in those waters when the Chinese began shooting at us."

Chaney nodded. "I've heard the rumors, the stories. The Israeli papers were filled with Israeli troubles, but now and then outside news was given some space."

"You'll hear the truth someday; it will jolt you. Washington hasn't released the figures, but when they do you'll get a stiff jolt in the belly. A lot of things are kept undercover in undeclared wars. Some of the things work their way into the open after a while, but others never do." Another sidelong glance, measuring Chaney. "Do you remember when the Chinese lobbed that missile on the port city we were working? That port below Saigon?"

"No one can forget that."

"Well, mister, our side retaliated in kind, and the Chinese lost two railroad towns that same week—Keiyang and Yungning. Two holes in the ground, and several hundred square miles of radioactive cropland. Their missile was packing a low-yield A, it was all they could manage at the time, but we hit *them* with two Harrys. You will please keep that under your hat until you read about it in the papers—if you ever do."

Chaney digested the information with some alarm. "What did they do, to retaliate for *that?*"

"Nothing—yet. But they will, mister, they will! As soon as they think we're asleep, they'll clobber us with something. And hard."

Chaney had to agree. "I suppose you've had more than one tour of duty in the South China Sea?"

"More than one," Saltus told him. "On my last tour,

I had two good ships torpedoed under me. Not one, but two, and Chinese subs were responsible both times. Those bastards can really shoot, mister—they're good."

"A Lieutenant Commander is equal to what?"

"A Major. Old William and me are buddies under the skin. But don't be impressed. If it wasn't for this war I'd be just another junior grade Lieutenant."

The desire for further conversation fell away and they walked in pensive silence to the commissary. Chaney recalled with distaste his contributions to Pentagon papers concerning the coming capabilities of the Chinese. Saltus seemed to have confirmed a part of it.

Chaney went first through the serving line but paused for a moment at the end of it, balancing the tray to avoid spilling coffee. He searched the room.

"Hey—there's Katrina!"

"Where?"

"Over there, by that far window."

"I don't believe in waiting for an invitation."

"Push on, push on, I'm right behind you!"

Chaney discovered that he *had* spilled his coffee by the time they reached her table. He had tried to move too fast, but still lost out.

Arthur Saltus was there first. He promptly sat down in the chair nearest the young woman and transferred his breakfast dishes from the tray to the table. Saltus put his elbows on the table, peered closely at Katrina, then half turned to Chaney.

"Isn't she lovely this morning! What would your friend Bartlett say about this?"

Chaney noted the tiny line of disapproval above her eyes. "Her very frowns are fairer far, than the smiles of other maidens are."

"Hear! Hear!" Saltus clapped his hands in approval, and stared back impudently at nearby diners who had turned to look. "Nosey peasants," was his loud whisper.

Kathryn van Hise struggled to maintain her reserve. "Good morning, gentlemen. Where is the Major?"

"Snoring," Arthur Saltus retorted. "We sneaked out to have breakfast alone with you."

"*And* these other two hundred characters." Chaney waved a hand at the crowded mess hall. "This is romantic."

"These peasants aren't romantic," Saltus disagreed. "They lack color and Old World charm." He stared bleakly at the room. "Hey—mister, we could practice on *them.* Let's run a survey on *them,* let's find out how many of them are Republicans eating fried eggs." Snap of fingers. "Better yet—let's find out how many Republican stomachs have been ruined eating these Army eggs!"

Katrina made a hasty sound of warning. "Be careful of your conversation in public places. Certain subjects are restricted to the briefing room."

Chaney said: "Quick! Switch to Aramaic. These peasants will never catch on."

Saltus began to laugh but just as suddenly shut it off. "I only know one word." He seemed embarrassed.

"Then don't repeat it," Chaney warned. "Katrina may have studied Aramaic—she reads everything."

"Hey—that's not fair."

"I do unfair things, I retaliate in kind, Commander. Last night, I sneaked into the briefing room while you were all asleep." He turned to the young woman. "I know your secret. I know one of the alternative targets."

"Do you, Mr. Chaney?"

"I do, Miss van Hise. I raided the briefing room and turned it inside out—a very thorough search, indeed. I found a secret map hidden under one of the telephones—the red phone. The alternative target is the Qumran monastery. We're going back to destroy the embarrassing scrolls—rip them from their jars and burn them. There." He sat back with barely concealed amusement.

The woman looked at him for a space, and Chaney had a sudden, intuitive torment. He felt uneasy.

When she broke her silence, her voice was so low it would not carry to the adjoining tables.

"You are almost right, Mr. Chaney. One of our alternatives *is* a probe into Palestine, and you were also selected for the team because of your knowledge of that general area."

Chaney was instantly wary. "I will have nothing to do with those scrolls. I'll not tamper with them."

"That will not be necessary. They are not an alternate target."

"What *is*?"

"I don't know the correct date, sir. Research has not been successful in determining the precise time and place, but Mr. Seabrooke believes it will be a profitable alternate. It is under active study." She hesitated and dropped her gaze to the table. "The general location in Palestine is or was a site known as the Hill of Skulls."

Chaney rocked in his chair.

In the long silence, Arthur Saltus groped for an understanding. "Chaney, what—?" He looked to the woman, then back to the man. "Hey—let *me* in on it!"

Chaney said quietly: "Seabrooke has picked a very hot alternative. If we can't go up *there* for the survey, our team is going *back* to film the Crucifixion."

FIVE

BRIAN CHANEY was the last of the four participants to return to the briefing room. He walked.

Kathryn van Hise had offered them a ride as they quit the mess hall and Arthur Saltus promptly accepted, scrambling into the front seat of the olive green sedan to sit close beside her. Chaney preferred the exercise. Katrina turned in the seat to look back at him as the car left the parking lot, but he was unable to read her expression: it may have been disappointment—and then again it may have been exasperation.

He suspected Katrina was losing her antipathy for him, and that was pleasing.

The sun was already hot in the hazy June sky and Chaney would have liked to go in search of the pool, but he decided against it only because he knew better than to be tardy a second time. As a satisfying substitute, he contented himself with watching the few women who happened to pass; he approved of the sharply abbreviated skirt that was the current style and, given another opportunity, would have included a forecast in his tables—but the stodgy old Bureau was likely to dismiss the subject matter as frivolous. Skirts had been climbing steadily for many years and now they were frequently one with the delta pants: a heady delight to the roving male eye. But with predictable military conservatism, the WAC skirts were not nearly as brief as those worn by civilians.

Happily, Katrina was a civilian.

The massive front door of the concrete building opened easily under his pull, moving on rolamite tracks. Chaney walked into the briefing room and stopped short at sight of the Major. A furtive signal from Saltus warned him to silence.

Major Moresby faced the wall, his back to the room and to Chaney. He stood at the far end of the long table, between the end of the table and the featureless wall with his fists knotted behind his back. The nape of his neck was flushed. Kathryn van Hise was busy picking up papers that had fallen—or been thrown—from the table.

Chaney closed the door softly behind him and advanced to the table, inspecting a stack of papers before his own chair. His reaction was one of sharp dismay. The papers were photo-copies of his second scroll, the lesser of the two Qumran scrolls he had translated and published. There were nine sheets of paper faithfully reproducing the square Hebrew lettering of the *Eschatos* document from its opening line to its close. If he didn't know better, Chaney would have thought the Major was enraged at his temerity for tacking a descriptive Greek title on a Hebrew fantasy.

"Katrina! What are we doing with *this*?"

She finished the task of picking up the fallen pages and stacked them neatly on the table before the Major's chair.

"They are a part of today's study, sir."

"No!"

"Yes, sir." The woman slipped into her own chair and waited for Chaney and the Major to sit down.

The man did, after a moment. He glared at Chaney.

Chaney said: "Is this another of Seabrooke's idiotic ideas?"

"The matter is germane, Mr. Chaney."

"That matter is *not* germane, Miss van Hise. This has absolutely nothing to do with the Indic report, with the statistical tables, with the future surveys—nothing!"

"Mr. Seabrooke thinks otherwise."

Angrily: "Gilbert Seabrooke has holes in his head; his Bureau has holes in its measuring jars. Please tell him I said so. He should know better than to—" Chaney came to a full stop and glared at the young woman. "Is this *another* reason why I was chosen for the survey team?"

"Yes, sir. You are the only authority."

Chaney repeated the Aramaic word, and Saltus laughed despite himself.

She said: "Sir, Mr. Seabrooke believes it may have some slight bearing on the future survey, and we should be familiar with it. We should be familiar with every facet of the future that comes to our attention."

"But this has nothing to *do* with a future Chicago!"

"It may, sir."

"It may not! This is a fantasy, a fairy tale. It was written by a dreamer and told to his students—or to the peasants." Chaney sat down, containing his anger. "Katrina: this is a waste of time."

Saltus broke in. "More *midrash,* mister?"

"*Midrash,*" Chaney agreed. He looked at the Major. "It has no biblical connection, Major. None whatever. This is a minor piece of prophecy fitted into a fantasy;

it's the story of a man who lived twice—or of twins, the text isn't clear—who swept dragons from the sky. If the Brothers Grimm had discovered it first, they would have published it."

Katrina said stubbornly: "We are to study it."

Chaney was equally stubborn. "The turn of the century is only twenty-two years away but this document is addressed to the far future, to the end of the world. It depicts the end—the last days. I called it *Eschatos,* meaning 'The End of Things.' Does Seabrooke really think the end of the world is only twenty-two years away?"

"No, sir, I'm sure he doesn't believe that, but he has instructed us to study it thoroughly in preparation for the probe. There may be a tenuous connection."

"What tenuous connection? Where?"

"Those references to the blinding yellow light filling the sky, for one. That may be an allusion to the war in Southeast Asia. And there were other references to a cooling climate, and a series of plagues. The dragons may have a military connotation. Mr. Seabrooke mentioned specifically your point on Armageddon, in relation to the Arab-Israeli war. There are a number of incidents, sir."

Chaney permitted himself an audible groan.

Saltus said: "Hoist by your own petard, mister. I feel for you."

Chaney knew his meaning. The reviewers and the Moresbys of the world didn't *want* to believe his English translation of the Revelations scroll, but it appeared to be authentic. Now, Seabrooke was making noises like he wanted to believe *Eschatos,* or was willing to believe it.

Impatiently: "The blinding yellow light in the sky has *nothing* to do with the Asian war. In Hebrew fiction it was a romantic promise of health, wealth, of peace and prosperity for all. The yellow light is a benign sun, spilling contentment on the earth. The old prophet was saying simply that at last the earth belonged to men, to all men, and eternal peace was at hand. Utopia. No more than that.

"That utopia was to come *after* the end of things, after the last days, when a brand new world under a golden sun would be given to the peoples of Israel. It is a prophecy as old as time. It has nothing to do with our war in Asia, or the color of any soldier's skin." Chaney pointed to the door. "How cold is it out there now? *This* is swimming weather. And where are the plagues? Have you ever seen a dragon?"

Saltus: "And where is Armageddon?"

"The proper name is Har-Magedon. It's a mountain in Israel, Commander, the mountain of Megiddo rising above the Plain of Esdraelon. And the prophecies are a little too late—*all* the prophecies. Any number of decisive battles have already happened there and vanished into history. It was a favorite locale for the old fictioneers; it had such a bloody history it was firmly fixed in the native mind, it was a good site for still another story."

"Mister, you sure know how to throw cold water."

"Commander, I believe in being realistic; I believe in facts, not fantasy. I believe in statistics and firmly rooted continuities, not prophecies and dreams." Chaney stabbed the copied document with his finger. "The man who wrote this was a dreamer, and something of a plagiarist. Several passages were lifted from Daniel, and there is a hint of Micah."

"Do you think it's a fake?"

"No, definitely not. I had to make sure of that at the beginning. The scroll was found in the usual way: by university students searching old jars, in cave Q12. It was wrapped in the usual rotting linen of a type woven at Qumran, and that linen was submitted to the carbon-14 dating process—the tests were made at the Libby Institute in Chicago. Repeated tests established an age of nineteen hundred years, plus or minus seventy, for the linen.

"But we don't accept *that* as proof that the scroll inside the linen is of the same age. There are other methods of dating a manuscript." He bent over the copies and placed a finger on the opening line. "This text is written with square letters and contains no vowels—none at all. It reads from right to left down the page, right to left across the scroll. Square lettering came into use about the third century before Christ; before that a more flowing script was used but afterwards a square was common."

Chaney caught a movement from the corner of his eye. Major Moresby unbent, to peer closely at the copies.

"The Hebrew language used at that time had only twenty-two letters, and they were all consonants. Vowels hadn't been invented, and wouldn't be for another six or seven hundred years. This text contains the twenty-two standard consonants but nowhere on the scroll—above or below the lines, or within the words, or the margins—is there a sign to indicate where a consonant becomes a vowel. That was significant." He glanced at Moresby and discovered he had the man's close attention. "But there were other clues to work with. This scribe was familiar with the writings of Daniel, and of Micah. The text is not pure Hebrew; several Aramaic touches have slipped in—a word or a phrase having more impact than a Hebrew equivalent. The old Greek word *eschatos* doesn't appear, but it should have. I was surprised to find it missing, for the scribe had a knowledge of Greek drama, or melodrama." Chaney made a gesture. "The earliest date was about 100 B.C. It was not written before that.

"Setting a closing date isn't nearly as difficult, because the scribe betrays the limit of his knowledge. He was not alive and writing in 70 A.D. The text contains three direct references to a Temple, a great white Temple which appears to be the center of all important activity. There were many temples in Palestine and in the surrounding lands, but only one *Temple*: the holiest of holy places, the Temple of Jerusalem. In this story the Temple is still standing, still in existence, and is the center of all activity. But in history *that* Temple stopped. The Roman armies invaded Judaea and destroyed it utterly in 70 A.D. In the course of putting down a Hebrew revolt they tore it apart to the last stone, and the Temple was no more."

Major Moresby said: "That was foretold."

Chaney ignored him. "So the date of composition was pinned down: not earlier than 100 B.C. and not later than 70 A.D. A satisfactory agreement with the radiocarbon tests. I'm satisfied the scroll is authentic, but the tale it tells is not—the story is pure fiction, built on symbols and myths known to the ancient Hebrews."

Arthur Saltus eyed the copies and then the woman. "Do we have to read all this, Katrina?"

"Yes, sir. Mr. Seabrooke has requested it."

Chaney said: "A waste of time, Commander."

Saltus grinned at him. "The Great White Chief has spoken, mister. I don't want to go back to that bucket in the South China Sea."

"Indic won't have me back—they sold me to the Great White Chief." Brian Chaney pushed the photo-copied papers aside and reached for the hefty Indic report. He opened a page at random and found himself reading figures pertaining to a West German election three years earlier.

He remembered that election; people in his section had followed it with interest and had tried to place bets on it, without takers. Just before the report was closed and submitted to the Bureau, the National Democratic party had captured four point three percent of the popular vote—only seven-tenths of one percent short of the minimum needed to gain entrance to the Bundestag. The party had been accused of Neo-Nazism, and Chaney wondered if it had managed to overcome the Hitler image and win the necessary five percent in the last few years. In peacetime, Israeli papers would have carried the news; he would have noticed it. Perhaps they had published subsequent election news, despite their paper shortages and their domestic troubles—perhaps he had missed it. His nose had been buried in the translations for a long time. As the noses of Saltus and Moresby were buried in *Eschatos* now. . . .

Chaney had often wondered about the anonymous scribe who had concocted that story. The long work on the scroll had imparted the feeling of almost knowing the man, of almost reading his mind. He sometimes thought the man had been a novice practicing his art—a probationer not yet tamped into the mold, or perhaps he was a defrocked priest who had lost his office because of his nonconformity. The man had never hesitated to employ Aramaic vernacular, where Aramaic was more colorful than his native Hebrew, and he told his story with zest, with poetic freedom.

Eschatos:

The sky was blue, new, and clear of dragons (winged serpents) when the man who was two men (twins?) lived on (under?) the earth. The man who was two men was at peace with the sun and his children multiplied (the tribes or families about him grew in size with the passage of time). He was known and welcomed in the white Temple, and may have dwelt there. His work took him frequently to distant Har-Magedon, where he was equally well known to those who lived on the mountain and those who tilled the plain below; he mingled with these peoples and instructed (counseled, guided) them in their daily lives; he was a wise man. He had a guest room (or house) with (alongside?) a mountain family and needed only to touch the tent rope (make sign) for food and water; it was supplied him without payment. (Form of repayment for his services?)

The man who was two men labored on the mountain. His task (performed at unknown intervals) was an onerous one, and consisted of standing on the mountain top and sweeping the skies clean of muck (impurities, debris left over from the Creation) which tended to gather there. The mountain people were required to assist him in his work, in that they furnished him with ten *cor* of water (nine hundred gallons) drawn from an inexhaustible well (or cistern) near the base of the mountain; and each time the job was finished in the dark and light of a single day (from one sunset to the next). This task had been put to him by the nomadic Egyptian prophet (Moses?) by more than five times the Year of Jubilee (more than two hundred and fifty years earlier); and it was a sign and a promise the prophet gave to his children, the tribes: for so long as the skies were clean the sun would remain quiet, dragons would not hover, and the bitter cold that immobilized old men would be kept in its proper place at a distance.

The new prophet who came after the Egyptian (Aaron?) approved the pact, and it was continued; after him, Elijah approved the pact, and it was continued; and after him, Zephaniah approved the pact, and it was continued; after him, Micah approved the pact (chronological error) and it was continued. It is now. The skies were swept and the peoples prospered.

The man who was two men was a wondrous figure. He was a son (lineal descendant) of David.

His head was of the finest gold and his eyes were brilliant (word missing; probably gems), his breast and arms were of purest silver, his body was bronze, his legs were of iron, and his feet were of iron mixed with clay (entire description borrowed from Daniel). The man who was two men did not grow old, his age never changed, but on a day when he was working at his appointed task he was struck down by a sign. A stone was dislodged from the mountain and rolled down on him, crushing his feet and grinding the clay to dust, which blew away in the wind and he fell to earth grievously hurt. (Again, a whole incident borrowed from Daniel.) Work stopped. The mountain people carried him down to the plains people and the plains people carried him to the white Temple, where the priests and the physicians put him down in his injury (buried him?).

The first Year of Jubilee passed, and the second (a century), but he did not appear at his place on the mountain. His room (house) was not made ready for him, for the new children had forgotten; the people did not fetch water and the well (cistern) ran low; the skies were not cleansed. Debris gathered above Har-Magedon. The first dragon was seen there, and another, and they spawned in the muck until the skies were dark with their wings and loud with their thunder. A chilling cold crept over the land and there was ice on the streams. The tribes were thin (depopulated) and were hungry; they fought one another for food, and it came to pass that touching the tent rope was no more honored in the land, and kinsman and traveler alike were turned away or driven into the desert for the jackals. The messengers (?) stopped and there was no more traffic between tribes and the towns of the tribes, and the roads were covered with weed and grass.

The elders lost the faith of their fathers and built a wall around the tribe, and then another and another, until the walls were a hundred and a hundred in number and every house was set apart from its neighbor, and families were set apart from one another. The elders caused great walls to be built and they did not traffic; the cities fell poor and made war on one another, and the sun was not quiet.

A plague came down from the muck above Har-Magedon, a dropping from the dragons to cover the land like a foul mist before dawn. The plague was a vile sickness of the eye, of the nose, of the throat, of the head, of the heart and the soul of a man, and his skin fell; the plague did make men over into a likeness of the four beasts, and they were loathsome in their misery and their brothers fled in terror before them.

And with this the voice of Micah cried out, saying, this was the end of the days; and the voice of Elisha cried out, saying, this was the end of the days; and the spirit and ghost of Ezekiel cried out, and was seen within the gates of the city, telling the lamentations and mourning, for this was the end of the days.

And it was so.

(The following line of text consisted of but a single word, an Aramaism indicating darkness, or time, or generation. It could be translated as Interregnum.)

The man who was two men rose up from his bed (tomb?) in the underworld, and was angry at what he found in the land. He broke the earth of the Temple (emerged from his tomb below? or within?) and came forth in fury to banish the dragons from the mountain. He raised up his rod and struck the walls, bidding the families to go free and live; he gave food and comfort to the traveler and counseled him, and guided his hand to the tent rope; he bade his kinsman enter his (room? house?) and take rest; he labored without stop to undo the sore misery on the land.

When the sun was quiet again, the man who was two men worked to refill the well (cistern) and he swept the skies clear of debris. The dragons fled from their foul nests, and the plague fled with them to another part of the world. The man turned his eye up to the Temple and there was a great, blinding yellow light filling the heavens from the rim of the world to the rim:

and it was a sign and a promise from the holy prophets to the laborer that the world was made new again, and was at peace with itself. Flowers bloomed and there was fruit on the vine. The sun was quiet.

The man who was two men rested in his earth-place (tomb?) and was content.

Brian Chaney pulled himself from his reverie to look down the table at his companions.

Arthur Saltus was reading the photo-copied pages in a desultory manner, his interest barely caught by the narrative. Major Moresby was scribbling in a notebook—his only support to a retentive memory—and had gone back to the beginning of the translation to read it a second time. Chaney suspected he was hooked. Kathryn van Hise was across the table from him, sitting motionless with her fingers interlaced on the tabletop. The young woman had been surreptitiously watching him while he day-dreamed, but turned her glance down when he looked directly at her.

Chaney wondered what she really thought of all this? Apart from her superior's opinions, apart from the stance officially adopted by the Bureau, what did *she* think? At breakfast she had exhibited some embarrassment—it may have been alarm—at the prospect of filming the alternate target, filming the Crucifixion, but other than that he'd found no sign of her personal beliefs or attitudes toward the future survey. She had revealed pride and triumph in the engineers' accomplishments and she was fanatically loyal to her employer—but what did *she* think? Did she have any mental reservations?

He failed utterly to understand Seabrooke's interest in the second scroll.

Every scholar recognized it as *midrash;* there had been no controversy over the second scroll and had it been published alone he would have escaped the notoriety. He thought Gilbert Seabrooke something of a lunatic to even introduce it into the briefing room. There was no meat here for the survey. There was nothing in the *Eschatos* relating to the coming probe of the turn of the century; the story was firmly rooted in the first century before Christ and did not look or hint beyond 70 A.D. Actually it didn't peer beyond its own century. It made no claim or pretense to genuine prophecy as did, say, the Book of Daniel—whose scribe pretended to be alive about five hundred years before he was born, only to betray himself by his faulty grasp of history. Gilbert Seabrooke was reading imaginary lines between the lines, grabbing at rays of yellow light and the droppings of dragons.

One of the three telephones rang.

Kathryn van Hise jumped from her chair to answer and the three men turned to watch her.

The conversation was short. She listened carefully, said *Yes, sir* three or four times, and assured the caller that the studies were proceeding at a satisfactory pace. She said *Yes, sir* a final time and hung up the instrument. Moresby was half out of his chair in anticipation.

Saltus said: "Well, come *on,* Katrina!"

"The engineers have concluded their testing and the vehicle is now on operational status. Field trials will begin very soon, gentlemen. Mr. Seabrooke suggested that we take the day off as a token of celebration. He will meet us at the pool this afternoon."

Arthur Saltus yelled, and was halfway to the door.

Brian Chaney dropped his copy of the *Eschatos* scroll into a wastebasket and prepared to follow him.

He looked to the woman and said: "Last one in is a wandering Egyptian."

SIX

Brian Chaney came up from a shallow dive and paddled to the edge of the pool; he clung to the tiled rim for a space and attempted to wipe the gentle sting of chlorine from his eyes. The sun was hot, and the air warmer than the water. Two of his companions played in the water behind him while a third—the Major—sat in the shade and stared solemnly at a chess board, waiting for anyone to come along and challenge him. The pieces were set out. The recreation area held a few others beside themselves but none seemed interested in chess.

Chaney glanced over his shoulder at the pair playing in the water, and felt the smallest pain of jealousy. He climbed from the pool and reached for a towel.

Gilbert Seabrooke said: "Afternoon, Chaney."

The Director of Operations sat nearby under a gaudy beach umbrella, sipping a drink and watching the bathers. It was his first appearance.

Chaney stretched the towel over his back and ran across the hot tiles. "Good afternoon. You're the red telephone." They shook hands.

Seabrooke smiled briefly. "No; that's our line to the White House. Please don't pick it up and call the President." A wave of the hand extended an invitation to the other chair beneath the umbrella. "Refreshments?"

"Not just yet, thanks." He studied the man with an open curiosity. "Has someone been carrying tales?" His glance went briefly to the woman in the water.

Seabrooke's smooth reply attempted to erase the sting. "I receive daily reports, of course; I try to keep on top of every activity on this station. And I'm quite used to people misunderstanding my motives and actions." Again the smallest of stingy smiles. "I make it a practice to explore every possible avenue to attain whatever goal is in view. Please don't be upset by my interest in your outside activities."

"They have no relation to *this* activity."

"Perhaps, and perhaps not. But I refuse to ignore them for I am a methodical man."

Chaney said: "And a persistent one."

Gilbert Seabrooke was tall, thin, taut, and looked like that well-known fellow in the State Department—or perhaps it was that other fellow who sat on the Supreme Court. He wore the carefully cultivated statesman image. His hair was silver gray and parted precisely in the middle, with the ends brushed backward at a conservative angle; his eyes appeared gray, although upon closer inspection they were an icy blue-green; the lips were firm, not used to laughter, while the chin was strong and clean with no hint of a double on the neckline. He carried his body as rigidly erect as a military man, and his pipe jutted out straight to challenge the world. He was Establishment.

Chaney had vague knowledge of his political history.

Seabrooke had been governor of one of the Dakotas—memory refused to reveal which one—and was only narrowly defeated in his bid for a third term. The man quickly turned up in Washington after the defeat and was appointed to a post in Agriculture: his party took care of its faithful. Some years later he moved to another post in Commerce, and after several years he dropped into a policy-making office in the Bureau of Standards. Today he sat beside the pool, directing everything on station.

Chaney asked: "How's the battle going?"

"Which battle?"

"The one with the Senate subcommittee. I suspect they're counting the dollars and the minutes."

The tight lips quavered, almost permitting a smile. "Eternal vigilance results in a healthy exchequer, Chaney. But I *am* having some little difficulty with those people. Science tends to frighten those who are infrequently exposed to it, while the practitioners of science are often the most misunderstood people in the world. The project could be different if more imagination were brought into play. If our researches were directly connected to the hostilities in Asia, if they would result in practical military hardware, we would be drowning in funds." A gesture of discontent. "But we must fight for every dollar. The military people and their war command priority."

Chaney said: "But there *is* a connection."

"I said this would be different if more imagination were brought into play," Seabrooke reminded him dryly. "At this point, imagination is sadly lacking; the military mind often does not recognize a practical use until that use is thrust under the nose. You may see an application and I believe I see one, but neither the Pentagon nor the Congress will recognize it for another dozen years. We must pinch pennies and depend upon the good will of the President for our continued existence."

"Ben Franklin's rocking chair didn't catch on for the longest time," Chaney said. But he saw a military application, and hoped the military never discovered it.

Seabrooke watched the woman in the water, following her lithe form as she raced away from Arthur Saltus.

"I understand that you experienced some difficulty in making up your mind."

Chaney knew his meaning. "I'm not an unduly brave man, Mr. Seabrooke. I have my share of brass and bravado when I'm standing on familiar ground, but I'm not a really brave man. I doubt that I could do what either of *those* men do every day, in their tours of duty." A tiny fear of the future turned like a worm in his mind. "I'm not the hero type—I believe discretion is the better part of valor, I want to run while I'm still able."

"But you stayed on in Israel under fire."

"I did, but I was scared witless all the while."

Seabrooke turned. "Do you believe Israel will be defeated? Do you believe this will end at Armageddon?"

Flatly: "No."

"You don't find it suggestive—?"

"No. That land has been a battleground for something like five thousand years—ever since the first Egyptian army marching north met the first Sumerian army marching south. Doom-criers marched with them, but don't fall into that trap."

"But those old biblical prophets are rather severe, rather disturbing."

"Those old prophets lived in a hard age and a hard land; they almost always lived under the boot of an invader. Those old prophets owed allegiance to a government and a religion which were at odds with every other nation within marching distance; they invited punishment by demanding independence." He repeated the warning. "Don't fall into that trap. Don't try to take those prophets out of their age and fit them into the twentieth century. They are obsolete."

Seabrooke said: "I suppose you're right."

"I can predict the downfall of the United States, of every government on the North American continent. Will you hang a medal on me for that?"

Seabrooke was startled. "What do you mean?"

"I mean that all this will be dust in ten thousand years. Name a single government, a single nation which has endured since the birth of civilization—say, five or six thousand years ago."

Slowly: "Yes. I see the point."

"Nothing endures. The United States will not. If we are fortunate we may endure at least as long as Jericho."

"I know the name, of course."

Chaney doubted it. "Jericho is the oldest town in the world, the city half as old as time. It was built in the Natufian period, but has been razed or burned and then rebuilt so many times that only an archeologist can tell the number. But the town is still there and has been continuously inhabited for at least six thousand years. The United States should be as lucky. We *may* endure."

"I fervently hope so!" Seabrooke declared.

Chaney braced him. "Then drop this *Eschatos* nonsense and worry about something worthwhile. Worry about our violent swing to the extreme right; worry about these hippy-hunts; worry about a President who can't control his own party, much less the country."

Seabrooke made no comment.

Brian Chaney had pivoted in his chair and was again watching Kathryn van Hise playing in the water. Her tanned flesh, only partially enclosed in a topless swim suit, was the target of many eyes. Those transparent plastic cups some women now wore in place of a bra or a halter was only one of the many little jolts he'd known on his return to the States. Israeli styles were much more conservative and he had half forgotten the American trend after three years' absence. Chaney looked at the woman's wet body and felt something more than a twinge of jealousy; he wasn't entirely sure the cups were decent. The swing to the ultra-conservative right was bound to catch up with feminine clothing sooner or later, and then he supposed legs would be covered to the ankle and the transparent cups and blouses would be museum pieces.

There would likely be other reactions in the coming years which would make some of *his* forecasts obsolete; the failure to anticipate a weak Administration was already throwing parts of the Indic report open to question. His recommendation for a renewable term trial marriage would probably be ignored—the program itself might be repealed before it got started if the howls frightened Congress. The vociferous minority might easily swell to a majority.

To move off an uncomfortable spot of dead silence, he asked casually: "The TDV is operational?"

"Oh, yes. It has been operational since an early hour

this morning. The years of planning and building and testing are done. We are ready to forge ahead."

"What took you so long?"

Seabrooke turned heavily to look at him. Blue-green eyes were hard. "Chaney, nine men have already died by that vehicle. Would you have cared to be the tenth?"

Shock. *"No."*

"No. Nor would anyone else. The engineers had to test again and again until every last doubt was erased. If any doubt *had* remained, the project would have been canceled and the vehicle dismantled. We would have burned the blueprints, the studies, the cuff-notes, everything. We would have wiped away every trace of the vehicle. You know the rule: two objects cannot occupy the same space at the same time."

"That's elementary."

A curt nod. "It is so elementary that our engineers overlooked it, and nine men died when the vehicle returned to its point of origin, its precise second of launch, and attempted to occupy the same space." His voice dropped. "Chaney, the most dreadful sight I have ever seen was the crash of an airliner on a Dakota hillside. I was with a hunting party less than a mile away and watched it fall. I was among the first to reach the wreckage. There was no possibility of anyone surviving—none." Hesitation. "The explosion in our laboratory was the second worst sight. I was not there—I was in another building—but when I reached the laboratory I found a terrible repetition of that hillside catastrophe. No man, no single piece of equipment was left intact. The room was shattered. We lost the engineer traveling with the vehicle and eight others on duty in the laboratory. The vehicle returned to the exact moment, the exact millisecond of its departure and destroyed itself. It was an incredible disaster, an incredible oversight—but it happened. Once."

After a space, Seabrooke picked up the thread of his recital. "We learned a bitter lesson. We rebuilt the laboratory with thicker, reinforced walls and we rebuilt the vehicle; we programmed a new line of research accenting the safety factor. That factor settled itself at just sixty-one seconds, and we were satisfied."

Chaney said: "They've been counted for me, again and again. I'll lose a minute on every trip."

"A passenger embarking for any distant point, *you*, will leave at twelve o'clock, let us say, and return not sooner than sixty-one seconds after twelve. The amount of elapsed time in the field will not affect the return; if you stayed there ten years you would return sixty-one seconds *after* you launched. If we could not be absolutely certain of that we would close shop and admit defeat."

"Thank you," Chaney said soberly. "I like my skin. How are you protecting those men now?"

"By reinforced walls and remote observation. The engineers work in an adjoining room but five feet of steel and concrete will separate you. They operate and observe the TDV by closed circuit television; indeed, they observe not only the operations room itself but the corridor to it and the storeroom and fallout shelter: everything on that level of basement."

Curiously: "How do you really *know* the vehicle is moving? Is it displacing anything?"

"It does not move, does not travel in the sense of passing through space. The vehicle will always remain in its original location, unless we choose to move it elsewhere. But it does operate, and in operation it displaces temporal strata just as surely as those people in the pool are displacing water by plunging into it."

"How did you prove that?"

"A camera was mounted in the fore of the vehicle, looking through a port into the operations room. A clock and a day-calendar hang on a wall in direct line of sight of that camera. The camera has not only photographed past hours and dates but has taken pictures of the wall *before* the clock was placed there. We know the TDV has probed at least twelve months into the past."

"Any effect on the monkeys?"

"None. They are quite healthy."

"What have you done to prevent another accident—a different kind of an accident?"

Sharply: "Explain that."

Chaney said carefully: "What will happen if that machine probes back into the past before the basement was dug? What will happen if it burrows into a bed of clay?"

"That simply will not be *allowed* to happen," was the quick reply. "The lower limit of displacement is December 30, 1941. A probe beyond that date is prohibited." The Director emptied his glass and put it aside. "Chaney, the site has been carefully researched to determine a lower limit; every phase of this operation has been researched so that nothing is left to chance. The first building on the site was a crude structure resembling a cabin. It burned to the ground in February, 1867."

"You went back that far?"

"We were prepared to go farther if necessary; we

had access to records dating back to the Black Hawk war in 1831. A farmhouse *with* a basement was built on the site during the summer of 1901, and remained in place until demolition in 1941 when the government acquired this land for an ordnance depot. It has since been government owned and occupied, and the site remained vacant until the laboratory was built. The engineers were very careful to locate that basement. Today the TDV floats in a sealed tank of polywater three feet above the original basement floor, in a space that could have been occupied by nothing else. We even pinpointed the former location of the furnace and the coal room."

"And so the deadline is 1941? Why not 1901?"

"The lower limit is December 30, 1941, well after the date of demolition. The safety factor above all."

"I'd like to see that tank of polywater."

"You will. It is necessary that you become quite familiar with every aspect of the operation. Have you been visiting the doctor for your physicals?"

"Yes."

"Have you had weapons training?"

"No. Will *that* be necessary?"

Seabrooke said: "The safety factory, Chaney. It's wise to anticipate. The training may be wasted, but it's still wise to prepare yourself in every way."

"That sounds pessimistic. Wasted in what way?"

"Excuse me; you've been out of the country. All weapons for civilians will probably be prohibited in the near future. President Meeks favors that, you know."

Chaney said absently: "That will please the Major. He doesn't believe civilians have enough sense to point a gun in the right direction."

He was looking across the pool. Katrina had left

the water and was now perched on the tiled rim of the opposite side, freeing her hair from the confines of a plastic cap. Arthur Saltus was as close as their two wet suits would permit, but none of the loungers about the pool were staring at him. Two other women in the water weren't drawing half the attention—but neither were they as exposed as Katrina. Military codes extended to the swimming pool whether WACS liked it or not.

Chaney continued to stare at the woman—and at Saltus hard by—but a part of his mind dwelt on Gilbert Seabrooke, on Seabrooke's matter-of-fact statements. He thought about the machine, the TDV. He *tried* to think about the TDV. Every effort to visualize it was a failure. Every attempt to understand its method of operation was a similar failure—he lacked the engineering background to comprehend it. It worked: he accepted that. His own ears told him that every time they rammed through a test.

Drawing an enormous amount of power and piloted by a remote guidance, the vehicle displaced—what? Temporal strata. Time layers. The machine didn't move through space, it didn't leave the basement tank, but it—or the camera mounted in the nose—peered and probed into time while photographing a clock and a calendar. Soon now, it would transmit humans into tomorrow and those humans were expected to do more than merely look through the nose at a clock. (But it had also killed nine men when it doubled back on itself.) Despite an effort to control it, his skin crawled. The cold shock would not leave him.

Chaney said shortly: "You picked a hell of a crew."

"Why do you think so?"

"Not an engineer in the lot—not a hard scientist in

the lot. Moresby and I love each other like a cobra and a mongoose. I think I'm the mongoose. Want to try again?"

"I know what I'm doing, Chaney. The engineers and the physical scientists will come later, when the probes demand engineers and physical scientists. When did the first geologist reach the moon? The first selenographer? *This* survey demands your kind of man, and Moresby, and Saltus. You and Moresby were chosen because each of you is supreme in your field, and because you are natural opposites. I like to think the pair of you are delicate balances, with Saltus the neutral weight in center. And I say again, I know what I am doing."

"Moresby thinks I'm some kind of a nut."

"Yes. And what do you think of him?"

Sudden glee: "*He's* some kind of a nut."

Seabrooke permitted himself a wintry smile. "Forgive me, but there is a measure of truth to both suppositions. The Major *also* has a hobby which has embarrassed him."

Chaney groaned aloud. "Those damned prophets!" He looked around at the Major. "Why doesn't he collect toy soldiers, or be the best chess player in the world?"

"Why don't you write cookbooks?"

Chaney glanced down at his chest. "See how neatly the blade entered between the ribs? Notice that the haft stands out straight and true? A marksman's thrust."

Seabrooke said: "You like to read the past, while the Major prefers to read the future. I will admit yours is the more valuable vocation."

"Another futurist. You collect futurists."

"He places an inordinate faith in prognostication. He begins with so simple an act as reading his horoscope in the daily papers, and conducting himself accordingly. After his arrival here he admitted to Kathryn the mission was no surprise to him, because a certain horoscope had advised him to prepare himself for a momentous change in his daily affairs."

Chaney said: "*That* is as old as time; the earliest Egyptians, the Sumerians, the Akkadians, all were crazy about astrology. It's the most enduring religion."

"I suppose you are familiar with the small booklets known as farmer's almanacs?"

A nod. "I know of them."

"Moresby buys them regularly, not only to learn how their minute prophecies may affect him but to anticipate the weather a year in advance. I will admit I have looked into that last, and the Major has a remarkable record of correlating military operations with weather conditions—when he's stationed in the United States, you understand. One would suppose the weather works for him. And on some previous military posts, he has been known to plant a garden in strict accordance with the guidelines laid down in those almanacs—phases of the moon and so forth."

Skeptically: "Did the spinach come up?"

The firm lips twitched and toyed with a smile, then controlled themselves. "Finally, there is his library. Moresby owns a small collection of books, perhaps forty or fifty in all, which he moves with him from post to post. Books by such people as Nostradamus, Shipton, Blavatsky, Forman, and that Cromwell woman in Washington. He has an autographed copy by someone named Guinness; he met the author at some lecture or other. I inquired into that because of the security angle but

Guinness proved harmless. Just recently he added your volume to the collection."

Chaney said: "He wasted his money."

"Do you also believe I've wasted mine?"

"If you were looking for prophetic visions, yes. If you were interested in a biblical curiosity, no. The future should bring some great debates on that Revelations scroll; a dozen or so applecarts have been upset."

Seabrooke peered at him. "But do you see how I'm using Moresby?"

"Yes. Just as you're using me."

"Quite so. I like to think I've assembled the best possible team for the most important undertaking of the twentieth century. There are no real and solid guidelines to the future, there are only speculative studies and pseudo-speculative literature. We're making use of both, and making use of trustworthy men who are actively involved in both. One or both of you will have a solid foot on the ground when you surface twenty-two years hence. What more can we do, Chaney?"

"You've taken hold of a wolf by the ears. You might look around for a way to let go—an escape route."

A moment of thoughtful silence. "A wolf by the ears. Yes, I have done that. But Chaney, I have no desire to let go; I am fascinated by this thing, I will *not* let go. This step is comparable to the very first rocket into space, the very first orbital flight, the very first man on the moon. I could not let go if I wanted to!"

Chaney was impressed by the vehemence, the passionate eagerness. "Why don't *you* go up to the future?"

Seabrooke said quietly: "I tried. I volunteered, but I was pushed aside." His voice betrayed the hurt. "I was washed out in the first physical examination by a heart murmur. Once again this is comparable to space flight, Chaney. Old men, disabled men, feeble men will never know the TDV. We have been shut out."

The man's gaze wandered back to Katrina, and Chaney joined him in the watchfulness. Her skimpy suit was beginning to dry under the June sun and some of the more interesting rubs and contours were smoothing out, losing the revealing contours beneath. Beside her, skin touching skin, Arthur Saltus monopolized her attention.

Chaney felt that he had been shut out.

After a while he asked a question that had been playing in the back of his mind.

"Katrina said you had a couple of alternatives in mind, if this future probe didn't work. What alternates?" And he waited to see if the woman had reported a breakfast table conversation to the Director.

"A confidence, Chaney?"

"Certainly."

"I know the President a bit better than you do."

"I'll grant you that."

"I know what he will not buy."

Chaney had a premonition. "He won't buy your alternatives? Either of them?"

"Buy them? He will be outraged by them. Shock waves will be felt all this distance from Washington." Seabrooke hit the table and his empty glass was upset. "I wanted to visit the future, see the future, *smell* the future, but I was rejected the first day by the medics; I was shipwrecked before I got aboard and that hurt me more than I can say. The only other way left to me, Chaney, was to see that future through your eyes—your camera, your tapes, your observations and reactions. I can live in it through you and Moresby and Saltus, and I am *determined* to do that! There is nothing else left to me.

"To that end, I prepared two alternatives to submit to the President. I made sure each of the alternate probes would be unacceptable to him, and he would direct me to proceed with the original plan. I want the future!"

Chaney asked: "Outrageous?"

A short nod. "The President is a religious man; he practices his faith. He will never permit a probe to the scene of the Crucifixion with film and tape."

"No—he won't do that." Chaney considered it. "But because of political consequences, not religious ones. He's afraid of the people and afraid of the politicians."

"If that be true, the second alternative would be more frightening."

Warily: "Where—or what?"

"The second alternative is Dallas in November, 1963. I propose to record the Kennedy assassination in a way not done before. I propose to station a cameraman on the sixth floor of that book depository, overlooking the route; I propose to station a second cameraman in that grove atop the knoll, to settle a controversy; I propose to station a third cameraman—*you*—on the curb alongside the Kennedy car, at the precise point necessary to record the shots from the window or the trees. We will have an accurate filmed record of the crime, Chaney."

SEVEN

THE TDV was a keen disappointment.

Brian Chaney knew dismay, disillusionment. Perhaps he had expected too much, perhaps he had expected a sleek machine gleaming with chrome and enamel and glass, still new from an assembly line; or perhaps he had expected a mechanical movie monster, a bulging leviathan sprouting cables like writhing tentacles and threatening to sink through the floor of its own massive weight. Perhaps he had let his imagination run away with him.

The vehicle was none of those things. It was a squat, half-ugly can with the numeral 2 chalked on the side. It was unromantic. It was strictly functional.

The TDV resembled nothing more than an oversized oil drum hand-fashioned from scrap aluminum and pieces of old plastic—materials salvaged from a scrap pile for this one job. Chaney thought of a Model-T Ford he'd seen in a museum, and a rickety biplane seen in another; the two relics didn't seem capable of moving an inch. The TDV was a plastic and aluminum bucket resting in a concrete tank filled with polywater, the whole apparatus occupying a small space in a nearly bare basement room. The machine didn't seem capable of moving a minute.

The drum was about seven feet in length, and of a

circumference barely large enough to accommodate a fat man lying down; the man inside would journey through time flat on his back; he would recline full-length on a webwork sling while grasping two hand-rails near his shoulders, with his feet resting on a kick-bar at the bottom of the drum. A small hatch topside permitted entry and egress. The upper end of the drum had been cut away—it appeared to be an afterthought—and the opening fitted with a transparent bubble for observing the clock and the calendar. A camera and a sealed metal cube rested in the bubble. Several electric cables, each larger than a swollen thumb, emerged from the bottom end of the vehicle and snaked across the basement floor to vanish into the wall separating the operations room from the laboratory. A stepstool rested beside the polywater tank.

The contrivance looked as if it had been pieced together in a one-man machine shop on the backlot.

Chaney asked: "*That* thing works?"

"Most assuredly," Seabrooke replied.

Chaney stepped over the cables and walked around the vehicle, following the invitation of an engineer. The clock and the calendar were securely fastened to a nearby wall, each protected by a clear plastic bubble. Above them—like perched and hovering vultures—were two small television cameras looking down on the basement room. A metal locker, placed near the door and securely fastened to the wall, was meant to contain their clothing. Light fixtures recessed in a high ceiling bathed the room in a cold, brilliant light. The room itself seemed chilly and strangely dry for a basement; it held a sharp smell that might be ozone, together with an unpleasant taste of disturbed dust.

Chaney put the flat of his hand against the aluminum hull and found it cold. There was a minute discharge of static electricity against his palm.

He asked: "How did the monkeys run it?"

"They didn't, of course," the engineer retorted with annoyance. (Perhaps he lacked a sense of humor.) "This vehicle is designed for dual operation, Mr. Chaney. All the tests were launched from the lab, as you will be on the out-stage of the journey. We will kick you forward."

Chaney searched that last for a double meaning.

The engineer said: "When the vehicle is programmed for remote, it can be literally kicked to or away from its target date by depressing the kickbar beneath your feet. We will launch you forward, but you will effect your own return when the mission is completed. We recall only in an emergency."

"I suppose it will wait up there for us?"

"It will wait there for you. After arrival on target the vehicle will lock on point and remain there until it is released, by you or by us. The vehicle cannot move until propelled by an electrical thrust and that thrust must be continuous. The tachyon generators provide the thrust against a deflecting screen which provides the momentum. The TDV operates in an artificially created vacuum which precedes the vehicle by one millisecond, in effect creating its own time path. Am I making myself clear?"

Chaney said: "No."

The engineer seemed pained. "Perhaps you should read a good book on tachyon deflector systems."

"Perhaps. Where will I find one?"

"You won't. They haven't been written."

"But it all sounds like perpetual motion."

"It isn't, believe me. This baby eats power."

"I suppose you *need* that nuclear reactor?"

"All of it—it serves this lab alone."

Chaney revealed his surprise. "It doesn't serve the station outside? How much does it take to kick this thing into the future?"

"The vehicle requires five hundred thousand kilos per launch."

Chaney and Arthur Saltus whistled in unison. Chaney said: "Is that power house protected? What about wiring? Transformers? Electrical systems are vulnerable to about everything: sleet storms, drunken drivers ramming poles, outages, one thing after another."

"Our reactor is set in concrete, Mr. Chaney. Our conduits are underground. Our equipment is rated for at least twenty years continuous service." A wave of the hand to indicate superior judgment, superior knowledge. "You needn't concern yourself; our future planning is complete. There will be power to spare for the next five hundred years, if need be. The power *will* be available for any launch and return."

Brian Chaney was skeptical. "Will cables and transformers last five hundred years?"

Again the quick annoyance. "We don't expect them to. All equipment will be replaced each twenty or twenty-five years according to a prearranged schedule. This *is* a completely planned operating system."

Chaney kicked at the concrete tank and hurt his toe. "Maybe the tank will leak."

"Polywater doesn't leak. It has the consistency of thin grease, and is suspended in capillary tubes. This is ninety-nine percent of the world's supply right here." He followed Chaney's lead and kicked the tank. "No leak."

"What does the TDV push against? That polywater?"

The engineer looked at him as if he were an idiot. "It *floats* on the polywater, Mr. Chaney. I *said* the thrust against a screen, a molybdenum screen provides the momentum to displace temporal strata."

Chaney said: "Ah! I see it now."

"I don't," Arthur Saltus said mournfully. He stood at the nose of the vehicle with his nose pressed against the transparent bubble. "What guides this thing? I don't see a tiller or a wheel."

The engineer gave the impression of wanting to leave the room, of wanting to hand over the instruction tour to some underling. "The vehicle is guided by a mercury proton gyroscope, Mr. Saltus." He pointed past the Commander's nose to a metal cube within the bubble, nestled alongside the camera. "That instrument. We borrowed the technique from the Navy, from their program to guide interplanetary ships in long-flight."

Arthur Saltus seemed impressed. "Good, eh?"

"Superior. Gyroscopes employing mercury protons are not affected by motion, shock, vibrations, or upset; they will operate through any violence short of destruction. *That* unit will take you there and bring you back to within sixty-one seconds of your launch. Rely on it."

Saltus said: "How?" and Major Moresby seconded him. "Explain it, please. I am interested."

The engineer looked on Moresby as the only partly intelligent non-engineer in the room. "Sensing cells in the unit will relay back to us a continuous signal indicating your time path, Mr. Moresby. It will signal any deviation from a true line; if the vehicle wavers we will know it immediately. Our computer will interpret and correct immediately. The computer will send forward the proper corrective signals to the tachyon deflector system and restore the vehicle to its right time path, all in less than a second. You will not be aware of the deviation or the correction, of course."

Saltus: "Do you guarantee we'll hit the target?"

"Within four minutes of the annual hour, Mr. Saltus. This system does not permit a tracking error greater than plus or minus four minutes per year. That is *on* target. The Soviet couldn't do any better."

Chaney was startled. "Do they have one?"

"No," Gilbert Seabrooke interposed. "That was a figure of speech. We all have pride in our work."

Seniority was all. Major Moresby made the first trial test, and then Commander Saltus.

When his turn came, Chaney undressed and stored his clothing in the locker. The hovering presence of the engineer didn't bother him but the prying eyes of the two television cameras did. He couldn't know who was on the other side of the wall, watching him. Wearing only his shorts—the one belated concession to modesty—and standing in his bare feet on the concrete floor, Chaney fought away the impulse to bolster his waning ego by thumbing his nose at the inquisitive cameras. Gilbert Seabrooke probably wouldn't approve.

Following instructions, he climbed into the TDV.

Chaney wriggled through the hatch, lowered himself onto the sling-like bed, and promptly banged his head against the camera mounted inside the bubble. It hurt.

"Damn it!"

The engineer said reprovingly: "Please be more careful of the camera, Mr. Chaney."

"You could hang that thing *outside* the bucket."

Inching lower onto the flimsy bed, he discovered that when his feet reached the kickbar there was insufficient room to turn his head without striking either the camera or the gyroscope, nor could he push out his elbows. He squinted up at the engineer in protest but the man's face disappeared from the opening as the hatch was slammed shut. Chaney had a moment of panic but fought it away; the drum was no worse than a cramped tomb—and better in one small respect: the transparent bubble admitted light from the ceiling fixtures. Still following the detailed instructions, he reached up to snug the hatch and was immediately rewarded by a blinking green bull's eye above his head. He thought that was nice.

Chaney watched the light for a space but nothing else happened.

Aloud: "All right, *move* it." The sound of his voice in the closed can startled him.

Twisting around at the expense of a strained neck muscle and another glancing blow off the camera, he peered through the bubble at the outside room but saw no one. It was supposed to be empty during a launch. He guessed that his companions were in the lab beyond the wall, watching him on the monitors as he had watched them. The sounds had been thunderously loud in there, causing acute pain to his eardrums.

Chaney's gaze came back to the green light against the hull above his head, and discovered that a red light beside it was now blazing, blinking in the same monotonous fashion as its brother. He stared at the two lights and wondered what he was supposed to do next. Instructions hadn't gone beyond that point.

He was aware that his knees were raised and that his legs ached; the interior of the bucket wasn't designed for a man who stood six feet four *and* had to share the space with a camera and gyroscope. Chaney lowered his knees and stretched out full length on the webbed sling, but he had forgotten the kickbar until his bare feet struck it. The red light winked out.

After a while someone rapped on the plastic bubble, and Chaney twisted around to see Arthur Saltus motioning for him to come out. He opened the hatch and sat up. When he was in a comfortable position, he found that he could rest his chin on the rim of the hatch and look down into the room.

Saltus stood there grinning at him. "Well, mister, what did you think of *that?*"

"There's more room in a Syrian coffin," Chaney retorted. "I've got bruises."

"Sure, sure, civilian, tight quarters and everything, but what did you *think* of it?"

"Think of what?"

"Well, the–" Saltus stopped to gape in disbelief. "Civilian, do you mean to sit there like an idiot and tell me you weren't watching that clock?"

"I watched the lights; it was like Christmas time."

"Mister, they ran you through your test. You saw *ours*, didn't you? You checked the time?"

"Yes, I watched you."

"Well, you jumped into the future! One hour up!"

"The hell I did."

"The hell you didn't, civilian. What did you think you were doing in there–taking a nap? You were supposed to watch the clock. You went up an hour, and then you kicked yourself back. That stuffy old engineer was mad—you were supposed to wait for *him* to do it."

"But I didn't hear anything, feel anything."

"You *don't* hear anything in there; just out here, on the outside looking in. Man, we heard it! Pow, pow, the airhammer. And the guy was supposed to tell you there was no sense of motion: just climb in, and climb out. Shoot an hour." Saltus made a face. "Civilian, sometimes you disappoint me."

"Sometimes I disappoint myself," Chaney said. "I've missed the most exciting hour of my life. I guess it was exciting. I was looking at the lights and waiting for something to happen."

"It did happen." Saltus stepped down from the stool. "Come on out of there and get dressed. We have to listen to a lecture from old windbag in the lab—and after that we inspect the ship's stores. The fallout shelter, food and water and stuff; we might have to live off the stores when we get up there to the brink of 2000. What if everything is rationed, and we don't have ration cards?"

"We can always call Katrina and ask for some."

"Hey—Katrina will be an old woman, have you thought of that? She'll be forty-five or fifty, maybe—I don't know how old she is now. An *old* woman—damn!"

Chaney grinned at his concept of ancient age. "You won't have time for dating. We have to hunt Republicans."

"Guess not—nor the opportunity. We're not supposed to go looking for anybody when we get up there; we're not supposed to look for her or Seabrooke or even us. They're afraid we'll find *us*." He made a weary gesture.

"Get your pants on. Damned lecture. I hate lectures—I always fall asleep."

A team of engineers lectured. Major Moresby listened attentively. Chaney listened with half an ear, attention wandering to Kathryn van Hise who was seated at one side of the room. Arthur Saltus slept.

Chaney wished the information given him had been printed on the usual mimeographed papers and passed around a table for study. That method of dissemination was the more effective for him; the information stayed with him when he could read it on a printed page and refer back to the sentence or the paragraph above to underscore a point. It was more difficult to call back a spoken reference without asking questions, which interrupted the speaker and the chain of thought and the drone which kept Saltus sleeping. The ideal way would be to set down the lecture in Aramaic or Hebrew and hand it to him to translate; *that* would insure his undivided attention to learn the message.

He gave one eye and one ear to the speaker.

Target dates. Once a target date was selected and the pertinent data was at hand, computers determined the exact amount of energy needed to achieve that date and then fed the amount into the tachyon generator in one immense surge. The resulting discharge against the deflector provided momentum by displacing temporal strata ahead of the vehicle along a designated time path; the displaced strata created a vacuum into which the vehicle moved toward the target date, always under the guidance of the mercury proton gyroscope. (Chaney thought: perpetual motion.)

The engineer said: "You can be no more than eighty-eight minutes off the designated hour of the target date, 2000. That is four minutes per year; that is to be anticipated. But there is another significant time element to be noted in the field, one that you must *not* forget. Fifty hours. You may spend up to fifty hours in the field on any date, but you may *not* exceed that amount. It is an arbitrary limit. To be sure, gentlemen, the safety of the displaced man is of first importance up to a point. Up to a point." He stared at the sleeping Saltus. "After that point the repossession of the vehicle will be of first importance."

"I read you," Chaney told him. "We're expendable; the bucket isn't."

"I cannot agree to that, Mr. Chaney. I prefer to say that at the expiration of fifty hours the vehicle will be recalled to enable a second man to go forward, if that is deemed advisable, to effect the recovery of the first."

"*If* he can be found," Chaney added.

Flatly: "You are not to remain on target beyond the arbitrary fifty-hour limit. We have only one vehicle; we don't wish to lose it."

"That is quite sufficient," Moresby assured him. "We can do the job in half that time, after all."

Upon completion of their assignment, each of them would return to the laboratory sixty-one seconds after the original launch, whether they remained on target one hour or fifty. The elapsed time in the field did not affect their return. They would be affected only by the elapsed time while *in* the field; those few hours of natural aging could not be recaptured or neutralized of course.

The necessities and some few of the luxuries of life were stored in the shelter: food, medicines, warm clothing, weapons, money, cameras and recorders, shortwave radios, tools. If storage batteries capable of giving service for ten or twenty years were developed in the near future, they would also be stocked for use. The radios were equipped to send and receive on both military and civilian channels; they could be powered by electricity available in the shelter or by batteries when used with a conversion unit. The shelter was fitted with lead-in wires, permitting the radios to be connected to an outside antenna, but once outside on the target minitennas built into the instruments would serve for a range of approximately fifty miles. The shelter was stocked with gasoline lanterns and stoves; a fuel tank was built into an outside wall.

After emerging from the vehicle, each man was to close the hatch and carefully note the time and date. He was to check his watch against the wall clock for accuracy and to determine the plus-or-minus variation. Before leaving the basement area to enter his target date he was to equip himself from the stores, and note any sign of recent use of the shelter. He was forbidden to open any other door or enter any other room of the building; in particular, he was forbidden to enter the laboratory where the engineers would be preparing his return passage, and forbidden to enter the briefing room where someone might be waiting out the arrival and departure.

He was to follow the basement corridor to the rear of the building, climb a flight of stairs and unlock the door for exit. He would be instructed where to locate the two keys necessary to turn the twin locks of the door. Only the three of them would ever use that door.

Chaney asked: "Why?"

"That has been designated the operations door. No other personnel are authorized to use it: field men only."

Beyond the door was a parking lot. Automobiles would be kept there continuously for their exclusive use; they would be fueled and ready on any target date. They were cautioned not to drive a new model car until they became thoroughly familiar with the controls and handling of it. Each man would be furnished the properly dated papers for gate passage, and was to carry a reasonable sum of money sufficient to meet anticipated expenses.

Saltus was awake. He poked at Chaney. "You can fly to Florida in fifty hours—have a swim and still get back in time. Here's your chance, civilian."

"I can walk to Chicago in fifty," Chaney retorted.

Their mission was to observe, film, record, verify; to gather as much data as possible on each selected date. Observations should also be made (and a permanent record left in the shelter) that would benefit the next man on his target. They were to bring in with them all exposed films and tapes but the instruments were to be stored in the shelter for the following man to use. A number of small metal discs each weighing an ounce would be placed in the vehicle before launch; the proper number of discs was to be thrown overboard before returning to compensate for the tapes and films being brought back.

Were there any questions?

Arthur Saltus stared at the engineer with sleepy eyes. Major Moresby said: "None at the moment, thank you." Chaney shook his head.

Kathryn van Hise claimed their attention. "Mr. Chaney, you have another appointment with the doctor in half an hour. When you are finished there, please come to the rifle range; you really should begin weapons training."

"I'm not going to run around Chicago shooting up the place—they have enough of that now."

"This will be for your own protection, sir."

Chaney opened his mouth to continue the protest, but was stopped. The sound was something like a massive rubber band snapped against his eardrums, something like a hammer or a mallet smashing into a block of compressed air. It made a noise of impact, followed by a reluctant sigh as if the hammer was rebounding in slow motion through an oily fluid. The sound hurt.

He looked around at the engineers with a question, and found the two men staring at each other with blank astonishment. With a single mind they deserted the room on the run.

Saltus said: "*Now* what the hell?"

"Somebody went joyriding," Chaney replied. "They'd better count the monkeys—one may be missing."

Katrina said: "There were no tests scheduled."

"Can that machine take off by itself?"

"No, sir. It must be activated by human control."

Chaney had a suspicion and glanced at his watch. The suspicion blossomed into conviction and despite himself he failed to suppress a giggle. "That was me, finishing my test. I hit that kickbar by accident just an hour ago."

Saltus objected. "My test didn't make a noise like that. William didn't."

Chaney showed him the watch. "You said I went up an hour. That's *now*. Did you kick yourself back?"

"No—we waited for the engineers to pull us back."

"But I kicked; I propelled myself from *here*, from a minute ago." He looked at the door through which the two men had run. "If that computer has registered a power loss, I did it. Do you suppose they'll take it out of my pay?"

They were outside in the warm sunshine of a summer afternoon. The Illinois sky was dark and clouded in the far west, promising a night storm.

Arthur Saltus looked at the storm clouds and asked: "I wonder if those engineers were sweeping bilge? Do you think they really know what they're talking about? Power surges and time paths and water that won't leak?"

Chaney shrugged. "A hair perhaps divides the false from the true. They have the advantage."

Saltus gave him a sharp glance. "You're borrowing again—and I think you've changed it to boot."

"A word or two," Chaney acknowledged. "Do you recall the rest of it? The remaining three lines of the verse?"

"No."

Chaney repeated the verse, and Saltus said: "Yes."

"All right, Commander. That machine down there is our Alif; the TDV is an Alif. With it, we can search for the treasure house."

"Maybe."

"No maybes: we *can*. We can search out *all* the treasure houses in history. The archeologists and the historians will go crazy with joy." He followed the man's gaze to the west, where he thought he heard low thunder. "If this wasn't a political project it wouldn't be wasted on Chicago. The Smithsonian would have a different use for the vehicle."

"Hah—I can read your mind, civilian! You wouldn't go up at all, you'd go back. You'd go scooting back to the year Zero, or some such, and watch those old scribes make scrolls. You've got a one-track mind."

"Not so," Chaney denied. "And there was no year Zero. But you're right about one thing: I wouldn't go up. Not with all the treasure houses of history waiting to be opened, explored, cataloged. I wouldn't go up."

"Where then, mister? Back where?"

Chaney said dreamily: "Eridu, Larsa, Nippur, Kish, Kufah, Nineveh, Uruk . . ."

"But those are just old—old cities, I guess."

"Old cities, old towns, long dead and gone—as Chicago will be when its turn comes. They are the treasure houses, Commander. I want to stand on the city wall at Ur and watch the Euphrates flood; I want to know how *that* story got into Genesis. I want to stand on the plains before Uruk and see Gilgamesh rebuild the city walls; I want to *see* that legendary fight with Enkidu.

"But more, I want to stand in the forests of Kadesh and see Muwatallis turn back the Egyptian tide. I think you'd both like to see that. Muwatallis was out-manned, out-wheeled, lacking everything but guts and intelligence; he caught Ramses' army separated into four divisions and what he did to them changed the course of Western history. It happened three thousand years ago but if the Hittites *had* lost—if Ramses had beaten Muwatallis—we'd likely be Egyptian subjects today."

Saltus: "I can't speak the language."

"You would be speaking it—or some local dialect—if Ramses had won." A gesture. "But that's what *I'd* do if I had the Alif and the freedom of choice."

Arthur Saltus stood lost in thought, looking at the western cloudbank. The thunder was clearly heard.

After a space he said: "I can't think of a blessed thing, mister. Not one thing I'd want to see. I may as well go up to Chicago."

"I stand in awe before a contented man," Chaney said. "The dust bin of history is no more than that."

EIGHT

BRIAN CHANEY was splashing in the pool the next morning before most of the station personnel had finished their breakfasts. He swam alone, enjoying the luxury of solitude after his customary walk from the barracks. The early morning sun was blindingly bright on the water, a contrast from the night just past: the station had been raked by a severe thunderstorm during the night, and blown debris still littered the streets.

Chaney turned on his back and filled his lungs with air, to float lazily on the surface of the pool. He was contented. His eyes closed to shut out the brightness.

He could almost imagine himself back on the Florida beach—back to that day when he loafed at the water's edge, watching the gulls and the distant sail and doing nothing more strenuous than speculating on the inner fears of the critics and readers who had damned him and damned his translation of the Revelations scroll. Yes, and back to the day before he'd met Katrina. Chaney hadn't been aware of a personal vacuum then, but when they parted—when this mission was finished—he would be aware of one. He would miss the woman. Parting company with Katrina would hurt, and when he went back to the beach he'd be keenly aware of the new vacuum.

He had been unnecessarily rude to her when she first approached him, and he regretted that now; he had believed her to be only another newspaper woman there to badger him. He wasn't on civilized speaking terms with newspaper people. Nor did Chaney like to admit to jealousy—a childish emotion—but Arthur Saltus had aroused in him some response suspiciously close to jealousy. Saltus had moved in and boldly taken possession of the woman, another hurt.

But that wasn't the only hurt.

His trigger finger was sore, stiff, and his shoulder hurt like sin; they had assured him it was a light rifle but after an hour of firing it, Chaney wholly disbelieved them. Even in his sleep the bullying figure of the Major stood over him, needling him: "Squeeze it, squeeze it, don't yank—don't jerk—squeeze it!" Chaney squeezed it and four or five times out of ten managed to hit the target. He thought that remarkable, but his companions did not. Moresby was so disgusted he tore the rifle from Chaney's grasp and put five shots through the bull's eye in the space between one breath and the next.

The hand gun was worse. The Army model automatic seemed infinitely lighter when compared to the rifle, but because he could not use his left hand to lift and steady the barrel he missed the target eight times out of ten. The two good shots were only on the rim of the target.

Moresby muttered: "Give the civilian a shotgun!" and stalked away.

Arthur Saltus had taught him camera techniques.

Chaney was familiar with the common hand cameras and with the mounted rigs used in laboratories to copy documents, but Saltus introduced him to a new world. The holograph camera was new. Saltus said that film had been relegated to the cheap cameras; the holograph instruments used a thin ribbon of embossed nylon which would withstand almost any abuse and yet deliver a recognizable picture. He scoured a nylon negative with sandpaper, then made a good print. Adequate lighting was no longer a problem; the holograph would produce a satisfactory picture taken in the rain.

Chaney experimented with a camera strapped to his chest, with the lens peering through a buttonhole in his jacket where a button should be; there was another that fitted over his left shoulder, with the lens appearing to be a lodge emblem attached to his lapel—a remote cable ran down the inside of his coat sleeve and the plunger nestled in the palm of his hand. A fat belt buckle held a camera. A bowler hat concealed a camera. A folded newspaper was actually a motion picture camera in camouflage, and a smart looking attaché case was another. Microphones for the tape recorders—worn under the coat, or in the pocket—were buttons or emblems or tie clasps or stays tucked inside shirt collars.

He usually managed a decent picture—it was difficult to produce a poor one with the holograph instruments, but Saltus was often dissatisfied, pointing out this or that or the other thing which would have resulted in a sharper image or a more balanced composition.

Katrina was photographed hundreds of times during the practice. She appeared to endure it with patience.

Chaney expelled a burst of air and started to sink. He flipped over on his stomach and swam under water to the edge of the pool. Grasping the tiled rim, he hauled himself out of the water and stared up in surprise at the grinning face of Arthur Saltus.

"Morning, civilian. What's new in ancient Egypt?"

Chaney peered past him. "Where is—?" He stopped.

"I haven't seen her," Saltus responded. "She wasn't in the mess hall—I thought she was here with *you.*"

Chaney wiped his face with a towel. "Not here. I've had the pool to myself."

"Hah—maybe old William is beating our time; maybe he's playing chess with her in a dark corner somewhere." Saltus grinned at that thought. "Guess what, mister?"

"What now?"

"I read your book last night."

"Shall I run for cover, or stand up for a medal?"

"No, no, not *that* one. I'm not interested in those old scrolls. I mean the other book you gave me, the one about the desert tribes—old Abraham, and all. Damn but that man made some fine pictures!" He sat down beside Chaney. "Remember that one of the Nabataean well or cistern or whatever it was, down there at the foot of the fortress?"

"I remember it. Well built. It served the fortress through more than one siege."

"Sure. The guy made that one with natural lighting. No flash, no sun reflectors, nothing, just natural light; you can see the detail of the stonework and the water level. And it was on film, too—he wasn't using nylon."

"You can determine that by examination?"

"Well, of course! *I* can. Listen, mister, that's good photography. That man is good."

"Thank you. I'll tell him next time I see him."

Saltus said: "Maybe I'll read your book someday. Just to find out why they're shooting at you."

"It doesn't have pictures."

"Oh, I can read all the easy words." He stretched out his legs and stared up at the underside of the gaudy beach umbrella. A spider was beginning a web between the metal braces. "This place is dead this morning."

"What's to do? Other than a rousing game with the Major, or another session at the rifle range?"

Saltus laughed. "Shoulder hurt? That will wear away. Say, if I could find Katrina, I'd throw her into the pool and then jump in with her—that's where the action is!"

Chaney thought it wisest not to answer. His gaze went back to the sun-bright waters of the pool, now empty of swimmers and slowly regaining placidity. He remembered the manner in which Saltus had played there with Katrina, but the memory wasn't a pleasant one. He hadn't joined in the play because he felt self-conscious for the first time in his life, because his physique was a poor one compared to the muscular body of the Commander, because the woman seemed to prefer the younger man's company to his. That was hurtful to admit.

Chaney caught a quick movement at the gate.

"The Major has found us."

Major Moresby hustled into the recreation area and strode toward the pool, seeking them. Halfway across the patio he found them beneath the umbrella and turned hard. He was breathing heavily and his face flushed with excitement.

"Get up off your duff!" he barked at the Commander.

And to Chaney: "Get your clothes on. Urgent. They want us in the briefing room *now*. I have a car waiting."

"Hey—what goes?" Saltus was out of the chair.

"We do. Somebody has made the big decision. Damn it, Chaney, move!"

"The field trials?" Saltus demanded. "The field trials? This morning? Now?"

"This morning, now," Moresby acknowledged. "Gilbert Seabrooke brought the decision; they roused me out of bed. We're moving up, after all!" He turned on Chaney. "Will you haul your ass out of that chair, civilian? Move it! I'm waiting, everybody is waiting, the vehicle is cranked up and waiting."

Chaney jumped from the chair, heart pounding against his rib cage.

Moresby: "Katrina said to use the car. You are *not* to waste time walking, and that is an order."

Chaney's reflexes were slower, but he was already racing for the bath house to change. They ran with him. "I'm not walking."

"Where are we going?" Saltus demanded breathlessly. "I mean when? *When* in Joliet? Did you get the word?"

"Katrina gave the word. You won't like it, Art."

Arthur Saltus stopped abruptly in the doorway and Chaney collided with him.

"Why won't I like it?"

"Because it's a political thing, a damned political thing, after all! Katrina said the decision came down early this morning from the White House—from *him*. We should have expected something like that."

Slow repeat: "Why won't I like it?"

Moresby said with disdain: "We're going up two years to a date in November. November 6, 1980, a Thursday. The President wants to know if he'll be re-elected."

Arthur Saltus stared in open-mouthed astonishment. After a space of disbelief he turned to Chaney.

"What was that word again, mister? In Aramaic?"

Brian Chaney told him.

Brian Chaney
Joliet, Illinois
6 November 1980

If we open a quarrel between the past
and the present,
We shall find that we have lost the future.

— Winston Churchill

NINE

CHANEY HAD NO forewarning of something amiss.

The red light blinked out. He reached up to unlock the hatch and throw it open. The green light went dark. Chaney grasped the two handrails and pulled himself to a sitting position, with his head and shoulders protruding through the hatchway. He was alone in the room, as he expected to be. He struggled through the hatch and climbed over the side, easing himself down the hull until his feet touched the stool. The vehicle felt icy cold. Chaney reached up to slam shut the hatch, then cast a curious glance at the monitoring cameras. He hoped those future engineers approved his obedience to the ritual.

Chaney looked at his watch: 10:03. That was expected. He had kicked off less than a minute ago, the third and last to move up. He sought out the calendar and clock on the wall to verify the date and the time: *6 Nov 80*. The clock read 7:55. A thermometer had been added to the instrument group to record outside temperature: 31 degrees F.

Chaney hesitated, unsure of his next move. The time was not right; it should have been ten o'clock, plus or minus eight minutes. He made a mental note to tell the engineers what he thought of their guidance system.

The first of the field trials had been launched at a few minutes past nine, with Major Moresby claiming his due. Thirty minutes later Arthur Saltus followed the Major into the future, and thirty minutes after him Chaney climbed into the bucket and was kicked off. All arrivals on target were supposed to be identical with departure times, plus or minus eight minutes. Chaney had expected to surface about ten and find the others waiting for him. They were scheduled to regroup in the fallout shelter, equip themselves, and travel to the target city in separate automobiles to effect a wider coverage of the area.

Katrina had given each of them explicit instructions and then wished them well.

Saltus had said: "Aren't you coming down to see us off?"

She'd replied: "I will wait in the briefing room, sir."

The wall clock moved to 7:56.

Chaney abandoned his irresolution. Rounding the hull of the vehicle, he opened the locker and reached for the suit hung there only minutes before. Small surprise. His suit had been cleaned and pressed and was now hanging in a paper sheath provided by the dry cleaner. Next to his were similar packages belonging to Moresby and Saltus. His name was written across the sheath and he recognized the woman's handwriting. *He* was first in: seniority.

Chaney ripped away the paper and dressed quickly, aware of the chill in the room. The white shirt he found in the locker was a new one and he looked with some interest at the wavy, patterned collar. Style, 1980. The sheath was jammed back into the locker as a mocking message.

Leaving the vehicle room, Chaney strode down the well-lighted corridor to the fallout shelter, conscious of the cameras watching his every step. The basement, the entire building, was cloaked in silence; the lab engineers would avoid contact with him as he must avoid them—but they had the advantage: they could examine a quaint specimen from two years in the past while he could only speculate on who was on the other side of the wall. Their door was shut. Chaney pushed the shelter door open and the overhead lights flashed on in automatic response. The room was empty of life.

Another clock above a workbench read 8:01.

Chaney strode into the shelter to stop, turn, stare, inspect everything open to his gaze. Except for a few new objects on the workbench the room was precisely the same as he'd last seen it, a day or two before. He was expected. Three tape recorders had been removed from the stores and set out on the bench, along with an unopened box of fresh tape; two still cameras designed to be worn over the shoulder were there, together with a motion picture camera for Arthur Saltus and new film for all three instruments. Three long envelopes rested atop the cameras, and again he recognized Katrina's handwriting.

Chaney tore his open, hoping to find a personal note, but it was curiously cool and impersonal. The envelope gave up a gate pass and identification papers bearing the date, 6 November 1980. A small photograph of his face was affixed to the identification. The brief note advised him not to carry arms off the station.

He said aloud: "Saltus, you've shut me out!" This evidence suggested the woman had made a choice in the intervening two years—unless he was imagining things.

Chaney prepared himself for the outside. He found a heavy coat and a rakish cap in the stores that were good fits, then armed himself with camera, recorder, nylon film and tape. He took from a money box what he thought would be an adequate supply of cash (there was a shiny new dime and several quarters bearing the date 1980; the portraits on the coins had not been changed), and a drawer yielded a pen and notebook, and a flashlight that worked. A last careful survey of the room suggested nothing else that would be useful to him, and he made ready to leave.

A clock told 8:14.

Chaney scrawled a quick note on the back of his torn

envelope and propped it against the motion picture camera: *Arrived early for a swim. Will look for you laggards in town. Protons are perfidious.*

He stuffed the ID papers in his pocket and quit the shelter. The corridor was as silent and empty as before. Chaney climbed the stairway to the operations door and stopped with no surprise to read a painted sign.

> DO NOT CARRY WEAPONS BEYOND THIS DOOR. FEDERAL LAW PROHIBITS THE POSSESSION OF FIREARMS BY ALL EXCEPT LAW ENFORCEMENT OFFICERS, AND MILITARY PERSONNEL ON ACTIVE DUTY. DISARM BEFORE EXITING.

Chaney fitted two keys into the twin locks and shoved. A bell rang somewhere behind him. The operations door rolled easily on rolamite tracks. He stepped outside into the chill of 1980. The time was 8:19 on a bleak November morning and there was a sharp promise of snow in the air.

He recognized one of the three automobiles parked in the lot beyond the door: it was the same car Major Moresby had driven a short while ago—or two years ago—when he hustled Chaney and Saltus from the pool to the lab. The keys were in the ignition lock. Walking to the rear of the vehicle, he stared for a moment at the red and white license plate to convince himself he *was* where he was supposed to be: Illinois 1980. Two other automobiles parked beyond the first one appeared to be newer, but the only visible change in their design appeared to be fancy grills and wheel caps. So much for public taste and Detroit pandering.

Chaney didn't enter the car immediately.

Moving warily, half fearful of an unexpected meeting, he circled the laboratory building to reconnoiter. Nothing seemed changed. The installation was just as he remembered it: the streets and sidewalks well repaired and clean—policed daily by the troops on station—the lawns carefully tended and prepared for the approach of winter, the trees now bare of foliage. The heavy front door was closed and the familiar black and yellow fallout shelter sign still hung above it. There was no guard on duty. On an impulse, Chaney tried the front door but found it locked—and that was a commentary of some kind on the usefulness of the fallout shelter below. He continued his inspection tour all the way around again to the parking lot.

Something *was* changed behind the lot.

Chaney eyed the space for a moment and then recognized the difference. What had been nothing more than a wide expanse of lawn two years ago was now a flower garden; the flowers were wilted with the nearness of winter and many of the dead blossoms and vines had been cleared away, but in the intervening two years someone—Katrina?—had caused a garden to be planted in an otherwise empty plot of grass.

Chaney left a sign for Major Moresby. He placed a shiny new quarter on the concrete sill of the locked door. A moment later he turned the key in the ignition and drove off toward the main gate.

The gatehouse was lighted on the inside and occupied by an officer and two enlisted men in the usual MP uniforms. The gate itself was shut but not locked. Beyond it, the black-topped road stretched away into the distance, aiming for the highway and the distant city. A white line had been newly painted—or repainted—down the center of the road.

"Are you going off station, sir?"

Chaney turned, startled by the sudden question. The officer had emerged from the gatehouse.

He said: "I'm going into town."

"Yes, sir. May I see your pass and identification?"

Chaney passed over his papers. The officer read them twice and studied the photograph affixed to the ID.

"Are you carrying weapons, sir? Are there any weapons in the car?"

"No, to both."

"Very good, sir. Remember that Joliet has a six o'clock curfew; you must be free of the city limits before that hour or make arrangements to stay overnight."

"Six o'clock," Chaney repeated. "I'll remember. Is it the same in Chicago?"

"Yes, sir." The officer stared at him. "But you can't enter Chicago from the south since the wall went up. Sir, are you going to Chicago? I will have to arrange for an armed guard."

"No—no, I'm not going there. I was curious."

"Very well, sir." He waved to a guard and the gate was opened. "Six o'clock, sir."

Chaney drove away. His mind was not on the road. The warning indicated that a part of the Indic report had correctly called the turn: the larger cities had taken harsh steps to control the growing lawlessness, and it was likely that many of them had imposed strict dusk-to-dawn curfews. A traveler not out of town before dusk would need hotel accommodations to keep him off the streets. But the reference to the Chicago wall puzzled him. *That* wasn't foreseen, nor recommended. A wall to separate what from what? Chicago had been a problem since the migrations from the south in the 1950s—but a wall?

The winding private road led him to the highway. He pulled up to a stop sign and waited for a break in traffic on route 66. Across the highway, an officer in a parked state patrol car eyed his license plate and then glanced up to inspect his face. Chaney waved, and pulled into traffic. The state car did not leave its position to follow him.

A second patrol car was parked at the outskirts of town, and Chaney noted with surprise that two men in the back seat appeared to be uniformed national guardsmen. The bayonet-tipped rifles were visible. His face and his license were given the same scrutiny and their attention moved on to the car behind him.

He said aloud (but to himself): "Honest, fellas, *I'm* not going to start a revolution."

The city seemed almost normal.

Chaney found a municipal parking lot near the middle of town and had to search for the rare empty space. He was outraged to learn it cost twenty-five cents an hour to park, and grudgingly put two of Seabrooke's quarters into the meter. A clerk sweeping the sidewalk before a shuttered store front directed him to the public library.

He stood on the steps and waited until nine o'clock for the doors to open. Two city squad cars passed him while he waited and each of them carried a guardsman riding shotgun beside the driver. They stared at him and the clerk with the broom and every other pedestrian.

An attendant in the reading room said: "Good morning. The newspapers aren't ready."

She hadn't finished the chore of rubber-stamping the library name on each of the front pages, or of placing the steel rods through the newspaper centerfolds. A hanging rack stood empty, awaiting the dailies. An upside-down headline read: JCS DENIED BAIL.

Chaney said: "No hurry. I would like the Commerce and Agriculture yearbooks for the past two years, and the Congressional Record for six or eight weeks." He knew that Saltus and the Major would buy newspapers as soon as they reached town.

"All the governmental publications are in aisle two, on your left. Will you need assistance?"

"No, thanks. I know my way through them."

He found what he wanted and settled down to read.

The lower house of Congress was debating a tax reform bill. Chaney laughed to himself and noted the date of the Record was just three weeks before election. In some few respects the debate seemed a filibuster, with a handful of representatives from the oil and mineral states engaging in a running argument against certain of the proposals on the pious grounds that the so-called reforms would only penalize those pioneers who risk capital in the search for new resources. The gentleman from Texas reminded his colleagues that many of the southwestern fields had run dry—the oil reserves exhausted—and the Alaskan fields were yet ten years from anticipated capacity. He said the American consumer was facing a serious oil and gasoline shortage in the near future; and he got in a blow at the utility people by reminding that the hoped-for cheap power from nuclear reactors was never delivered.

The gentleman from Oregon once injected a plea to repeal the prohibition on cutting timber, claiming that not only were outlaw lumberjacks doing it, but that foreign opportunists were flooding the market with cheap wood. The presiding officer ruled that the gentleman's remarks were not germane to the discussion at hand.

The Senate appeared to be operating at the customary hectic pace.

The gentleman from Delaware was discussing the intent of a resolution to improve the lot of the American Indian, by explaining that his resolution would direct the Bureau of Indian Affairs to act on a previous resolution passed in 1954, directing them to terminate government control of the Indians and return their resources to them. The gentleman complained that no worthwhile action had been taken on the 1954 resolution and the plight of the Indian was as sorry as ever; he urged his fellows to give every consideration to the new resolution, and hoped for a speedy passage.

The sergeant-at-arms removed several people from the balcony who were disturbing the chamber.

The gentleman from South Carolina inveighed against a phenomenon he called "an alarming tide of ignorants" now flowing from the nation's colleges into government and industry. He blamed the shameful tide on "the radical-left revamping and reduction of standard English courses by misguided professors in our institutions of higher learning," and urged a return to the more rigorous disciplines of yesteryear when every student could "read, write, and talk good American English in the tradition of their fathers."

The gentleman from Oklahoma caused to be inserted in the Record a complete news item circulated by a press wire service, complaining that the nation's editors had either ignored it or relegated it to the back pages, which was a disservice to the war effort.

GRINNELL ASSESSES ARMS

Saigon (AP): General David W. Grinnell arrived in Saigon Saturday to assess what progress South Asian Special Forces have made in assuming a bigger share of the fighting chores.

Grinnell, making his third visit to the war zone in two years, said he was keenly interested in the course of the so-called Asian Citizen Program, and planned to talk to the fighting men in the countryside to find out first-hand how things were going.

With additional American troop commitments pegged in part on the effectiveness of South Asian Special Forces (SASF), Grinnell's visit sparked rumors of a fresh troop build-up in the hard hit northern sectors. Unofficial estimates set a figure of two million Americans now in combat in the Asian Theater, which the military command refuses to confirm or deny.

Asked about new arrivals, Grinnell said: "That is something the President will have to decide at the proper time." General Grinnell will confer with American military and civilian officials on all fighting fronts before returning to Washington next week.

Chaney closed the record with a sense of despair and pushed the stack aside. Wanting to lose himself in less depressing but more familiar matters, he opened a copy of the current Commerce yearbook and sought out the statistical tables that were his stock in trade.

The human lemmings hadn't changed their habits. A bellwether indicating the migration patterns from one area to another was the annual ton-miles study of interstate shipments of household goods; the family that removed together grooved together. The flow continued into California and Florida, as he had forecast, and the adjoining tables revealed corresponding increases in tonnage for consumer durables and foodstuffs not indigenous to those states. The shipment of automobiles (assembled, new) into California had sharply decreased, and that surprised him. He had supposed that the proposal to ban automobiles in the state by 1985 would only result in an accelerated flow—a kind of hoarding—but the current figures suggested that state officials had found a way to discourage hoarding and depress the market at the same time. Prohibitive taxation, most likely. New York City should note the success of the program.

Chaney began filling his notebook.

The measured tolling of a bell somewhere outside the library brought him up from the book with surprise, and a flurry of aged men from the newspaper racks toward the door underscored the passage of time. It was the noon hour.

Chaney put away the government publications and cast a speculative eye on the attendant. A girl had replaced the older woman on duty earlier. He studied her for a space and decided on an approach least likely to arouse suspicion.

"Excuse me."

"Yes?" The girl looked up from a copy of *Teen Spin.*

Chaney consulted his notebook. "Do you remember the date of the Chicago wall? The *first* date—the earliest beginning? I can't pin it down."

The girl stared into the air above his head and said: "I think it was in August . . . no, no, it was the last week of July. I'm pretty sure it was the last of July." Her gaze came down to his. "We have the news magazines on file if you want me to get it for you."

Chaney caught the hint. "Don't bother; I'll look. Where are those files?"

She pointed behind him. "Fourth aisle, next to the windows. They may not be in chronological order."

"I'll find them. Thank you." Her head was already bending over the magazine as he turned away.

The Chicago wall ran down the middle of Cermak Road.

It stretched from Burnham Park on the lakefront (where it consisted only of barbed wire), westward to Austin Avenue in Cicero (where it finally ended in another loose skein of barbed wire in a white residential neighborhood). The wall was built of cement and cinder blocks; of wrecked or stolen automobiles, burned-out shells of city buses, sabotaged police cars, looted and stripped semi-trailer trucks; of upended furniture, broken concrete, bricks, debris, garbage, excretion. Two corpses were a part of it between Ashland and Paulina Street. The barrier began going up on the night of July twenty-ninth, the third night of widespread rioting along Cermak Road; it was lengthened and reinforced every night thereafter as the idea spread until it was a fifteen-mile barricade cutting a city in two.

The black community south of Cermak Road had begun the wall at the height of the rioting, as a means of preventing the passage of police and fire vehicles. Both blacks and belligerent whites completed it. The corpses near Paulina Street had been foolish men who attempted to cross it.

There was no traffic over the wall, nor through it, nor along the north-south arteries intersecting Cermak Road. The Dan Ryan Expressway had been dynamited at 35th Street and again at 63rd Street; the Stevenson Expressway was breached at Pulaski Road. Aerial reconnaissance reported that nearly every major street in the sector was blocked or otherwise unfit for vehicular traffic; fires raged unchecked on South Halsted, and cattle had been loosed from their pens in the stockyards. Police and Army troops patrolled the city above the wall, while black militants patrolled below it. The government made no effort to penetrate the barrier, but instead appeared to be playing a waiting game. Rail and highway traffic from the east and south was routed in a wide swing around the zone, entering the city above the wall to the west; civilian air traffic was restricted to higher elevations. Road blocks were thrown up at the Indiana line, and along Interstate 80.

Chicago above the wall counted three hundred dead and two thousand-plus injured during the rioting and the building of the barricade. No one knew the count below the wall.

By the second week of August, troops had encircled the affected area and had dug in for a siege; none but authorized personnel were permitted to enter and none but white refugees were permitted to leave. Incomplete figures placed the number of emerging refugees at about six hundred thousand, although that figure was well below the known white population living in the rebellious zone. Attempts were being made daily—with small success—to rescue white families believed to be still alive in the area. Penetration was not possible from the north but search parties from the western and southern boundaries made several sallies into the area, sometimes working as far north as Midway Airport. Refugees were being relocated to downstate cities in Illinois and Indiana.

North Chicago was under martial law, with a strict dusk-to-dawn curfew. Violaters moving on the streets at night were shot on sight and identified the following day, when the bodies could be removed. South Chicago had no curfew but shootings continued day and night.

At the end of October with the election only a week away, the northern half of the city was relatively quiet; firing across the wall under cover of darkness had fallen off to nuisance shooting, but the police and troops had been issued new orders not to fire unless fired upon. City water service into the zone continued but electricity was curtailed.

On the Sunday morning before election, a party of about two hundred unarmed blacks had approached Army lines at Cicero Avenue and asked for sanctuary. They were turned back. Washington announced the siege was effective and was already putting an end to the rebellion. Hunger and pestilence would destroy the wall.

Chaney strode across the room to the newspaper rack.

Thursday morning editions confirmed their projections

published the day before: President Meeks had carried all but three states and won re-election by a landslide. A local editorial applauded the victory and claimed it was earned by "the President's masterful handling of the Chicago Confrontation."

Brian Chaney emerged from the library to stand on the steps under a cold November sun. He knew a sense of fear, of confusion—an uncertainty of where to turn. A city police cruiser passed the building, with an armed guardsman riding beside the driver.

Chaney knew why they both stared at him.

TEN

HE WANDERED aimlessly along the street looking in store windows which were not boarded over, and at parked automobiles along the curb. None of the obviously newer cars were much changed from the older models parked ahead and behind; it was a personal satisfaction to see Detroit edging away from the annual model change and back to the more sensible balance of three decades ago.

Chaney stopped by the post office to mail a postcard to an old friend at the Indiana Corporation, and found the cost had climbed to ten cents. (He also made a mental note *not* to tell Katrina. She would probably claim he had fouled up the future.)

A grocery store window was entirely plastered over with enormous posters proclaiming deep price cuts on every item: ten thousand and one cut-rate bargains from wall to wall. Being a curious futurist, he walked in to inspect the bargains. Apples were selling at two for a quarter, bread at forty-five cents a pound loaf, milk at ninety-nine cents a half gallon, eggs at one dollar a dozen, ground beef at a dollar and twenty-nine cents a pound. The beef was well larded with fat. He bent over the meat counter to check the price of his favorite steak and discovered it was two dollars and forty-nine cents a pound. On an impulse, he paid ninety cents for an eight-ounce box of something called *Moon Capsules* and found them to be vitamin-enriched candies in three flavors. The advertising copy on the back panel claimed that NASA fed the capsules to the astronauts living on the moon, for extra jump-jump-jumping power.

The store boasted an innovation that was new to him. A customers' lounge was fitted out with soft chairs and a large television, and Chaney dropped into a chair to look at the colored glass eye, curious about the programming. He was quickly disappointed. The television offered him nothing but an endless series of commercials featuring the products available in the store; there was no entertainment to break their monotony. He timed the series: twenty-two commercials in forty-four minutes, before an endless tape began repeating itself.

Only one made a lasting impression.

A splendidly beautiful girl with glowing golden skin was stretched out nude on a pink-white cloud; a sensuous cloud of smoke or wisp formed and changed and reformed itself to caress her saffron body with loving tongues of vapor. The girl was smoking a golden cigarette. She lay in dreamy indolence, eyes closed, her thighs sometimes moving with euphoric languor in response to a kiss of cloud. There was no spoken message. At spaced intervals during the two minutes, five words were flashed across the screen beneath the nude: *Go aloft with Golden Marijane.*

Chaney decided the girl's breasts were rather small and flat for his tastes.

He quit the store and returned to his car, finding an overtime parking ticket fastened to the windshield. The fine was two dollars, if paid that same day. Chaney scribbled a note on a page torn from his notebook and put it inside the envelope in lieu of two dollars; the ticket was then dropped into a receptacle fastened to a nearby meter post. He thought the local police would appreciate his thought.

That done, he wheeled out of the lot and retraced his route toward the distant station. The sunset curfew was yet some hours away but he was done with Joliet—nearly done with 1980. It seemed much colder and inhospitable than the temperature would suggest.

A state patrol car parked on the outskirts watched him out of town.

The gatehouse was lighted on the inside and occupied by an officer and two military policemen; they were not the same men who had checked him out earlier in the day but the routine was the same.

"Are you coming on station, sir?"

Chaney looked across the hood of his car at the gate just beyond the bumper. "Yes, I thought I would."

"May I see your pass and identification?"

Chaney gave up the necessary papers. The officer

read them twice and studied the photograph affixed to one, then raised his eyes to compare the photograph to the face.

"You have been visiting in Joliet?"

"Yes."

"But not Chicago?"

"No."

"Did you acquire weapons while you were off-station?"

"No."

"Very well, sir." He waved to the guard and the gate was opened for him. "Please drive through."

Brian Chaney drove through and steered the car to the parking lot behind the laboratory building. The other two automobiles were absent, as was the shiny quarter marker.

He unloaded the paraphernalia from his pockets and from under his coat, only to realize with dismay that he hadn't taken a single photograph: not one fuzzy picture of a scowling policeman or an industrious side-walk sweeper. That omission was apt to be received with something less than enthusiasm. Chaney fitted a tape cartridge into the recorder and flipped open his notebook; he thought he could easily fill two or three tapes with an oral report for Katrina and Gilbert Seabrooke. His personal shorthand was brief to the extreme—and unreadable by anyone else—but long experience in the tank enabled him to flesh out a report that was a reasonable summary of the Commerce and Agriculture yearbooks. Facts were freely interspersed with opinions, and figures with educated guesses, until the whole resembled a statistical and footnoted survey of that which Seabrooke wanted: a solid glimpse forward.

On the last tape he repeated all that he remembered

from the pages of the Congressional Record, and after a pause asked Katrina if she knew what General Grinnell was doing now? The old boy got around a lot.

Chaney left the gear on the seat and got out of the car to stretch his legs. He looked at the western sky to measure the coming of darkness, and guessed that he had an hour or two before sunset. His watch read 6:38 but it was two hours faster than the clock in the basement; the engineering limit of fifty hours was far away.

The inquisitive futurist decided on a tour.

Walking with an easy stride he followed the familiar route to the barracks but was surprised to find it dark—padlocked. That gave him pause. The building deserted? Was he gone from this place? Moresby, Saltus, himself, gone from the station?

This day, this hour, this *now* was two years after the successful tests of the TDV, two years after the animals had stopped riding into time and men had taken their places; this was two years after the launching of the field trials and the scheduled launch of the Chicago survey. All that work was over and done—mission completed. Wasn't it then reasonable to assume the team was disbanded and returned to their own corners of the world? Moresby, Saltus, himself, now working elsewhere? (Perhaps he should have sent that postcard to himself at Indic.)

Neither Gilbert Seabrooke nor Katrina had ever dropped a hint of future plans for the team; he had assumed they would be disbanded when the Chicago probe was concluded and he hadn't considered staying on. He couldn't imagine himself wanting to stay on. Well—with *one* reservation, of course. He *would* entertain the idea of a probe into the opposite direction: it would be sheer delight to poke and peer and pry into old Palestine before the arrival of the Roman Tenth Legion—well before their arrival.

He found himself on E Street.

The recreation area appeared not to have changed at all. The post theater wasn't yet opened, its parking lot was empty. The officers' club was already brightly lit and filled with music, but the second club nearby for enlisted men was dark and silent. The pool area was closed for the winter and its gate secured by a lock. Chaney peered through the fencing but saw nothing more than a deserted patio and a canvas covering stretched over the pool. The chairs and benches together with the tables and umbrellas had been stored away, leaving nothing but memories clashing with a cold November evening.

He turned away from the fence to begin an aimless wandering about the station. It seemed normal in every respect. Automobiles passed him, most of them going to the commissary; he was the only man on foot. The sound of an aircraft brought his head up, his eyes searching the sky. The plane was not visible—he supposed it was above the thickening cloud cover—but he could follow its passage by the sound; the craft was flying an air corridor between Chicago and St. Louis, a corridor which paralleled the railroad tracks below. In a few minutes it was gone. A drop of moisture struck his upturned face, and then another, the first few flakes of promised snow. The smell of snow had been in the air since morning.

Chaney turned about to retrace his steps.

Three automobiles waited side by side in the parking lot behind the lab. His companions were back, neither of them languishing in a Joliet jail—but he suspected it would be terribly easy to get into jail. Chaney lifted the hood of the nearest car and laid his hand on the motor block. He almost burned the skin from his palm. The hood was snapped shut, and he gathered up the gear from the seat of his own car.

The twin keys were fitted into the locks of the operations door and turned. A bell rang somewhere below as the door eased open.

"Saltus! Hello, down there—Saltus!"

The hurtful sound hit him with near physical impact. The sound was something like a massive rubber band snapped against his eardrums, something like a hammer smashing into a block of compressed air. It struck and rebounded with a tremulous sigh. The vehicle kicked back following its time path to home base. The sound hurt.

Chaney jumped through the door and pulled it shut behind him.

"Saltus?"

A sandy-haired muscular figure stepped through the open doorway of the fallout shelter below.

"Where the hell have *you* been, civilian?"

Chaney went down the steps two or three at a time. Arthur Saltus waited at the bottom with a handful of film.

"Out there—out there," Chaney retorted. "Knocking around this forsaken place, staring through the fences, sniffing at the cracks and peeping in windows. I couldn't find a spoor. I think we're gone from here, Commander

—dismissed and departed, the barracks padlocked. I hope we get a decent bonus."

"Civilian, have you been drinking?"

"No—but I could use one. What's in the stores?"

"You've been drinking," Saltus said flatly. "So what happened to you? We looked all over town."

"You didn't look in the library."

"Oh, hell! You would, and we didn't. Research stuff. What did you think of 1980, mister?"

"I don't like it, and I'll be liking it even less when I'm living in it. That milquetoast was re-elected and the country is going to hell in a handbasket. A forty-eight state sweep! Did you see the election results?"

"I saw them, and by this time William has passed the news to Seabrooke and Seabrooke is calling the President. He'll celebrate tonight. But *I'm* not going to vote for him, mister—I *know* I didn't vote for him. And if I'm living Stateside then—now—I'm going to choose one of those three states that voted for the other fellow, old What's-his-name, the actor fellow."

"Alaska, Hawaii, and Utah."

"What's Utah like?"

"Dry, lonely, and glowing with radioactivity."

"Make it Hawaii. Will you go back to Florida?"

Chaney shook his head. "I'll feel safer in Alaska."

Quickly: "You didn't get into trouble?"

"No, not at all; I walked softly and carried a sweet smile on my face. I was polite to a mousy librarian. I didn't sass the cops or buy any pork in a grocery store." He laughed at a memory. "But someone will have to explain a parking ticket when they trace the license number back to this station."

Saltus looked his question.

Chaney said: "I got a ticket for overtime parking. It was an envelope affair; I was supposed to put two dollars in the envelope and drop it in a collection box. I didn't. Commander, I struck a blow for liberty. I wrote a note."

Saltus eyed him. "What was in the note?"

"We shall overcome."

Saltus tried to stifle startled laughter, but failed. After a space he said: "Seabrooke will fire you, mister!"

"He won't have the chance. I expect to be far away when 1980 comes. Did you read the papers?"

"Papers! We bought *all* the papers! William grabbed up every new one he could find—and then read his horoscope first. He was down in the mouth; he said the signs were bad—negative." Saltus turned and waved toward newspapers spread out on the workbench. "I was photographing those when you came in. I'd rather copy them than read them onto a tape; I can blow the negs up to life size when we get back—larger than life, if they want them that way."

Chaney crossed to the bench and bent over to scan a page under the camera lens. "I didn't read anything but the election results, and an editorial."

After a moment he said excitedly: "Did you read this? China invaded Formosa—captured it!"

"Get the rest, read the rest of it," Saltus urged him. "That happened weeks ago, and *now* there's hell to pay in Washington. Canada has formally recognized the take-over and is sponsoring a move to kick Formosa out of the United Nations—give the seat to China. There's talk of breaking off diplomatic relations and stationing troops along the Canadian border. Civilian, that will be a real mess! I don't give a damn for diplomats and diplomatic relations, but we need another hostile like we need an earthquake."

Chaney tried to read between the lines. "China *does* need Canadian wheat, and Ottawa *does* like Chinese gold. That's been a thorn in Washington's side for thirty years. Are you a stamp collector?"

"Me? No."

"Not too many years ago, American citizens were forbidden to buy Chinese stamps from Canadian dealers; it was a crime to purchase or possess. Washington was being silly." He fell silent and finished reading the news story. "If these facts are reliable, Ottawa has made a whopping deal; they will deliver enough wheat to feed two or three Chinese provinces. The cash price wasn't made public, and that's significant—China bought more than wheat. Diplomatic recognition and Canadian support for a seat in the United Nations were probably included in the sale contract. That's smart trading, Commander."

"They're damned good shots, too. I told you that. I hate their guts but I don't downgrade them." He flipped a newspaper page and repositioned his camera. "What time did you get in this morning? How come you were early?"

"Arrival was at 7:55. I don't know why."

"Old William was upset, mister. We were supposed to be first but you fouled up the line of seniority."

Chaney said impatiently: "I can't explain it; it just happened. That gyroscope isn't as good as the engineers claimed it to be. Maybe the mercury protons need fixing, recharging or something. Did you hit the target?"

"Dead on. William was three or four minutes off. Seabrooke won't like it, I'll bet."

"I wasn't jumping with joy; I expected to find you and the Major waiting for me. And I wonder now what will happen on a long launch? Can those protons even *find* 2000?"

"If they can't, mister, you and me and old William will be wandering around in a fog without a compass; we'll just have to kick backwards and report a scrub."

The camera was moved again and another page copied.

"Hey—did you see the girls?"

"Two librarians. They were sitting down."

"Mister, you missed something good. They wear their hair in a funny way—I can't describe it—and their skirts aren't long enough to cover their sterns. Really, now, in November! Most of them wore long stockings to keep their legs warm while their sterns were freezing, and most of the time the stockings matched their lipstick: red and red, blue and blue, whatever. This year's fad, I guess. Ah, those girls!" He moved the camera and turned a page.

"I talked to them, I took pictures of them, I coaxed a phone number, I took a blonde lovely to lunch—it only cost eight dollars for the two of us. That's not too much, everything considered. The people here are just like us, mister. They're friendly, and they speak English. That town was one sweet liberty port!"

"But they should be like us," Chaney protested. "They're only two years away."

"That was a joke, civilian."

"Excuse me."

"Didn't they have jokes in the tank?"

"Of course they did. One of the mathematicians came up with proof that the solar system didn't exist."

Saltus turned around to stare. "Paper proof?"

"Yes. It filled three pages, as I recall. He said that if he faced the east and recited it aloud, everything would go *poof.*"

"Well, I hope he doesn't do that; I hope to hell he doesn't make a test run just to see if it works. I've got a special reason." Saltus studied the civilian for a long space. "Mister, do you know how to keep your mouth shut?"

Cautiously: "Yes. Is this a confidence?"

"You can't even tell William, or Katrina."

Chaney was uneasy. "Does it involve me? My work?"

"Nope—you have nothing to do with it, but I want a promise you'll keep quiet, no matter what. *I'm* not going to report it when I go back. It's something to keep."

"Very well. I'll keep it."

Saltus said: "I stopped in at the courthouse and had a look at the records—the vital statistics stuff—your kind of stuff. I found what I was looking for last March, eight months ago." He grinned. "My marriage license."

It was a kick in the stomach. "Katrina?"

"The one and only, the fair Katrina. Mister, I'm a married man! Me, a married man, chasing the girls and even taking one to lunch. Now, how will I explain that?"

Brian Chaney remembered the note found propped against his camera: it *had* sounded cool, impersonal, even distant. He recalled the padlocked barracks, the emptyness, the air of desertion. He and Major Moresby were gone from this place.

He said: "Let us therefore brace ourselves to our duties, be they favorable or not. John Wesley, I think."

Chaney kept his face turned away to mask his emotions; he suspected the sharp sense of loss was reflected on his face and he didn't care to stumble through an explanation or an evasion. He put away the heavy clothing worn on the outside and then replaced the unused camera and the nylon films. The reels of tape were removed from the recorder, and the recorder put back in the stores. As an afterthought, he replaced the identification papers and the gate pass in the torn envelope—alongside Katrina's note—and propped the envelope on the bench where she would find it.

Saltus had finished his task and was removing film from the copying camera. He had left the newspapers flung over the bench in disarray.

Chaney gathered them up into an orderly pile. When he had finished the housekeeping chore, a right-side-up headline said: JCS DENIED BAIL.

"Who is JCS? What did he do?"

Saltus stared in disbelief. "Damn it, civilian, didn't you do *anything* out there?"

"I didn't bother with the papers."

Incredulously: "What the hell—are you blind? Why do you think the cops were patrolling the town? Why do you think the state guards were riding shotgun?"

"Well—because of that Chicago business. The wall."

"Bigod!" Arthur Saltus stalked across the room to face him, suddenly impatient with his naivete. "No offense, mister, but sometimes I think you never left that ivory tower, that cloud bank in Indiana. You don't seem to know what's going on in the world—you've got your nose buried too deep in those damned old tables. Shape up, Chaney! Shape up before you get washed out." He jabbed a long index finger at the newspapers stacked on the bench. "This country is under martial law. JCS is the Joint Chiefs of Staff. General Grinnell,

General Brandon, Admiral Elstar, the top dogs. They tried to pull a fast one but got caught, they—that French word."

"Which French word?"

"For take-over."

Chaney was stunned. "Coup."

"*That's* the word. Coup. They marched into the White House to arrest the President and the Vice President, they tried to take over the government at gun point. Our own government, mister! You hear about that sort of thing down in South America all the time, but now, right here in *our* country!" Saltus stopped talking and made a visible effort to control himself. After a moment he said again: "No offense, mister. I lost my temper."

Chaney wasn't listening. He was running across the basement room to the stacked newspapers.

It happened not at the White House, but at the Presidential retreat at Camp David.

A power failure blacked out the area shortly before midnight on Monday night, election eve. The President had closed his re-election campaign and flown to Camp David to rest. An emergency lighting system failed to operate and the Camp remained in darkness. Two hundred troops guarding the installation fell back upon the inner ring of defenses according to a prearranged emergency plan, and took up positions about the main buildings occupied by the President, the Vice President, and their aides. They elected not to go underground as there was no indication of enemy action. Admiral Elstar was with the Presidential party, discussing future operations in the South Asian seas.

Thirty minutes after the blackout, Generals Grinnell and Brandon arrived by car and were admitted through the lines. At General Grinnell's command, the troops about-faced and established a ring of quarantine about the buildings; they appeared to be expecting the order. The two generals then entered the main building—with drawn weapons—and informed the President and the Vice President they were under military arrest, together with all civilians in the area. Admiral Elstar joined them and announced that the JCS were taking control of the government for an indefinite period of time; he expressed dissatisfaction with civilian mismanagement of the country and the war effort, and said the abrupt action was forced upon the Joint Chiefs. The President appeared to take the news calmly and offered no resistance; he asked the members of his party to avoid violence and cooperate with the rebellious officers.

The civilians were herded into a large dining room and locked in. As soon as they were alone the aides brought out gas masks which had previously been concealed there; the party donned the masks and crawled under heavy dining tables to wait. Mortar fire was heard outside.

Electric power was restored at just one o'clock. The firing stopped.

FBI agents also wearing masks breached the door from the opposite side and informed the President the rebellion was ended. The Joint Chiefs of Staff and the disloyal troops had been taken under cover of a gas barrage, by an undisclosed number of agents backed by Federal marshals. Casualties among the troops were held to a minimum. The Joint Chiefs were unharmed.

Helicopters ferried the Presidential party back to Washington, where the President requested immediate reactivation of the TV networks to announce the news of the attempted coup and its subsequent failure. Congress was called into an emergency session, and at the request of the President declared the country under martial law. The affair was done.

A White House spokesman admitted that the plot was known well in advance, but refused to reveal the source of the tip. He said the action was allowed to go as far as it did only to ascertain the number and the identities of the troops who supported the Joint Chiefs. The spokesman denied rumors that those troops had been nerve-gassed. He said the plotters were being charged with treason and were being held in separate jails; he would not disclose the locations other than to say they were dispersed away from Washington. The spokesman declined to answer questions regarding the number of FBI agents and Federal marshals involved in the action; he shrugged off unofficial reports that thousands had been mustered.

The only reliable information known was that large numbers of them had lain in concealment about Camp David for several days prior to the action. The spokesman would say only the two groups had courageously rescued the President and his party.

Brian Chaney was unaware that the lights dimmed and the hurtful rubber band smashed against his eardrums; he didn't hear the massive mallet smash into the block of compressed air and then rebound with a soft, oily sigh. He didn't know that Arthur Saltus had left him until he turned around and found himself alone.

Chaney stared around the empty shelter and shouted aloud: "Saltus!"

There was no answer.

He strode to the door and shouted into the corridor. "Saltus!"

Booming echoes, and then silence. The Commander was emerging from the vehicle at home base.

"Listen to the word from the ivory tower, Saltus! Listen to me! What do you want to bet the President didn't risk *his* precious skin under a dining room table? What do you want to bet that he sent a double to Camp David? He's no Greatheart, no Bayard; he couldn't be certain of the outcome." Chaney stepped into the corridor.

"*We* tipped him off, you idiot—*we* passed the word. *We* told him of the plot and of his re-election. Do you really think he has the guts to expose himself? Knowing that he would be re-elected the next day for another four-year ride? Do you think that, Saltus?"

Monitoring cameras looked at him under bright lights.

In the closed-off operations room, the TDV came back for him with an explosive burst of air.

Chaney turned on his heel and walked into the shelter. The newspapers were stacked, the gear was stored away, the clothing was neatly hung on racks. He had arrived and was preparing to leave with scarcely a trace of his passage.

The torn envelope caught his eye—the instructions from Katrina, and his identification papers, his gate pass. Cool, impersonal, distant—impassive, reserved. The wife of Arthur Saltus giving him last minute instructions for the field trial. She still lived on station; she still worked for the Bureau and the secret project—and unless the Commander had been reassigned to the war theater he was living with her.

But the barracks were dark, padlocked.

Brian Chaney knew the strong conviction that he was gone—that he and the Major had left the station. He didn't believe in crystal balls, in clairvoyance, hunches, precognition—Major Moresby could have all that claptrap to add to his library of phony prophets, but this one conviction was deeply fixed in his mind.

He was not *here* in November, 1980.

ELEVEN

CHANEY SENSED a subtle change in relationships. It was nothing he could clearly identify, mark, pin down, but a shade of difference was there.

Gilbert Seabrooke had sponsored a victory party on the night of their return, and the President telephoned from the White House to offer his congratulations on a good job well done. He spoke of an award, a medal to convey the grateful appreciation of a nation—even though the nation could not be informed of the stunning breakthrough. Brian Chaney responded with a polite *thank you,* and held his tongue. Seabrooke hovered nearby, watchful and alert.

The party wasn't as successful as it might have been. Some indefinable element of spontaneity was missing, some elusive spark which, when struck, changes over an ordinary party into a memorable evening of pleasure. Chaney would remember the celebration, but not with heady delight. He passed over the champagne in favor of bourbon, but drank that sparingly. Major Moresby seemed withdrawn, troubled, brooding over some inner problem, and Chaney guessed he was already preoccupied with the startling power struggle which was yet two years away. Moresby had made a stiff, awkward little speech of thanks to the President, striving to assure him without words of his continued loyalty. Chaney was embarrassed for him.

Arthur Saltus danced. He monopolized Katrina, even to the point of ignoring her whispered suggestions that he give unequal time to Chaney and the Major. Chaney didn't want to cut in. On another evening, another party before the field trials, he could have cut in as often as he dared, but now he sensed the same subtle change in Kathryn van Hise which was sensed in the others. The mountain of information brought back from Joliet, November 1980, had altered many viewpoints and the glossy overlay of the party could not conceal that alteration.

There was a stranger at the party, the liaison agent dispatched by the Senate subcommittee. Chaney discovered the man surreptitiously watching him.

The briefing room offered the familiar tableau.

Major Moresby was again studying a map of the Chicago area. He used a finger to mark the several major routes and backroads between Joliet and the metropolis; the finger also traced the rail line through the Chicago suburbs to the Loop. Arthur Saltus was studying the photographs he'd brought back from Joliet. He seemed particularly pleased with a print of an attractive girl standing on a windy street corner, half watching the cameraman and half watching for a car or a bus coming along the street behind. The print revealed an expert's hand in composition and cropping, with the girl limned in sunny backlighting.

Kathryn van Hise said: "Mr. Chaney?"

He swung around to face her. "Yes, Miss van Hise?"

"The engineers have given me firm assurance *that* mistake will not happen again. They have used the time since your return to rebuild the gyroscope. The cause has been traced to a vacuum leakage but that has been repaired. The error is to be regretted, but it will not happen again."

"But I *like* getting there first," he protested. "That's the only way I can assert seniority."

"It will not happen again, sir."

"Maybe. How do they *know* it won't?"

Katrina studied him.

"The next targets will each be a year apart, sir, to obtain a wider coverage. Would you care to suggest a tentative date?"

He betrayed surprise. "We may choose?"

"Within reason, sir. Mr. Seabrooke has invited each of you to suggest an appropriate date. The original plan of the survey must be followed, of course, but he would welcome your ideas. If you would rather not suggest a date, Mr. Seabrooke and the engineers will select one."

Chaney looked down the table at Major Moresby.

"What did you take?"

Promptly: "The Fourth of July, 1999."

"Why that one?"

"It has significance, after all!"

"I suppose so." He turned to Saltus. "And you?"

"My birthday, civilian: November 23rd, 2000. A nice

round number, don't you think? I thought so anyway. That will be my fiftieth birthday, and I can't think of a better way to celebrate." His voice dropped to a conspiratorial whisper. "I might take a jug with me. Live it up!"

Chaney considered the possibilities.

Saltus broke in. "Now, look here, mister—don't tell Seabrooke you want to visit Jericho on the longest day of summer, ten thousand years ago! *That* will get you the boot right through the front gate. Play by the rules. How would you like to spend Christmas in 2001? New Year's Eve?"

"No."

"Party-pooper. Wet blanket. What do you want?"

"I really don't care. Anything will do."

"Pick *something*," Saltus urged.

"Oh, just say 2000-plus. It doesn't much matter."

Katrina said anxiously: "Mr. Chaney, is something wrong?"

"Only that," he said, and indicated the photographs heaped on the table before Arthur Saltus, the new packets of mimeographed papers neatly stacked before each chair. "The future isn't very attractive right now."

"Do you wish to withdraw?"

"*No*. I'm not a quitter. When do we go up?"

"The launch is scheduled for the day after tomorrow. You will depart at one-hour intervals."

Chaney shuffled the papers on the table. "I suppose these will have to be studied now. We'll have to follow up."

"Yes, sir. The information you have developed on the trials has now become a part of the survey, and it is desirable that each segment be followed to its conclusion. We wish to know the final solutions, of course, and so you must trace these new developments." She hesitated. "*Your* role in the survey has been somewhat modified, sir."

He was instantly wary, suspicious. "In what way?"

"You will not go into Chicago."

"Not— But what the hell *am* I supposed to do?"

"You may visit any other city within range of your fifty-hour limit: Elgin, Aurora, Joliet, Bloomington, the city of your choice, but Chicago is now closed to you."

He stared at the woman, knowing humiliation. "But this is ridiculous! The problem may be cleared away, all but forgotten twenty-two years from now."

"It will not be forgotten so easily, sir. It *will* be wise to observe every precaution. Mr. Seabrooke has decided you may not enter Chicago."

"I'll resign—I'll quit!"

"Yes, sir, you may do that. The Indic contract will be returned to you."

"I *won't* quit!" he said angrily.

"As you wish."

Saltus broke in. "Civilian—sit down."

Chaney was surprised to discover himself standing. He sat down, knowing a mixture of frustration and humbled pride. He knotted his fingers together in his lap and pressed until they hurt.

After a space he said: "I'm sorry. I apologize."

"Apology accepted," Saltus agreed easily. "And don't let it trouble you. Seabrooke knows what he's doing—he doesn't want you naked and shivering in some Chicago jail, and he *doesn't* want some damned fool chasing you with a gun."

Major Moresby was eyeing him.

"I don't quite read you, Chaney. You've got more guts than I suspected, or you're a damned fool."

"When I lose my temper I'm a damned fool. I can't help myself." He felt Katrina watching him and turned back to her. "What am I supposed to do up there?"

"Mr. Seabrooke wishes you to spend the greater part of your time in a library copying pertinent information. You will be equipped with a camera having a copying lens when you emerge on target; your specific assignment is to photograph those books and periodicals which are germane to the information discovered in Joliet."

"You want me to follow the plots and the wars and the earthquakes through history. Make a copy of everything—steal a history book if I have to."

"You may purchase one, sir, and copy the pages in the room downstairs."

"That sounds exciting. A really wild visit to the future. Why not bring back the book with me?"

She hesitated. "I will have to ask Mr. Seabrooke. It seems reasonable, if you compensate for the weight."

"Katrina, I want to go outside and see *something*—I don't want to spend the time in a hole."

She said again: "You may visit any other city within range of your fifty-hour limit, sir. If it is safe."

Morosely: "I wonder what Bloomington is like."

"Girls!" Saltus answered. "One sweet liberty port!"

"Have you been there?"

"No."

"Then what are you talking about?"

"Just trying to cheer you up, civilian. I'm helpful that way." He picked up the photograph of the girl on the

Joliet street corner and waggled it between thumb and forefinger. "Go up in the summertime. It's nicer then."

Chaney looked at him with a particular memory in the front of his mind. Saltus caught it and actually blushed. He dropped the photograph and betrayed his fleeting guilt by sneaking a sidelong glance at Katrina.

She said: "We hope for a thorough coverage, sir."

"I wish I had more than fifty hours in a library. A decent research job requires several weeks, even months."

"It may be possible to return again and again, at proper intervals of course. I will ask Mr. Seabrooke."

Saltus: "Hey—what about that, Katrina? So what happens *after* the survey? What do we do next?"

"I can't give you a meaningful answer, Commander. At this point in the operation nothing beyond the Chicago probe is programmed. Nothing more could be programmed until we knew the outcome of these first two steps. A final answer cannot be made until you return from Chicago."

"Do you *think* we'll do something else?"

"I would imagine that other probes will be prepared when this one is satisfactorily completed and the resultant data analyzed." But then she added a hasty postscript. "That is only my opinion, Commander. Mr. Seabrooke has said nothing of possible future operations."

"I like your opinion, Katrina. It's better than a bucket in the South China Sea."

Chaney asked: "What happened to the alternatives? To Jerusalem, and Dallas?"

Moresby broke in. "What's this?"

The young woman explained them to Moresby and Saltus. Chaney realized that only he had been told of both alternate programs, and he wondered now if he had let a cat out of the bag by mentioning them.

Katrina said: "The alternatives are being held in abeyance; they may never be implemented." She looked at Brian Chaney and paused. "The engineers are studying a new matter related to vehicle operations; there appears to be a question whether the vehicle may operate in reverse prior to the establishment of a power source."

"Hey—what's *that* in English?"

"It means I can't go back to old Jericho," Chaney told him. "No electricity back there. I *think* she said the TDV needs power all along the line to move anywhere."

Moresby: "But I understood you to say those test animals had been sent back a year or more?"

"Yes, sir, that is correct, but the nuclear reactor has been operating for more than two years. The previous lower limit of the TDV was December 30, 1941, but now that may have to be drastically revised. If it is found that the vehicle may not operate prior to the establishment of its power source, the lower limit will be brought forward to an arbitrary date of two years ago. We do not wish to lose the vehicle."

Chaney said: "One of those bright engineers should sit down to his homework—lay out a paradox graph, or map, or whatever. Katrina, if you keep this thing going, you're going to find yourself up against a wall sooner or later."

She colored and betrayed a minute hesitation before answering him. "The Indiana Corporation has been approached on the matter, sir. Mr. Seabrooke has proposed that all our data be turned over to them for a crash study. The engineers are becoming aware of the problems."

Saltus looked around at Chaney and said: "Sheeg!"

Chaney grinned and thought to offer an apology to Moresby and the woman. "That's an old Aramaic word. But it expresses my feelings quite adequately." He considered the matter. "I can't decide what I would rather do: stay here and make paradoxes, or go back there and solve them."

Saltus said: "Tough luck, civilian. I was almost ready to volunteer. *Almost*, I said. I *think* I'd like to stand on the city wall at Larsa with you and watch the Euphrates flood; I *think* I'd like– What?"

"The city wall at Ur, not Larsa."

"Well, wherever it was. A flood, anyway, and you said it got into the Bible. You have a smooth line, you *could* persuade me to go along." An empty gesture. "But I guess that's all washed out now–you'll never go back."

"I don't believe the White House would authorize a probe back that far," Chaney answered. "They would see no political advantage to it, no profit to themselves."

Major Moresby said sharply: "Chaney, you sound like a fool!"

"Perhaps. But if we *could* probe backward I'd be willing to lay you money on certain political targets, but nothing at all on others. What would the map of Europe be like if Attila had been strangled in his crib?"

"Chaney, after all!"

He persisted. "What would the map of Europe be like if Lenin had been executed for the anti-Czarist plot, instead of his older brother? What would the map of the United States be like if George the Third had been cured of his dementia? If Robert E. Lee had died in infancy?"

"Civilian, they sure as hell won't let you go back *anywhere* with notions like that."

Dryly: "I wouldn't expect a bonus for them."

"Well, I guess not!"

Kathryn van Hise stepped into the breach.

"Please, gentlemen. Appointments have been made for your final physical examinations. I will call the doctor and inform him you are coming now."

Chaney grinned and snapped his fingers. "*Now.*"

She turned. "Mr. Chaney, if you will stay behind for a moment I would like more information on your field data."

Saltus was quickly curious. "Hey—what's this?"

She paged through the pile of mimeographed papers until she found the transcript of Chaney's tape recording. "Some parts of this report need further evaluation. If you care to dictate, Mr. Chaney, I will take it in shorthand."

He said: "Anything you need."

"Thank you." A half turn to the others at the table. "The doctor will be waiting, gentlemen."

Moresby and Saltus pushed back their chairs. Saltus shot Chaney a warning glance, reminding him of a promise. The reminder was answered with a confirming nod.

The men left the briefing room.

Brian Chaney looked across the table at Katrina in the silence they left behind. She waited quietly, her fingers laced together on the table top.

He remembered her bare feet in the sand, the snug delta pants, the see-through blouse, the book she carried in her hand and the disapproving expression she wore on her face. He remembered the startlingly brief swim suit worn in the pool, and the way Arthur Saltus had monopolized her.

"That was rather transparent, Katrina."

She studied him longer, not yet ready to speak. He waited for her to offer the next word, holding in his mind the image of that first glimpse of her on the beach.

At length: "What happened up there, Brian?"

He blinked at the use of his given name. It was the first time she had used it.

"Many, many things—I think we covered it all in our reports."

Again: "What happened up there, Brian?"

He shook his head. "Seabrooke will have to be satisfied with the reports."

"This is not Mr. Seabrooke's matter."

Warily: "I don't know what else I can tell you."

"Something happened up there. I am aware of a departure from the norm that prevailed before the trials, and I think you are too. Something has created a disparity, a subtle disharmony which is rather difficult to define."

"The Chicago wall, I suppose. And the JCS revolt."

"They were shocks to us all, but what else?"

Chaney gestured, searching for an escape route. "I found the barracks closed, locked. I think the Major and myself have left the station."

"But not Commander Saltus?"

"He may be gone—I don't know."

"You don't seem very sure of that."

"I'm not sure of anything. We were forbidden to

open doors, look at people, ask questions. I didn't open doors. I know only that our barracks have been closed—and I don't think Seabrooke let us move in with him."

"What would you have done if it was permissible to open doors?"

Chaney grinned. "I'd go looking for you."

"You believe I was on the station?"

"Certainly! You wrote notes to each of us—you left final instructions for us in the room downstairs. I knew your handwriting."

Hesitation. "Did you find similar evidence of anyone else being on station?"

Carefully: "No. Your note was the only scrap."

"Why has the Commander's attitude changed?"

Chaney stared at her, almost trapped. "Has it?"

"I think you are aware of the difference."

"Maybe. Everybody looks at me in a new light. I'm feeling paranoiac these days."

"Why has your attitude changed?"

"Oh? Mine too?"

"You are fencing with me, Brian."

"I've told you everything I *can* tell you, Katrina."

Her laced fingers moved restlessly on the tabletop. "I sense certain mental reservations."

"Sharp girl."

"Was there some—some personal tragedy up there? Involving any one of you?"

Promptly: "No." He smiled at the woman across the table to rob his next words of any sting. "And, Katrina—if you are wise, if you are very wise, you won't ask any more questions. I hold certain mental reservations; I *will* evade certain questions. Why not stop now?"

She looked at him, frustrated and baffled.

He said: "When this survey is completed I want to leave. I'll do whatever is necessary to complete the work when we return from the probe, but then I'm finished. I'd like to go back to Indic, if that's possible; I'd like to work on the new paradox study, if that's permissible, but I don't want to stay here. I'm finished here, Katrina."

Quickly: "Is it because of something you found up there? Has something turned you away, Brian?"

"Ah— No more questions."

"But you leave me so unsatisfied!"

Chaney stood up and fitted the empty chair to the table. "Every thing comes to every man, if he but has the years. That sounds like Talleyrand, but I'm not sure. *You* have the years, Katrina. Live through just two more of them and you'll know the answers to all your questions. I wish you luck, and I'll think of you often in the tank—if they'll let me back in."

A moment of silence, and then: "Please don't forget your doctor's appointment, Mr. Chaney."

"I'm on my way."

"Ask the others to be here at ten o'clock in the morning for a final briefing. We must evaluate these reports. The probe is scheduled for the day after tomorrow."

"Are you coming downstairs to see us off?"

"No, sir. I will wait for you here."

Major William Theodore Moresby
4 July 1999

Dumah, beware!
Someone is crying out to me from Seir,
Watchman, how much of the night is gone?
Watchman, how much of the night is gone?
The watchman said:
Morning comes, and night again too.
If you would know more
Come back, come back, and ask anew.

— The First Book of Isaiah

TWELVE

MORESBY WAS METHODICAL.

The red light blinked out. He reached up to unlock the hatch and throw it open. The green light went dark. Moresby grasped the two handrails and pulled himself to a sitting position, with his head and shoulders protruding through the hatchway. He was alone in the lighted room, as he expected to be. The air was cool and smelled of ozone. Moresby struggled out of the hatch and climbed over the side; the step stool was missing as he slid down the hull to the floor. He reached up to slam shut the hatch, then quickly turned to the locker for his clothing. Two other suits belonging to Saltus and Chaney also hung there in paper sheaths waiting to be claimed. He noted the locker had collected a fine coat of dust. When he was fully dressed, he smoothed out the imaginary wrinkles in the Air Force dress uniform he had elected to wear.

Moresby checked his watch: 10:05. He sought out the electric calendar and clock on the wall to verify the date and time: *4 July 99*. The clock read 4:10, off six hours from his launching time. Temperature was an even 70 degrees.

Moresby decided the clock was in error; he would rely on his watch. His last act before leaving the room was to direct a smart salute toward the twin lenses of the monitoring cameras. He thought that would be appreciated by those on the other side of the wall.

Moresby strode down the corridor in eerie silence to the shelter; fine dust on the floor was kicked up by his feet. The shelter door was pushed open and the overhead lights went on in automatic response. He stared around, inspecting everything. There was no ready evidence that anyone had used the shelter in recent years; the stores were as neatly stacked as he had found them during his last inspection. Moresby lit a gasoline lantern to check its efficiency after so long a time; he watched its steady flame with satisfaction and then put it out. The supplies were dependable, after all. As an afterthought, he broke open a container of water to sample the quality: it tasted rather flat, insipid. But that was to be expected if the water had not been replaced this year. He considered that something of an oversight.

Three yellow cartons rested on the work bench—cartons which had not been there before.

He opened the first box and found a bullet-proof vest made from some unfamiliar nylon weave. The presence of the vests on the bench was significant. He slipped out of his military jacket only long enough to don the vest and then turned to work.

Moresby chose a tape recorder, inserted a cartridge, tested the machine, and crisply recorded those observations made thus far: the step stool was missing, the basement had collected dust, the water had not been refreshed, the clock-time of his arrival was off six hours and five minutes. He did not offer personal opinions on any observation. The recorder was put aside on the bench. His next act was to select a radio, connect the leads of the exterior antenna to the terminal screws on the chassis, and plug it into a wall socket. The tape recorder was moved to within easy listening distance and turned on. Moresby snapped on the radio and tuned in a military channel.

Voice: ". . . moving around the northwest corner in a southerly direction—moving toward you. Estimated strength, twelve to fifteen men. Watch them, Corporal, they're packing mortars. Over." The sound of gunfire was loud behind the voice.

Voice: "Roger. We've got a hole in the fence at the northwest—some bastard tried to put a truck through. It's still burning, maybe that'll stop them. Over."

Voice: "You *must* hold them, Corporal. I can't send you any men—we have a double red here. Out."

The channel fell silent, closing off the firefight.

Moresby was not given to panic or reckless haste. Feeling little surprise, he began methodically to equip himself for the target. An Army-issue automatic, together with its belt and extra ammunition, was strapped around his waist; he selected a rapid-fire rifle after examining its make and balance, then emptied several boxes of cartridges in his jacket pockets. All insignia marking him an officer were removed from his uniform, but there was little he could do now about the uniform itself.

The stores offered him no battle helmets or liners. Moresby slung a canteen of the insipid water over his shoulder and a pack of rations across his back. He decided against the tape recorder because of its extra bulk, but reached for the radio as he studied a map of Illinois. A sudden hunch told him the skirmish would be somewhere near Chicago; the Air Force had long been worried about the defense of that city because it was the hub of railroad and highway traffic—and there was the always-threatening problem of foreign shipping traversing the Great Lakes to tie up at Chicago ports. Surveillance of that shipping had always been inadequate.

He was reaching out to disconnect the antenna when the channel came alive.

Voice: "Eagle One! The bandits have hit us—hit us at the northwest corner. I count twelve of them, spread out over the slope below the fence. They've got two—damn it!—two mortars and they're lobbing them in. Over." The harsh, half-shrieking voice was punctuated by the dull thump of mortar fire.

Voice: "Have they penetrated the fence? Over."

Voice: "Negative—negative. That burning truck is holding them. I think they'll try some other way—blow a hole in the fence if they can. Over."

Voice: "*Hold* them, Corporal. They are a diversion; we have the main attack here. Out."

Voice: "Damn it, Lieutenant—" Silence.

Moresby reached again for the leads to sever the radio from the topside antenna, but was stopped by an idea. He switched to an alternate military channel, one of six on the instrument, and punched the *send* button.

"Moresby, Air Force Intelligence, calling Chicago or the Chicago area. Come in, Chicago."

The channel remained silent. He repeated himself, waited impatiently for the sweep hand of his watch to make a full circle, and then made a third attempt. There was no response. Another military channel was selected.

"Moresby, Air Force Intelligence, calling Chicago or the Chicago area. Come in please."

The radio crackled with static or small arms fire. A weak voice, dimmed by distance or a faulty power supply: "Nash here. Nash here, west of Chicago. Use caution. Come in, Moresby. Over."

He stepped up the gain. "Major William Moresby, Air Force Intelligence on special duty. I am trying to reach Joliet or Chicago. Please advise the situation. Over."

Voice: "Sergeant Nash, sir, Fifth Army, HQ Company. Chicago negative, repeat negative. Avoid, avoid. You can't get in there, sir—the lake is hot. Over."

Moresby was startled. "*Hot?* Please advise. Over."

Voice: "Give me your serial number, sir."

Moresby rattled it off, and repeated his question.

Voice: "Yes, sir. The ramjets called in a Harry on the city. We're pretty certain they called it in, but the damned thing fell short and dropped into the lake off Glencoe. You can't go in anywhere there, sir. The city has been fired, and that lake water sprayed everything for miles up and down the shoreline. It's *hot,* sir. We're picking up civilian casualties coming out, but there isn't much we can do for them. Over."

Moresby: "Did you get your troops out? Over."

Voice: "Yes, sir. The troops have pulled back and established a new perimeter. I can't say where. Over."

A wash of static rattled the small speaker.

Moresby wished desperately for fuller information, but he knew better than to reveal his ignorance by asking direct questions. The request for his serial number had warned him the distant voice was suspicious, and had he stumbled over the number contact would have been lost. It suggested these radio channels were open to the enemy.

Moresby: "Are you certain those devils called in the Harry? Over."

Voice: "Yes, sir, reasonably certain. Border Patrol uncovered a relay station in Nuevo Leon, west of Laredo. They think they've found another one in Baja California, a big station capable of putting a signal overseas. Navy pinned down a launching complex at Tienpei. Over."

Moresby, fuming: "Damn them! We can expect more of the same if Navy doesn't take it out quickly. Do you know the situation at Joliet? Over."

Voice: "Negative, sir. We've had no recent reports from the south. What is your location? Be careful in your answer, sir. Over."

Moresby took the warning. "Approximately eight miles out of Joliet. I am well protected at the moment. I've heard mortar fire but haven't been able to locate it. I think I will try for the city, Sergeant. Over."

Voice: "Sir, we've taken a fix on you and believe we

know your location. You are very well protected there. You have a strong signal. Over."

Moresby: "I have electricity here but I will be on battery when I leave cover. Over."

Voice: "Right, sir. If Joliet is closed to you, the O.D. suggests that you circle around to the northwest and come in here. Fifth Army HQ has been re-established west of the Naval Training Station, but you'll pass through our lines long before that point. Look for the sentries. Use care, sir. Be alert for ramjets between your position and ours. They are heavily armed. Over."

Moresby: "Thank you, Sergeant. I'll go for the target of opportunity. Over and out."

Moresby snapped off the radio and disconnected the leads. That done, he turned off the tape recorder and left it on the bench for his return.

He studied the map once again, tracing the two roads which led to the highway and the alternate highway into Joliet. The enemy would be well aware of those roads, as well as the railroad, and if their action reached this far south they would have patrols out. It wouldn't be safe to use an automobile; large moving targets invited trouble.

A last searching examination of the room gave him no other article he thought he would need. Moresby took a long drink of water from the stores and quit the shelter. The corridor was dusty and silent, yet bright under lights and the monitoring cameras. He eyed the closed doors along the passageway, wondering who was behind them—watching. Obeying orders, he didn't so much as touch a knob to learn if they were locked. The corridor ended and a flight of stairs led upward to the operations exit. The painted sign prohibiting the carrying of arms beyond the door had been defaced: a large slash of black paint was smeared from the first sentence to the last, half obliterating the words and voiding the warning. He would have ignored it in any event.

Moresby again noted the time on his watch and fitted the keys into first one lock and then the other. A bell rang below him as he pushed out into the open air.

The northeast horizon was bright with the approaching dawn. It was ten minutes before five in the morning. The parking lot was empty.

He knew he had made a mistake.

The first and second sounds he heard were the booming thump of the mortar to the northwest, and a staccato tattoo of small arms fire near at hand—near the eastern gate. Moresby slammed shut the door behind him, made sure it had locked itself, and fell to the ground all in one blurring motion. The nearness of the battle was a shock. He pushed the rifle out in front of his face and crawled toward the corner of the building, searching for any moving object.

He saw no moving thing in the space between the lab building and the nearest structure across the way. Firing was louder as he reached the corner and rounded it.

A strong wind drove over the roof of the laboratory, blowing debris along the company street and bowing the tops of the trees planted along the thoroughfare. The wind seemed to be coming from everywhere, from every direction, moaning with a mounting intensity as it raced toward the northeast. Moresby stared that way with growing wonder and knew he'd made another mistake in guessing the coming dawn. That was not the sun. The red-orange brightness beyond the horizon was fire and the raging wind told him Chicago was being caught up in an enormous firestorm. When it grew worse, when steel melted and glass liquefied, a man would be unable to stand upright against the great inward rush of the feeding winds.

Moresby searched the street a second time, searched the parking lot, then jumped suddenly to his feet and ran across the street to the safety of the nearest building. No shot followed him. He hugged the foundation wall, turned briefly to scan his back trail, and darted around a corner. Shrubbery offered a partial concealment. When he stopped to catch his breath and reconnoiter the open yard ahead, he discovered he had lost the military radio.

The continued booming of the mortars worried him. It was easy to guess the Corporal's guard holding the northwest corner was outnumbered, and probably pinned down. The first voice on the radio said *he* had a hell of a fight on his hands—"double red" was new terminology but quickly recognizable—down there near the gate or along the eastern perimeter, and men could not be spared for the defense of the northwestern corner. A wrong decision. Moresby thought that officer guilty of a serious error in judgment. He could hear light rifle fire at the gate—punctuated at intervals by a shotgun, suggesting civilians were involved in the skirmish—but those mortars were pounding the far corner of the station and they made a deadly difference.

Moresby left the concealing shrubbery on the run. There had been no other activity about the laboratory, no betraying movement of invader or defender.

He moved north and west, taking advantage of whatever cover offered itself, but occasionally sprinting along the open street to gain time—always watchfully alert for any other moving man. Moresby was painfully aware of the gap in intelligence: he didn't know the identity of the bandits, the ramjets, didn't know friend from foe save for the uniform he might be wearing. He knew better than to trust a man without uniform inside the fence: shotguns were civilian weapons. He supposed this damned thing was some civil uprising.

The mortar fired again, followed by a second shell. If that pattern repeated itself, they were side by side working in pairs. Moresby fell into a jogging trot to hold his wind. He worried about the Chinese thrust, about the Harry called in on Chicago. Who would bring *them* in on an American city? Who would ally himself with the Chinese?

In a surprisingly short time he passed a series of old barracks set back from the street, and recognized one of them as the building he had lived in for a few weeks—some twenty-odd years ago. It now appeared to be in a sorry state. He jogged on without pause, following the sidewalk he'd sometimes used when returning from the mess hall. The hot wind rushed with him, overtaking him and half propelling him along his way. That fire over the horizon was feeding on the wind, on the debris being sucked into it.

On a vagrant impulse—and because it lay in his direction—Moresby turned sharply to cut across a yard to E Street: the swimming pool was near at hand. He glanced at the sky and found it appreciably lighter: the real dawn was coming, bringing promise of a hot July day.

Moresby gained the fence surrounding the patio and the pool and stopped running, because his breath was spent. Cautiously, rifle ready, he moved through the entranceway to probe the interior. The recreation area was deserted. Moresby walked over to the tiled rim and looked down: the pool was drained, the bottom dry and littered with debris—it had not been used this summer. He expelled a breath of disappointment. The next to last time he'd seen the pool—only a few days ago, after all, despite those twenty years—Katrina had played in the blue-green water wearing that ridiculous little suit, while Art had chased her like a hungry rooster, wanting to keep his hands on her body. A nice body, that. Art knew what he was doing. And Chaney sat on the sun deck, mooning over the woman—the civilian lacked the proper initiative; wouldn't fight for what he wanted.

The mortars boomed again in the familiar one-two pattern. Moresby jumped, and spun around.

Outside the patio fence he saw the automobile parked at the curb a short distance up the street, and cursed his own myopic planning. The northwest corner was a mile or more away, an agonizing distance when on foot.

Moresby stopped in dismay at sight of the dashboard.

The car was a small one—painted the familiar olive drab—more closely resembling the German beetle than a standard American compact, but its dash was nearly bare of ornament and instrument controls. There was no key, only a switch indicating the usual on-off positions; the vehicle had an automatic drive offering but three options: park, reverse, forward. A toggle switch for headlights, another for the windshield wipers completed the instrument cluster.

Moresby slid in under the wheel and turned the switch on. A single idiot light blinked at him briefly and stayed out. Nothing else happened. He pushed the selector lever deeper into park, flicked the switch off and on again, but without result other than a repetitious blinking of the idiot light. Cursing the balky car, he yanked at the lever—pulling it into forward—and the car quickly shot away from the curb. Moresby fought the wheel and kicked hard on the brake, but not before the vehicle had ricocheted off the opposite curb and dealt a punishing blow to his spine. It came to a skidding stop in the middle of the street, throwing his chest against the wheel. There had been no audible sound of motor or machinery in motion.

He stared down at the dashboard in growing wonder and realized he had an electric vehicle. Easing off on the brake, he allowed the car to gather forward momentum and seek its own speed. This time it did not appear to move as fast, and he went down gently on the accelerator. The car responded, silently and effortlessly.

Moresby gunned it, running for the northwest fence. Behind him, the rattle of gunfire around the gate seemed to have lessened.

The truck was still burning. A column of oily black smoke climbed into the early morning sky.

Major Moresby abandoned the car and leaped for the ground when he was within fifty yards of the perimeter. A second hole had been torn in the fence, blasted by short mortar fire, and in his first quick scan of the area he saw the bodies of two aggressors sprawled in the same opening. They wore civilian clothing—dirty shirts and levis—and the only mark of identification visible on either corpse was a ragged yellow armband. Moresby inched toward the fence, seeking better information.

The mortar was so near he heard the cough before the explosion. Moresby dug his face into the dirt and waited. The shell landed somewhere behind him, up slope, throwing rocks and dirt into the sky; debris pelted the back of his neck and fell on his unprotected head. He held his position, frozen to the ground and waiting stolidly for the second mortar to fire.

It never fired.

After a long moment he raised his head to stare down the slope beyond the ruptured fence. The slope offered poor shelter, and the enemy had paid a high price for that disadvantage: seven bodies were scattered over the terrain between the fence and a cluster of tree stumps two hundred yards below. Each of those bodies was dressed alike: street clothing, and a yellow band worn on the left arm.

Ramjets.

Moresby slid his gaze away to study the terrain.

The land sloped gently away from his own position and away from the protective fence, dropping down two hundred yards before leveling off into tillable area. Flat land at the bottom looked as though it had been plowed in the spring, but no crop grew there now. A billboard stood at the base of the slope looking toward the main line of the Chicago and Mobile Southern Railroad, another five hundred yards beyond the plowed area. Thirty yards north of the billboard and five yards higher up the slope was a cluster of seven or eight tree stumps that had been uprooted from the soil and dumped to one side out of the way; the farmer had cleared his tillable area but hadn't yet burned the unwanted stumps. The wheel marks of an invading truck showed clearly on the field.

Moresby studied the billboard and then the stumps. If he were directing the assault he would place a mortar behind each one; they were the only available cover.

Moving cautiously, he brought up the rifle and put two quick shots through the billboard near its bottom. Another two shots followed, biting into the tall grass and weeds immediately below the board. He heard a shout, a cry of sudden pain, and saw a man leap from the weeds to run for the stumps. The bandit staggered as he ran, holding pain in his thigh.

He was a soft target. Moresby waited, leading him. When the running man was just halfway between the billboard and the nearest stump, he fired once—high, aiming for the chest. The falling body tumbled forward under its own headlong momentum and crashed to earth short of the stump.

The cough of the mortar was a grotesque echo.

Moresby delayed for a second—no more—and thrust his face into the dirt. There had been a furtive movement behind the stumps. The shell burst behind him, striking metal now instead of dirt, and he spun around on his belly to see the electric car disintegrate. Direct hit. Fragments rained down on him and he threw up his hands to protect his head and the back of his neck. His fingers stung.

The rain stopped. Moresby sat up and threw an angry brace of shots at the stumps, wanting to put the fear of God into the mortarman. He fell back quickly to await the cough of the second mortar. It did not come. A stillness; other than the headlong rush of the wind and the tiny sound of sporadic firing at the main gate. Moresby felt a sudden heady elation: that back-up mortar was out of action. *One down.* Deliberately sitting up, deliberately taking aim, he emptied the rifle at the offending tree stumps. There was no answering fire, despite the target he offered. He had nothing more than a mortar to contend with—a mortar manned by a civilian. A poor goddamned civilian.

Moresby discovered a trickle of blood on his fingers and knew the keen exuberance of battle. A shout declared his gleeful discovery. He rolled to the ground to reload his weapon and shouted again, hurling a taunt at the enemy.

He searched the area behind the fence for the defenders, the Corporal's guard he'd picked up on the radio. They should have joined him when he opened fire down slope. His searching glance picked out three men this side of the fence, near the burning truck, but *they* couldn't have joined in. The empty shoes and helmet liner of a fourth man lay on the scarred ground ten yards away. He caught a flicker of movement in a shell hole—it may have been no more than the bat of an eye, or the quiver of parched lips—and found the only survivor. A bloodless face stared over the rim of the hole at him.

Moresby scrabbled across the exposed slope and fell into the hole with the soldier.

The man wore Corporal's stripes on his only arm and clutched at a strap which had once been attached to a radio; the remainder of each had been blown away. He didn't move when Moresby landed hard beside him and burrowed into the bloodied pit. The Corporal stared helplessly at the place where Moresby had been, at the boiling column of oily smoke rising above the truck, at the coming sun, at the sky. His head would not turn. Moresby threw away his useless rations pack and tilted the canteen to the Corporal's mouth. A bit of water trickled between his lips but the greater part of it ran down his chin and would have been lost, had Moresby not caught it in his hand and rubbed it over the man's mouth. He attempted to force more between the lips.

The Corporal moved his head with a feeble negative gesture and Moresby stopped, knowing he was choking on the water; instead, he poured more into his open palm and bathed the Corporal's face, pulling down the wide eyelids with a wet caressing motion of his fingers. The bright and hurtful sky was shut out.

Wind roared across the face of the slope and over the plowed field below, sweeping toward the lakefront.

Moresby raised his eyes to study the slope and the field. A carelessly exposed foot and ankle were visible behind a tree stump. Calmly—without the haste that might impair his aim—he brought up his rifle and put a single slug into the ankle. He heard a bellowing cry of pain, and the curse directed at him. The target vanished from sight. Moresby's gaze came back to the empty shoes and helmet liner beyond the shell hole. He decided to move—knew he *had* to move now to prevent that mortar from coming in on him.

He fired again at the stumps to keep the mortarman down, then sprinted for the ruptured hole in the fence where the bodies of the two aggressors lay. He fell on his belly, fired another round and then jumped on all fours against the nearest body, burrowing down behind it as a shield against the mortarman. The raging wind blew over the hole.

Moresby plucked at the bandit's shirt, tearing away the armband and bringing it up to his eyes for a careful inspection.

It was no more than a strip of yellow cotton cloth cut from a bolt of goods, and bearing a crude black cross in India ink. There was no word, slogan, or other point of identification to establish a fealty. Black cross on yellow field. Moresby prodded his memory, wanting to fit that symbol into some known civilian niche. It *had* to fit into a neat little slot somewhere. His orderly mind picked and worried at the unfamiliar term: *ramjet.*

Nothing. Neither sign nor name were known prior to the launch, prior to 1978.

He rolled the stiffening body over on its back the better to see the face, and knew jarring shock. The black and bloodied face was still twisted in the agony of death. Two or more slugs had torn into the man's midsection, while another had ripped away his throat and showered his face with his own blood; it had not been instantaneous death. He had died in screaming misery alongside the man next to him, vainly attempting to break through the fence and take the defenders up the slope.

Major Moresby was long used to death in the field; the manner of this man's dying didn't upset him—but the close scrutiny of his enemy jolted him as he'd not been jolted before. He suddenly understood the crude black cross etched on the yellow field, even though he'd not seen it before today. This was a civilian rebellion—organized insurrection.

Ramjets were Negro guerrillas.

The mortar coughed down the slope and Major Moresby burrowed in behind the body. He waited impatiently for the round to drop somewhere behind him, above him, and then by God he'd *take* that mortar.

The time was twenty minutes after six in the morning, 4 July 1999. The rising sun burned the horizon.

A ramjet mortarman with a shattered ankle peered warily over a tree stump, and counted himself the victor.

Lieutenant Commander Arthur Saltus
23 November 2000

Yesterday this day's madness did prepare;
Tomorrow's silence, triumph, or despair:
Drink! for you know not whence you came, nor why;
Drink! for you know not why you go, nor where.

— Omar Khayyam

THIRTEEN

SALTUS WAS prepared to celebrate.

The red light blinked out. He reached up to unlock the hatch and throw it open. The green light went dark.

Saltus grasped the two handrails and pulled himself to a sitting position with his head and shoulders protruding through the hatchway. He was alone in the room as he expected to be, but he noted with mild surprise that some of the ceiling lights had burned out. Sloppy housekeeping. The air was chill and smelled of ozone. He struggled out of the hatch and climbed over the side; the step stool was missing and he slid down the hull to the floor. Saltus reached up to slam shut the hatch, then turned to the locker for his clothing.

Another suit belonging to Chaney hung there in its paper sheath waiting to be claimed. He noted the locker had collected a heavy amount of dust and a fine film of it had even crept inside. Wretched housekeeping. When Saltus was dressed in the civvies he had elected to wear, he took out a pint of good bourbon from its place of concealment in the locker and surreptitiously slipped the bottle into a jacket pocket.

He thought he was adequately prepared for the future.

Arthur Saltus checked his watch: 11:02. He sought out the electric calendar and clock on the wall to verify the date and time: *23 Nov 00.* The clock read 10:55. Temperature was a cold 13 degrees. Saltus guessed his watch was wrong; it had been wrong before. He left the room without a glance at the cameras, secretively holding his hand against the bottle to mask the pocket bulge. He didn't think the engineers would approve of his intentions.

Saltus walked down the corridor in eerie silence to the shelter; dust on the floor muffled his footfalls and he wondered if William had found that same dust sixteen months earlier. The old boy would have been annoyed. The shelter door was pushed open and the overhead lights went on in automatic response—but again, some of them were burned out. Somebody rated a gig for poor maintenance. Saltus stopped just inside the door, pulled the bottle from his pocket and ripped away the seal from the cap.

A shout rattled the empty room.

"Happy birthday!"

For a little while, he was fifty years old.

Saltus swallowed the bourbon, liking its taste, and wiped his mouth with the back of his hand; he stared around the shelter with growing curiosity. Somebody had been at the ship's stores—somebody had helped himself to the provisions set by for *him* and then had carelessly left the debris behind for *him* to find. The place was overrun with privateers and sloppy housekeepers.

He discovered a gasoline lantern on the floor near his feet and reached down quickly to determine if it was warm. It was not, but a jostling shake told him there was fuel remaining in the tank. Many boxes of rations had been cut open—emptied of their contents—and the cartons stacked in a disorderly pile along the wall near the door. A few water containers rested beside the cartons and Saltus grabbed up the nearest to shake it, test it for use. The can was empty. He took another long pull from his birthday bottle and roamed around the room, making a more detailed inspection of the stores. They weren't in the ship-shape order he remembered from his last inspection.

A sealed bag of clothing had been torn open, a bag holding several heavy coats and parkas for winter wear. He could not guess how many had been taken from the container.

A pair of boots—no, two or three pair—were missing from a rack holding several similar pairs. Another bundle of warm lined mittens appeared to have been disturbed, but it was impossible to determine how many were gone. Somebody had visited the stores in winter. That somebody should not have been the Major—he was scheduled for the Fourth of July, unless that gyroscope went crazy and threw him off by half a year. Saltus turned again to count the used ration boxes and the water cans: not enough of them had been emptied to support a big man like William for the past sixteen months—not unless he was living outside most of the time and supporting himself from the land. The used-up stores *might* have carried him through a single winter, supplementing game from outside. It seemed an unlikely possibility.

Saltus worked his way around the room to the bench. It was littered with trash.

Three yellow cartons rested on the bench top, cartons he'd not seen there on previous visits. The first one was empty, but he tore away the lid flaps of the next to discover a bullet-proof vest made of an unfamiliar nylon weave. He did not hesitate. The garment looked flimsy and unreliable but because Katrina always knew what she was doing, he put on the protective vest beneath his civilian jacket. Saltus sipped at his bourbon and eyed the mess on the bench. It wasn't like William to leave things untidy—well, not *this* untidy. Some of it was his work.

A tape recorder and another gasoline lantern were on the bench. A moment later he discovered empty boxes which had contained rifle cartridges, another box for the tape now in the recorder, an opened map, and the insignia removed from the Major's dress uniform.

Saltus thought he knew what that meant. He touched the lantern first but found it cold although the fuel tank was full, and then leaned over the bench to examine the recorder. Only a few minutes of tape had been spun off.

Saltus depressed the voice button, said: "Mark," and rewound the tape to its starting point.

Another push and the tape rolled forward.

Voice: "Moresby here. Four July 1999. Time of arrival 10:05 on my watch, 4:10 by the clock. Six hours and five minutes discrepancy. Dust everywhere, stool missing from operations room; shelter unoccupied and stores intact, but the water is stale. Am preparing for the target."

Brief period of miscellaneous sounds.

Arthur Saltus had another drink while he waited. He stared again at William's discarded military insignia.

Voice: ". . . moving around the northwest corner in a southerly direction—moving toward you. Estimated strength, twelve to fifteen men. Watch them, Corporal, they're packing mortars. Over." The sound of gunfire was loud behind the voice.

Voice: "Roger. We've got a hole in the fence at the northwest—some bastard tried to put a truck through. It's still burning; maybe that'll stop them. Over."

Voice: "You *must* hold them, Corporal. I can't send you any men—we have a double red here. Out."

The channel fell silent, closing off the firefight.

Arthur Saltus stared at the machine in consternation, knowing the first suspicions of what might have happened. He listened to the small sounds of Moresby working about the bench, guessing what he was doing; the sound of cartridges being emptied from boxes was quickly recognizable; a rattle of paper was the map being unfolded.

Voice: "Eagle one! The bandits have hit us—hit us at the northwest corner. I count twelve of them, spread out over the slope below the fence. They've got two—damn it!—two mortars and they're lobbing them in. Over." The harsh, half-shrieking voice was punctuated by the dull thump of mortar fire.

Voice: "Have they penetrated the fence? Over."

Voice: "Negative—negative. That burning truck is holding them. I think they'll try some other way—blow a hole in the fence if they can. Over."

Voice: "*Hold* them, Corporal. They are a diversion; we have the main attack here. Out."

Voice: "Damn it, Lieutenant—" Silence.

The pause was of short duration.

Voice: "Moresby, Air Force Intelligence, calling Chicago or the Chicago area. Come in, Chicago."

Arthur Saltus listened to Moresby's efforts to make radio contact with the world outside, and listened to the ensuing dialogue between Moresby and Sergeant Nash holding somewhere west of Chicago. He sucked breath in a great startled gasp when he heard the Chicago statement—it hit him hard in the belly—and listened in near-disbelief at the exchange which followed. Baja California clearly indicated the shortwave signals were being bounced to the Orient: *that* was where the Harrys were and *that* was where they had been called in from. The Chinese at last were retaliating for the loss of their two railroad towns. It was likely that now—sixteen months after the strike—Lake Michigan and the lands adjoining it were as radioactive as the farming area around Yungning. They had retaliated.

But who called it in? Who were the bandits? What in hell were ramjets? That was a kind of aircraft.

Voice: ". . . Fifth Army HQ has been re-established west of the Naval Training Station, but you'll pass through our lines long before that point. Look for the sentries. Use care, sir. Be alert for ramjets between your position and ours. They are heavily armed. Over."

Moresby thanked the man and went out.

The tape repeated a snapping sound that was Moresby shutting off his radio, and a moment later the tape itself went silent as he stopped the recorder. Arthur Saltus waited—listening for a postscript of some kind when William returned from his target and checked in. The tape went on and on repeating nothing, until at last his own voice jumped out at him: "Mark."

He was dissatisfied. He let the machine run through the end of the reel but there was nothing more. Moresby had not returned to the shelter—but Saltus knew he would *not* attempt to reach Fifth Army headquarters near Chicago, not in the bare fifty hours permitted him on target with a firefight underway somewhere outside. He might try for Joliet if the route was secure but he certainly wouldn't penetrate far into hostile territory with a deadline over his head. He had gone out; he hadn't come back inside.

But yet Saltus was dissatisfied. Something nagged at his attention, something that wasn't quite right, and he stared at the tape recorder for a long time in an effort to place the wrongness. Some insignificant little thing didn't fit smoothly into place. Saltus rewound the tape to the beginning and played it forward a second time. He put down the birthday bottle to listen attentively.

When it was finished he was certain of a wrongness;

something on the tape plucked at his worried attention.

And yet a third time. He hunched over the machine.

In order:

William making his preliminary report; two voices, worried over the bandits and the mortars at the northwest corner, plus the fighting at the main gate; William again, calling Chicago; Sergeant Nash responding, with a dialogue on the Chicago situation and an invitation to join them at the relocated headquarters. A farewell word of thanks from William, and a snap of the radio being shut off; a moment later the tape itself went silent when William turned off the recorder and left the shelter—

There—*that* was it.

The tape went dead when the recorder was turned off. There were no after-sounds of activity about the bench, no final message—there was nothing to indicate William had ever touched the recorder again. He had shut off the radio and the recorder in one-two order and quit the room. The tape should have ended there, stopped there. It did not. Saltus looked at his watch, squinting at the sweep hand. He ran the tape forward yet another time, from the point when William had shut it off to the point when *he* turned it on again and said: "Mark."

The elapsed time was one minute, forty-four seconds. Someone *after* William had done that. Someone else had opened the shelter, pilfered the stores, donned winter clothing, and listened to the taped report. Someone else had let the machine run on another minute and forty-four seconds before shutting it off and taking his leave. The visitor may have returned, but William never did.

Arthur Saltus felt that fair warning. He closed the corridor door and thumbed a manual switch to keep the shelter lights on. An Army-issue automatic was taken from the stores and strapped around his waist. Another mouth-filling pull from the bottle, and he rolled the tape back to his "Mark."

"Saltus checking in. That was my mark and this is my birthday, 23 November, in the nice round number year of 2000. I am fifty years old but I don't look a day over twenty-five—chalk it up to clean living. Hello, Katrina. Hello, Chaney. And hello to you, Mr. Gilbert Seabrooke. Is that nosey little man from Washington still knocking around back there?

"I arrived at 10:55 or 11:02 something, depending on which timepiece you read. I say something because I don't yet know if it's ack-emma or the other—I haven't put my nose outside to test the wind. I have lost all faith in engineers and mercury protons, but they'd better not cheat *me* out of my full birthday. When I walk out that door I want to see bright sunshine on the greensward—morning sunshine. I want birds singing and rabbits rabbiting and all that jazz.

"Katrina, the housekeeping is awfully sloppy around here: it's poor ship. Dust on the furniture, the floors, lights burned out, empty boxes littering the place—it's a mess. Strangers have been wandering in and out, helping themselves to the drygoods and pinching the groceries. I guess somebody found a key to the place.

"Everything you heard before my mark was William's report. He didn't come back to finish it, and he *didn't* go up to Chicago or anywhere near there—you can rely on that." The bantering tone was dropped. "He's outside."

Arthur Saltus began a straightforward recital of all that he'd found. He ticked off the missing items from the stores, the number of empty boxes stacked haphazardly along the wall, the used water cans, the two lanterns which had seen but little service—William may have tested the one found on the bench—the debris on the floor, the insignia, and the peculiarity of the tape being rolled forward. He invited his listeners to make the same time-delay test he'd made and then offer a better explanation if they didn't care for his.

He said: "And when you come up here, civilian, just double-check the stores; count the empties again to see if our visitor has been back. And hey—arm yourself, mister. You'd damned well better shoot straight if you have to shoot at all. Remember *something* we taught you."

Saltus flicked off the machine to prevent the tape from listening to him take a drink—as difficult as that might be—and then flicked it on again.

"I'm going topside to search for William—I'm going to try tailing him. Lord only knows what I'll find after sixteen months but I'm going to try. It's likely he did one of two things: either he'd go for Joliet to find out what he could about that Chicago thing, or he'd jump into the squabble if it was alongside.

"If the squabble was here—on the station—I think he'd run for the northwest corner to help the Corporal; he'd *have* to get into the fight." Short pause. "I'm going up to take a look at that corner, but if I don't find anything I'll run into Joliet. I'm in the same boat now with old William—I've got to know what happened to Chicago." He stared solemnly at the empty space in his bottle and added: "Katrina, this sure knocks hell out of your survey. All that studying for nothing."

Saltus stopped talking but let the machine run on.

He plugged in a radio and connected the leads to the outside antenna. After a period of band searching, he reported back to the tape recorder.

"Radio negative. Nothing at all on the GI channels." Another slow sweep of the bands. "That's damned funny, isn't it? Nobody's playing the top ten platters."

Saltus switched over to the civilian wavelengths and monitored them carefully. "The forty- and eighty-meter bands are likewise negative. Everybody is keeping their mouths shut. What do you suppose they're scared of?" He went back to a military channel and turned up the gain to peak, hearing nothing but an airy whisper. The lack of communications nettled him.

The *send* button was depressed.

"Navy boot, come in. Come in, boot, you know me—I caddied for the Admiral at Shoreacres. Saltus calling Navy boot. Over."

He reported himself two or three times on several channels.

The radio crackled a sudden command. "Get off the air, you idiot! They'll get a fix on you!" It went silent.

Saltus was so startled he turned off the radio.

To the tape recorder: "Chaney, did you hear that? There *is* somebody out there! They don't have much going for them—the power was weak, or they were a long ways off—but there *is* somebody out there. Scared spitless, too. The ramjets must have them on the run." He stopped to consider that. "Katrina, try to find out what a ramjet is. Our Chinese friends *can't* be here; they don't have the transport, and they couldn't get through the Pacific minefields if they did. And keep *that* under your hat, civilian—it's top secret stuff."

Arthur Saltus equipped himself for the target, always remembering to keep an eye on the door.

He helped himself to a parka and pulled the hood over his head; he removed the light shoes he'd been wearing the summer he left and found a pair of hiking boots the proper size. Mittens were tucked into a pocket. Saltus slung a canteen of water over one shoulder and a pack of rations on his back. He picked out a rifle, loaded it, and emptied two boxes of cartridges into his pockets. The map was of little interest—he knew the road to Joliet, he'd been there only last Thursday to look into a little matter for the President. The President had thanked him. He loaded a camera and found room to pack away a fresh supply of nylon film.

Saltus decided against taking a radio or recorder, not wanting to be further encumbered; it would be awkward enough as it was and all signs clearly indicated the survey was sunk without a trace. Chicago was lost, forbidden, and Joliet might be a problem. But there *was* something he could do with the recorder and William's brief message—something to insure its return to home base. A last searching examination of the room gave him no other thing he thought he would need. The lights were turned off.

Saltus took a long pull on his dwindling supply of bourbon and quit the shelter. The corridor was dusty and vacant, and he fancied he could see his own footprints.

He carried the tape recorder with its dangling cord back to the operations room where the vehicle waited in its polywater tank. A thorough search of the room failed to reveal an electric outlet; even the service for the clock and the calendar came through the wall behind the encased instruments, wholly concealed.

"Damn it!" Saltus spun around to stare up at the two glass eyes. "Why can't you guys do something right? Even your lousy proton gyroscope is—is sheeg!"

He strode out of the room, marched along the dusty corridor to the adjoining laboratory door, and gave it a resounding kick to advertise his annoyance. *That* ought to shake up the engineers.

His jaw dropped when the door swung open under the blow. Nobody slammed it shut again. Saltus edged closer and peered inside. Nobody shoved him back. The lab was empty. He walked in and stared around: it was his first sight of the working side of the project and the impression was a poor one.

Here too some of the ceiling lights had burned out, without being replaced. A bank of three monitoring sets occupied a wall bench at his left hand; one of them was blanked out but the remaining two gave him a blurred and unsatisfactory image of the room he had just quit. The vehicle was recognizable only because of its shape and its supporting tank. The two images lacked quality, as though the tubes were aged beyond caring. He turned slowly on the ball of his foot and scanned the room but found nothing to suggest recent occupancy. The tools and equipment were there—and still functioning—but the lab personnel had vanished, leaving nothing but dust and marks in the dust. A yellow bull's eye on a computer panel stared at him for an intruder.

Saltus put down the recorder and plugged it in.

He said without preamble: "Chaney, the treasure house is empty, deserted—the engineers are gone. Don't ask me why or where—there's no sign, no clue, and they didn't leave notes. I'm in the lab now but there's nobody here except the mice and me. The door was open, sort of, and I wandered in." He sipped whiskey, but this time didn't bother to conceal it from the tape.

"I'm going topside to look for William. Wait for me, Katrina, you lovely wench! Happy birthday, people."

Saltus pulled the plug from the receptacle, wrapped the cord around the recorder and walked back to the other room to drop the machine into the TDV. To compensate for the added weight, he pulled loose the heavy camera in the nose bubble and threw it overboard after first salvaging the film magazine. He hoped the liaison agent from Washington would cry over the loss. Saltus slammed shut the hatch and left the room.

The corridor ended and a flight of stairs led upward to the operations exit. The painted sign prohibiting the carrying of arms beyond the door had been defaced: a large slash of black paint was smeared from the first sentence to the last, half obliterating the words and voiding the warning.

Saltus noted the time on his watch and fitted the keys into the locks. A bell rang behind him as he pushed open the door. The day was bright with sunshine and snow.

It was five minutes before twelve in the morning. His birthday was only just begun.

An automobile waited for him in the parking lot.

FOURTEEN

Arthur Saltus stepped out warily into the snow. The station appeared to be deserted: nothing moved on any street as far as the eye could see.

His gaze came back to the parked automobile.

It was a small one resembling the German beetle and olive drab in color, but he tardily recognized it as an American make by the name stamped on each hub-cap. The car had been there since before the snow: there were no tracks of movement, of betrayal. A thinner coating of snow lay over the hood and roof of the vehicle and one window was open a crack, allowing moisture to seep inside.

Saltus scanned the parking lot, the adjoining flower garden and the frigid empty spaces before him but discovered no moving thing. He held himself rigid, alert, intently watching, listening, and sniffing the wind for signs of life. No one and nothing had left tell-tale prints in the snow, nor sounds nor smells on the wind. When he was satisfied of that, he stepped away from the operations door and eased it shut behind him, making sure it was locked. Rifle up, he inched toward a corner of the lab building and peered around. The company street was trackless and deserted, as were the walks and lawns of the structures across the street. Shrubbery was bent under the weight of snow. His foot struck a covered object when he took a single step away from the protective corner.

He looked down, bent, and picked a radio out of the snow. It had been taken from the stores below.

Saltus turned it over looking for damage but saw none; the instrument bore no marks to suggest it had been struck by gunfire, and after a hesitation he concluded that Moresby had simply dropped it there to be rid of the extra weight. Saltus resumed his patrol, intent on circling the building to make certain he was alone. The sun-bright snow was unmarred all the way around. He was relieved, and paused again to sample the bourbon.

The automobile claimed his attention.

The dash puzzled him: it had an off-on switch instead of the usual key, and but one idiot light; there were no gauges to give useful information on fuel, oil, water temperature, or tire pressures, nor was there a speedometer. Propelled by a sudden exciting idea, Saltus climbed out of the little car and raised the hood. Three large silver-colored storage batteries were lined up against a motor so compact and simple it didn't appear capable of moving anything, much less an automobile. He dropped the hood and got back into the seat. The switch was flipped to the *on* position. There was no sound but the idiot light briefly winked at him. Saltus very gently pulled the selector lever to drive position and the car obediently crept forward through the snow toward the empty street. He pushed down on the accelerator with growing exhilaration and deliberately threw the car into a skid on the snow-packed street. It lurched and swung in a giddy manner, then came back under control when Saltus touched the steering wheel. The little automobile was fun.

He followed a familiar route to the barracks where he'd lived with William and the civilian, swinging and dancing from side to side on the slippery surface because the car seemed to obey his every whim. It would spin in a complete circle and come to rest with the nose pointing in the proper direction, it would slide sideways without threatening to topple, it would bite into the snow and leap forward with a minimum of slippage if just one wheel had a decent purchase. He thought that four-wheel-drive electric cars should have been invented a century ago.

Saltus stopped in dismay at the barracks—at the place where the barracks had been. He very nearly missed the site. All the antiquated buildings had burned to their concrete foundations, nearly hiding them from sight. He got out of the car to stare at the remains and at the lonely shadows cast by the winter sun.

Feeling depressed, Saltus drove over to E Street and turned north toward the recreation area.

He parked the car outside the fence surrounding the patio and prowled cautiously through the entranceway to scan the interior. The unmarked snow was reassuring but it did not lull him into a false sense of security. Rifle ready, pausing every few steps to look and listen and smell the wind, Saltus advanced to the tiled rim of the pool and looked down. It was nearly empty, drained of water, and the diving board taken away.

Nearly empty: a half dozen long lumps huddled under the blanket of snow at the bottom, lumps the shape of men. Two GI helmet liners lay nearby, recognizable by their shapes despite the covering snow. A naked, frozen foot protruded through the blanket into the cold sunshine.

Saltus turned away, expelling a breath of bitter disappointment; he wasn't sure what he had expected after so long a time, but certainly not that—not the bodies of station personnel dumped into an uncovered grave. The GI liners suggested their identities and suggested they had been dumped there by outsiders—by ramjets. Survivors on station would have buried the bodies.

He remembered the beautiful image of Katrina in that pool—Katrina, nearly naked, scantily clad in that lovely, sexy swim suit—and himself chasing after her, wanting the feel of that wet and splendid body under his hands again and again. She had teased him, run away from him, knowing what he was doing but pretending not to be aware: *that* added to the excitement. And Chaney! The poor out-gunned civilian sat up on the deck and burned with a green, sulphurous envy, wanting to but not daring to. Damn, but that was a day to be remembered!

Arthur Saltus scanned the street and then climbed back into the car.

There were two large holes in the fence surrounding the station at the northwest corner. Action from outside had caused both penetrations. The shell of a burned-out truck had caused one of them, and that rusted shell still occupied the hole. A mortar had torn through the other. There was a shallow cavity in the earth directly beneath the second hole, a cavity scooped out by another exploding mortar round. Snow-covered objects that might be the remains of men dotted the slope on both sides of the fence. There was the recognizable hulk of a thoroughly demolished automobile.

Saltus probed the wreckage of the car, turning over wheels with shredded tires, poking among the jumble of machined parts, picking up to examine with mild wonder a windshield fashioned of transparent plastic so sturdy it had popped out of place and fallen undamaged several feet away from the hulk. He compared it to the windshield of his own car, and found it to be identical. The batteries had been carried away—or were entirely demolished; the little motor was a mass of fused metal.

As best he could, Saltus scraped snow from the ground in search of something to indicate that William Moresby had died here. He thought it likely that William had found his car in the parking lot—a twin to his own vehicle—and drove it north to the scene of the skirmish. To *here*. It would be a hell of a note if the man had died before he got out of the car. Old William deserved a better break than that.

He found nothing—not even a scrap of uniform in the debris, and for the moment that was encouraging.

Down the slope a cluster of tree stumps and a sagging billboard were visible. Saltus went down to see them. A snow-blanketed body lay smashed against a stump but that was all; there was no weapon with it. The blown remains of one mortar lay around in front of the billboard and from the appearance of the piece, he would guess that a faulty shell had exploded within the tube, destroying the usefulness of the weapon and probably killing the operator. There was no corpse here to back up that guess, unless it was the one hurled against the tree stump. The second of the two mortars mentioned on the tape was missing—taken away. The winners of *this* skirmish had to be the ramjets; they had picked up their remaining mortar and retired—or had penetrated the hole to invade the station.

Saltus picked his way back up the slope and walked through the hole in the fence. The snow pattern dipped gracefully, following the rounded rough-bottomed contour of the cavity. His foot turned on something unseen at the bottom of the hole and he struggled to save his balance. A cold wind blew across the face of the slope, numbing his fingers and stinging his face.

He began the distasteful task of scraping snow off each of the fallen man-objects, brushing away just enough to catch a glimpse of the rotting cloth of the uniform. The defenders had worn Army tans, and one of them still carried a GI dogtag around his neck; in another place he turned up a Corporal's stripes attached to a bit of sleeve, and not far away was an empty pair of shoes. William Moresby's dress blues were not found.

An oversight nagged at him.

Saltus retraced his steps down the slope, annoyed at the oversight and annoyed again by the futility of it: he uncovered the remains of civilians wearing nondescript civilian clothing, and one yellow armband. A faded black cross on a rotting patch of yellow goods meant nothing to him but he folded it away for later examination. Katrina would want to see it. The ramjets themselves were beyond identification; sixteen months of exposure had made them as unrecognizable as those other bodies above the fence line. The only thing new he'd learned was that civilians were the bandits on the tape, civilians equipped with mortars and some kind of central organization—maybe the same group that had called in the Harry on Chicago. Ramjets allied with the Chinese—or at least inviting their cooperation.

To Saltus the scene read civil war.

He stopped at the next thought, staring with hard surprise at the covered bodies. Ramjets blowing Chicago —in retaliation? Ramjets losing in Chicago twenty years ago, trapped behind their own wall, but striking back in harsh retaliation *now?* Ramjets working with the Chinese, welded together by a mutual hatred of the white establishment?

He picked again at the body against the stump, but the color of the man's skin was lost.

Arthur Saltus climbed the slope.

The world was strangely silent and empty—deserted. He'd seen no traffic on the distant highway nor on the nearer railroad; the sky was uncommonly bare of aircraft. He stayed continually on the alert for danger, but sighted no one, nothing—even animal tracks were missing from the snow. Deserted world—or more likely, a concealed world. That angry voice on the radio had ordered him to silence lest he betray his cover.

Saltus stayed only a few minutes longer on the cold upper slope, standing amid the debris of the smashed car. He hoped to God that William had jumped clear before the mortar smashed in. The old boy deserved at least a couple of whacks at the bandits before his doom prophets caught up to him.

He was finally convinced the Major had died there.

Saltus drove by the mess hall with little more than a passing glance. Like the barracks, the wooden parts of the structure were burned to the concrete block foundation. He thought it likely the ramjets had swept the station after the fence was breached, burning what was flammable and stealing or destroying the remainder. It was a blessing that the lab had been built to withstand war and earthquake, or he would have emerged into a room open to the sky and climbed down from the vehicle into snow. He hoped the bandits had long since starved to death—but at the same time remembered the pilfered stores in the shelter.

That bandit hadn't starved, but neither had he fed his fellows. How had he gotten through the locked door? He would need both keys and he would have to take them from William—but a direct hit on the car would have scattered the keys as thoroughly as the parts of the auto itself. Assuming possession of the keys, why hadn't the bandit thrown open the doors to his companions? Why hadn't the stores been looted, cleaned out, the lab ransacked? Was the man so selfish that he had fed only himself and let the rest go hang? Perhaps. But more than one pair of boots was missing.

Saltus turned a corner at a fast clip, skidding in the snow and then straightening his course toward the front gate. It was a small comfort to find the gatehouse still standing: concrete blocks were difficult to burn or destroy. The gate itself was torn open and twisted back out of the way. He drove through it and concentrated on the barely visible pattern of the road ahead; the smooth unbroken expanse of snow flanked by shallow ditches to either side guided him. Only last Thursday he and William had raced over the road hell-bent for a day in Joliet.

A bearded man leaped out of the gatehouse and put a shot through the rear window of the car.

Arthur Saltus didn't take the time to decide if he

was astonished or outraged—the shot did frighten him, and he reacted automatically to danger. Slamming the accelerator to the floor, he spun hard on the wheel and threw the car into a sickening skid. It lurched and swung around in a dizzy arc, coming to rest with its blunt nose aimed at the gatehouse. Saltus floored the accelerator. The rear wheels spun uselessly on the slick snow, found a purchase only when they had burned down to the pavement, then thrust the car forward in a burst of speed that caught him unprepared. It careened wildly through the gate. He rammed the nose hard against the gatehouse door and leaped clear, hugging the side of the vehicle.

Saltus pumped two quick shots through the sagging door, and was answered by a scream of pain; he fired again and then scrambled over the hood to crouch in the doorway. The screaming man lay on the floor tearing at his bloodied chest. A tall, gaunt black man was backed against the far wall taking aim at him. Saltus fired without raising the rifle, and then deliberately turned and put a finishing shot through the head of the man writhing on the floor. The screaming stopped.

For a moment the world was wrapped in silence.

Saltus said: "Now, what the hell—"

An incredibly violent blow struck him in the small of his back, robbing him of breath and speech, and he heard the sound of a shot from an unimaginable distance away. He stumbled and went to his knees while a raging fire burned up his spine into his skull. Another distant shot shattered the peace of the world, but this once he felt nothing. Saltus turned on his knees to meet the threat.

The ramjet was climbing over the hood of the little fun car to get at him.

Caught up like a man swimming in mud, Saltus raised the rifle and tried to take aim. The weapon was almost too heavy to lift; he moved in a slow, agonizing motion. The ramjet slid down the hood and jumped through the doorway, reaching for him or his rifle. Saltus squinted at the face but it refused to come into clear focus. Somebody behind the face loomed over him as large as a mountain; somebody's hands grasped the barrel of the rifle and pulled it away. Saltus squeezed the trigger.

The looming face changed: it disintegrated in a confusing jumble of bone, blood, and tissue, coming apart like William's electric car under a mortar barrage. The face out of focus disappeared while a booming thunder filled the gatehouse and rattled the broken door. A large piece of the mountain teetered over him, threatening to bury him when it came down. Saltus tried to crawl away.

The toppling body knocked him off his knees and knocked away his weapon. He went down beneath it, still fighting for breath and praying not to be crushed.

Arthur Saltus opened his eyes to find the daylight gone. An intolerable burden pinned him to the gatehouse floor and an overpowering hurt wracked his body.

Moving painfully but gaining only an inch or two at a time, he crawled from under the burden and tried to roll it aside. After minutes or hours of strenuous effort he climbed as far as his knees and threw off the knapsack hammering at his back; he spilled as much water as he drank before the canteen followed. His rifle lay on the floor at his knee, but he was astonished to discover that his hand and arm lacked the strength to pick it up. It may have taken another hour to draw the service automatic from under his coat and place it on the hood of the car.

An unbelievable time was spent in crawling over the same hood to get outside. The gun was knocked to the ground. Saltus bent over, touched it, fingered it, grew dizzy and had to abandon the weapon to save himself. He grabbed at the door handle and hauled himself upright. After a while he tried it again, and only managed to seize the gun and stand upright before the recurring wave of nausea struck him. His stomach doubled up and ejected.

Saltus climbed into the car and backed it off from the gatehouse door. Opening the near window to get the cold bracing air, he tugged at the drive selector and steered a tortuous course from gate to parking lot. The car glanced off one curb and skidded across the snow to jump the other curb; it would have thrown its occupant if it had been traveling at greater speed. Saltus had lost the strength to push down on the brake, and the little car stopped only when it slammed into the concrete wall of the laboratory. He was thrown against the wheel and then out into the snow. A spotted trail of blood marked his erratic path from the car to the door with the twin locks.

The door opened easily—so easily that a dim corner of his fogged consciousness nagged at him: had he inserted *both* keys into the locks before the door swung? Had he inserted *any* key?

Arthur Saltus fell down the flight of stairs because he could not help himself.

The gun was gone from his hand but he couldn't remember losing it; his bottle of birthday bourbon was gone from his pocket but he couldn't remember emptying it or throwing away the bottle; the keys to the door were lost. Saltus lay on his back on the dusty concrete, looking at the bright lights and looking up the stairs at the closed door. He didn't remember closing that door.

A voice said: "Fifty hours."

He knew he was losing touch with reality, knew he was drifting back and forth between cold, painful awareness and dark periods of feverish fantasy. He wanted to sleep on the floor, wanted to stretch out with his face on the cold concrete and let the raging fire in his spine burn itself out. Katrina's vest had saved his life—barely. The slug—more than one?—was lodged in his back, but without the vest it would have torn all the way through his chest and blown away the rib cage. Thanks, Katrina.

A voice said: "Fifty hours."

He tried to stand up, but fell on his face. He tried to climb to his knees, but pitched forward on his face. There was not much strength left to him. In time with the measured passing of an eternity, he crawled to the TDV on his belly.

Arthur Saltus struggled for an hour to climb the side of the vehicle. His awareness was slipping away in a sea of nauseous fantasy: he had the hallucinatory notion that someone pulled off his heavy boots—that someone removed the heavy winter garments and tried to take off his clothing. When at last he fell head first through the vehicle's open hatch, he had the fever-fantasy that someone out there had helped him over the side.

A voice said: "Push the kickbar."

He lay on his stomach on the webbing facing in the

wrong direction, and remembered that the engineers wouldn't recover the vehicle until the end of fifty hours. They had done that when William failed to return. Something was under him, hurting him, putting a hard new pressure on a rib cage already painfully sore. Saltus pulled the lump from beneath him and found a tape recorder. He pushed it toward the kickbar but it fell inches short of the goal. The hallucination slammed shut the hatch cover.

He said thickly: "Chaney . . . the bandits have burned the treasure house . . ."

The tape recorder was thrown at the kickbar.

The time was forty minutes after two in the morning, 24 November 2000. His fiftieth birthday was long past.

THE YEAR OF THE QUIET SUN

Brian Chaney
2000-plus

The meek, the terrible meek,
the fierce agonizing meek,
Are about to enter into their inheritance.

— Charles Rann Kennedy

FIFTEEN

CHANEY was apprehensive.

The red light blinked out. He reached up to unlock the hatch and throw it open. The green light went dark. Chaney grasped the two handrails and pulled up to a sitting position, with his head and shoulders protruding through the hatchway. He hoped he was alone in the room—the vehicle was in darkness. The air was sharply cold and smelled of ozone. He struggled out of the hatch and climbed over the side. Saltus had warned him the stool was gone so he slid cautiously to the floor, and clung to the polywater tank for a moment of orientation. The blackness around him was complete: he saw nothing, heard nothing but the hoarse sound of his own breathing.

Brian Chaney reached up to slam shut the hatch but then stopped himself—the TDV was his only lifeline to home base and it was wiser to keep that hatch open and waiting. He stretched out his hand to grope for the locker; he remembered its approximate location, and took a few hesitant steps in the darkness until he bumped into it. His suit hung in a dusty paper sheath, prepared by a dry cleaner now many years behind him, and his shoes were on the bottom beneath the suit. An automatic pistol—put there at the insistence of Arthur Saltus—now was an ungainly lump in the pocket of his jacket.

The weapon underscored his apprehension.

Chaney didn't bother to check his watch: it lacked an illuminated dial and there was nothing to be seen on the wall. He quit the darkened room.

He moved slowly down the corridor in a black eerie silence to the shelter; dust stirred up by his feet made him want to sneeze. The shelter door was found by touch and pushed open but the overhead lights failed in their automatic response. Chaney felt for the manual switch beside the door, flicked it, but stayed in darkness: the electric power was out and the lecturing engineer was a liar. He listened intently to the unseen room. He had no matches or lighter—the penalty paid by a non-smoker when light or fire was needed—and stood there for a moment of indecision, trying to recall where the smaller items were stored. He thought they were in metal lockers along the far wall, near the racks of heavy clothing.

Chaney shuffled across the floor, wishing he had that cocksure engineer here with him.

His feet collided with an empty carton, startling him, and he kicked it out of the way. It struck another object before it came to rest: Saltus had complained of sloppy housekeeping, and Katrina had written a memo.

After a period of cautious groping the ungainly bulge in his jacket pocket struck the leading edge of the bench, and he put forth both hands to explore the working surface. A radio—plugged in and wired to the antenna—a lantern, a few small empty boxes, a large one, a number of metal objects his fingers could not immediately identify, and a second lantern. Chaney barely hesitated over the objects and continued his probe. His roving fingers found a box of matches; the fuel tanks of both lanterns jostled with reassuring sounds. He lit the two lanterns and turned to look at the room. Chaney didn't like to think of himself as a coward but his hand rested in the gun pocket as he turned and peered into the gloom.

The raider had returned to pilfer the stores.

From the looks of the place the man must have spent the last few winters here, or had invited his friends in with him.

A third lantern rested on the floor near the door and he would have knocked that one over if he had stepped sideways in the darkness. A box of matches lay ready beside it. An incredible number of empty food cartons were stacked along a wall together with a collection of water cans, and he wondered why the man hadn't hauled the boxes outside and burned them to be rid of an untidy mess. Chaney counted the cans and boxes with growing wonder and tried to guess at the many years separating Arthur Saltus from his own recent arrival. *That* reminded him to look at his watch: five minutes before nine. He had the uneasy suspicion that the TDV had sent him askew once again. A plastic bag had been opened—as Saltus had reported—and a number of winter garments were missing from the racks. Several pairs of boots were gone from their shelves. The bundle of mittens was broken open and one had fallen to the floor, unnoticed in the darkness.

But there was no spilled food on the floor despite the litter of cartons and cans; every scrap had been taken up and used. Nor were there signs of mice or rats.

He whirled to the gun rack. Five rifles had been taken plus an undetermined number of the Army-issue automatics. He supposed—without count—that an appropriate amount of ammunition had gone with them. Major Moresby and Saltus would have accounted for two of the rifles.

The tiny metal objects on the workbench were the insignia Moresby had removed from his uniform, and Saltus had explained the reason for their removal in combat zones. The empty boxes had contained reels of tape, nylon film, and cartridges; the one remaining larger box was his bullet-proof vest. The map revealed the usual layer of dust. The radio was now useless—unless the supply of batteries had survived the intervening years.

Years: time.

Chaney picked up both lanterns and walked back to the room housing the TDV. He crossed to the far wall and bent down to read the calendar and clock. Each had stopped when the power line went out.

The clock read a few minutes of twelve noon, or twelve midnight. The calendar stopped measuring time on 4 Mar 09. Only the thermometer gave a meaningful reading: 52 degrees.

Eight and one half years after Arthur Saltus lived his disastrous fiftieth birthday, ten years after Major Moresby died in the skirmish at the fence, the nuclear power plant serving the laboratory failed or the lines were destroyed. They may have destroyed themselves for lack of replacement; the transformers may have blown out; the nuclear fuel may have been used up; any one or a hundred things could have happened to interrupt transmission. The power was gone.

Chaney had no idea how long ago it had failed: he knew only that he was somewhere beyond March 2009.

The outage may have happened last week, last month, last year, or at any time during the last hundred years. He hadn't asked the engineers the precise date of *his* target but had assumed they would fling him into the future one year following Saltus, to reconnoiter the station. The assumption was wrong—or the vehicle had strayed once more. Chaney ruefully concluded that it didn't matter, it really didn't matter at all. The ill-starred survey was nearly finished; it *would* be finished as soon as he made a final tour of the station and went back with his report.

He carried the lanterns back to the shelter.

The radio took his attention. Chaney dug out a sealed carton of batteries and fitted the required number into the conversion unit. The band selector was swept over the military channels and back again, without result. He turned up the gain to peak and held the instrument to his ear but it refused to give him even the airy whisper of dead air; the lack of hiss or static told him that the batteries had not survived the passage of time. Chaney dismissed the radio as of no further value and prepared himself for the target.

He was disappointed there was no note from Katrina, as he'd found on the field trial.

The bullet-proof vest went on first. Arthur Saltus had

warned him of that, had shown him the valued protection of that: Saltus lived only because he'd worn one.

Because he didn't know the season of the year—only the temperature—Chaney donned a pair of boots and helped himself to a heavy coat and a pair of mittens. He picked out a rifle, loaded it as Moresby had taught him to do, and emptied a box of cartridges in his pocket. The map was of no interest: the probes into Joliet and Chicago had been hastily cancelled and *now* he was restricted to the station itself. Check it out quickly and jump for home base. Katrina had said the President and his Cabinet were awaiting a final report before concluding a course of remedial action. They called it "formulating a policy of positive polarization," whatever that was.

A last tour of the station and the survey was ended; that much of the future would be known and mapped.

Chaney slung a canteen of water over his shoulder, then stuffed a knapsack with rations and matches and hung it from the other shoulder; he didn't expect to be outside long enough to use either one. He was pleased the aged batteries didn't work—that was excuse enough to leave radio and recorder behind—but he fitted film into the camera because Gilbert Seabrooke had asked for a record of the destruction of the station. The verbal description offered by Saltus had been a depressing one. One last searching examination of the room gave him no other article he thought he would need.

Chaney licked his lips, now dry with apprehension, and quit the shelter.

The corridor ended and a flight of stairs led up to the operations exit. The painted sign prohibiting the carrying of arms beyond the door had been defaced:

a large slash of black paint was smeared from the first sentence to the last, half obliterating the words and voiding the warning. Chaney noted the time, and set the two lanterns down on the top step to await his return. He fitted the keys into the twin locks and stepped out hesitantly into the open air.

The day was bright with sunshine but sharply chill. The sky was new, blue, and clear of aircraft; it looked freshly scrubbed, a different sky than the hazy polluted one he had known almost all his life. Patches of light frost clung to the protected spots not yet touched by the sun.

His watch read 9:30, and he guessed the time was about right—the bright morning outside was still new.

A two-wheeled cart waited in the parking lot.

Chaney eyed the crude apparition, prepared for almost anything but that. The cart was not too skillfully made, having been put together with used lumber, an axle, and a pair of wheels taken from one of the small electric cars Saltus had described. Strands of machine wire had been employed to hold the four sides together where nails failed to do an adequate job, and to fasten the bed to the axle; the tires were long rotted away and the cart rode on metal rims. No skilled carpenter had fitted it together.

The second object to catch his eye was a heaped mound of clay in the adjoining area that had once been a flower garden. Unusually tall grass and weeds grew everywhere, partially obscuring a view of the station and almost blocking sight of the yellow mound; the grass grew high around the parking lot, and beyond it, and in the open spaces surrounding the buildings across the street. Weeds and grass filled the near distance as far as the eye could see, and he was reminded of the buffalo grass said to have grown here when Illinois was an Indian prairie. Time had done that—time and neglect. The station lawns had long gone unattended.

Moving warily, stopping often to scan the area around him, Chaney approached the mound.

When he was yet a distance away he discovered a faint trail running from the edge of the lot, through the garden and toward the mound itself. The next discovery was equally blunt. Alongside the path—almost invisible in the high grass—was a water channel, a crude aqueduct made from guttering ripped from some building and twisted into shape to serve this purpose. Chaney stopped short in surprise and stared at the guttering and the nearby mound, already guessing at what he would find. He continued the stealthy approach.

He came suddenly into a clearing in the rampant grass and found the artifact: a cistern with a crude wooden lid. A bucket and a length of rope rested beside it.

Chaney slowly circled the cistern and the clay that had come from the excavation, to stumble over yet another channel made of the same guttering; the second aqueduct ran through the weeds and grass toward the lab building—probably to catch the run-off from the roof. The clay mound was not fresh. Struck with an overwhelming curiosity, he knelt down and pried away the lid to find a cistern half filled with water. The walls of the pit were lined with old brick and rough stone slabs but the water was remarkably clean, and he looked to see why. Filters made of screenwire torn from a window were fitted over the ends of each gutter to protect the cistern from incoming debris and small animals. The gutters themselves were free of leaves and trash, and an effort had been made to seal the joints with a tarry substance.

Chaney put down the rifle and bent to study the cistern in wonder. It was already recognizable.

Like the cart, it had not been fashioned by skilled hands. The shape of the thing—the lines of it—were easily familiar: the sides not quite perpendicular, the mouth not evenly rounded, and the shaft appearing to be larger near the bottom than at the top. It was odd, amateurish, and sunk without a plumb line—but it was a reasonably faithful copy of a Nabataean cistern and it might be expected to hold water for a century or more. In this place it was startling. Chaney replaced the lid and climbed to his feet.

When he turned around he saw the grave.

It shocked him. The site had been concealed from him until now by the high growth of the garden, but again a faint path led to it from the clearing at the cistern. The mound above the grave was low, aged, and covered by a short weedy grass; the cross above it was nailed together and coated with fading white paint. Dim lettering was visible on the crossarm.

Chaney moved in and knelt again to read it.

A ditat Deus K

The gatehouse door had been loosed from its hinges and taken away—perhaps to build the cart.

Chaney peered warily through the opening, alert for danger but dreading the possibility of it, then stepped inside for a closer examination. The room was bare. No trace remained of the men who had died there: bone, weapon, scrap of cloth, nothing. Some of the window glass had been knocked out but other panes were intact; the screenwire had been taken from two of the windows. An empty place.

He backed out and turned to stare at the gate.

It was shut and padlocked, effectively blocking admittance to all but a determined climber, and an effort had been made to repair the damage done to it. Chaney noted all that in a single glance and went forward to study the additional stoppers—the added warnings. Three grisly talismans hung on the outside of the gate facing the road: three skulls, taken from the bodies of the men who'd died in the gatehouse so long ago. The warning to would-be trespassers was strikingly clear.

Chaney stared at the skulls, knowing the warnings to be as old as time; he knew of similar monitions which had guarded towns in Palestine before the Roman conquest, monitions which had been used as late as the eighteenth century in some of the more remote villages of the Negev.

He saw no one in the area: the entrance and its approaches were deserted, the warning well taken. Weeds and waist-high grass grew in the ditches and the fields on either side of the road leading to the distant highway but the grass had not been disturbed by the passage of men. The blacktopped road was empty, the white line down the center long since weathered away and the asphalt surface badly damaged by the years. An automobile using that road now would be forced to move at a snail's pace.

Chaney photographed the scene and quit the area.

Walking north with an easy stride, he followed the familiar route to the barracks where he'd lived that short while with Saltus and Moresby. The site was almost passed over because it was covered by a tangle of weeds and grass; no buildings rose above the jungle.

Forcing his way through the tangle—and flushing from its nesting place a quick, furry thing he tardily recognized as a rabbit—Chaney stumbled upon the burned-out base of a building nearly lost in the undergrowth. He couldn't recognize it as his own barracks, nor point to the location of his small room if it *had* been the barracks; only the long narrow rectangle of the foundation suggested the kind of dwelling it was. Chaney peered over the wall. A narrow band of frost lined the cement blocks at the groundline on the north side, pointing up the chill in the air. Patches of blue wildflowers grew in the sunlight and—much to his surprise—other patches of wild, red strawberries sprouted everywhere along the sunnier side of the foundation. He thought to glance at the sky, measuring the progress of the sun and the season, then stared again at the strawberries. It *should* be early summer.

Chaney photographed it and went back to the street. An abandoned place. He continued north.

E Street was easily identified without the need of the rusted sign standing on a pole at a corner. He stayed alert, walking cautiously and listening hard for any sound around him. The station was quiet under the sun.

The recreation area was harshly changed.

Chaney crept silently in the entrance and across the broken concrete patio to the rim of the swimming pool. He looked down. A few inches of dirty water covered the bottom—residue from the rains—together with a poor collection of rusted and broken weapons and an appreciable amount of debris blown in by the wind: the pool had become a dumping ground for trash and armament. The sodden corpse of some small animal floated in a corner. A lonely place. Chaney very carefully put away the memory of the pool as he'd known it and backed away from the edge. The area now seemed unkempt, ugly, and not a scene to be compared with more pleasant times.

He left quickly, bearing north and west. The far corner was a mile or more away as he remembered the map of the station, but he thought he could walk the distance in a reasonable time.

Chaney found the motor pool before he'd progressed a half dozen long blocks. Less than twenty cars littered the great blacktopped lot, but not one was operable: they had been wantonly stripped of parts and many of them were no more than burned-out shells. The hood of every vehicle was propped open, and the batteries taken; not one of the small motors was left intact to provide him with an idea of the plant. Chaney poked about the lot because he was curious, and because Arthur Saltus had told him about the little electric cars. He wished he could drive one. There were no trucks on the lot nor had he seen one anywhere on the station, although a number of them had been working the post during his training period. He supposed they had been transferred to Chicago to meet the emergency—or had been stolen when the ramjets overran the station.

Chaney emerged from the lot and stopped abruptly on the street. It may have been an illusion brought on by tension, but he thought he glimpsed movement in the high grass across the street. He slipped the safety on the rifle and walked to the curb. Nothing was visible in the heavy undergrowth.

There were no holes in the fence at the corner.

The burned and rusted shell of a truck occupied a place that had once been a hole, but now that truck was a part of the repaired fence. Barbed wire had been strung back and forth across the opening, pulled taut over, under, and through the wreck itself in such fashion that the truck became an integral part of the barrier; yet other strands of wire were laced vertically through the fencing, making it impossible for even a small boy to crawl through. He went along the fence to examine the second hole. It had been repaired and rebuilt in as thorough a manner as the first, and an old cavity in the ground had been filled in. The barricade was intact, impenetrable.

Everywhere the weeds and grass grew tall, actually concealing the lower third of the fence from a man standing only a few feet away. Chaney was not surprised to find the same gruesome talismans guarding the northwest corner; he had expected to find them. The skeletal owners of the skulls were missing, but nowhere on the station had he seen a human body—someone had buried them all, friend and foe alike. The three skulls hung at the top of the fencing, glaring down at the plain below and at the rusted railroad beyond.

Chaney turned away.

He prowled through the high grass, looking for anything. Arthur Saltus had found no trace of the Major but yet Chaney could not help himself; he searched for any trifle that would indicate the man's presence on the scene. It was impossible to give up Major Moresby without some effort, some attempt to place him there.

From somewhere in the distance the shrill, playful shout of a child pierced the morning.

Chaney jumped with astonishment and nearly lost his footing on a chunk of metal buried in the grass. He turned quickly to scan the corner of the station he thought empty, then searched backward over the route he'd traveled from the motor pool. The child was heard again—and then a woman's voice calling to it. Behind him. Down the slope. Chaney felt an eager, mounting excitement as he spun about and ran to the fence. They were out there beyond the fence.

He found them at once: a man, a woman, and a child of three or four years, trudging along the railway tracks in the middle distance. The man was carrying nothing but a stout stick or club, while the woman was toting a bag. The youngster ran along behind them, playing some game of his own devising.

Chaney was so glad to see them he forgot his own danger and yelled at the top of his voice. The rifle was a burden and he dropped it, to wave both hands.

Ignoring the barbed wire, he climbed part way up the fence to show himself and gain their attention. He shouted again, and beckoned them to come toward him.

The result left him utterly dumbfounded.

The adult members of the family looked around with some surprise, stared up and down the tracks, across fields, and discovered him at last clinging to the fence alongside the talismans. They stood motionless, frozen by fear, for only a tick in time. The woman cried out as though in pain and dropped the bag; she ran to protect the child. The man sprinted after her—passed her—

and caught up the child in a quick scooping motion. The stick fell from his hands. He turned only once to stare at Chaney hanging on the fence and then raced away along the tracks. The woman stumbled—nearly fell—then ran desperately to keep pace with the man. The father shifted his small burden to one shoulder, then used his free hand to help the woman—urging her, hurrying her. They ran from him with all the speed and strength they possessed, the child now crying with consternation. Fear ran with them.

"Come back!"

He clung to the prickly fence and watched them out of sight. The billboard and high grasses hid them, shut them off, and the childish crying was hushed. Chaney hung there, his fingers curling through the holes of the fencing.

"Please come back!"

The northwest corner of the world stayed empty. He climbed down from the fence with bloodied hands.

Chaney picked up the rifle and turned away, plowing a path through the weeds and grass toward the distant road and the cluster of buildings at the heart of the station. He lacked the courage to look back. He had never known anyone to run from him—not even those beggar children who had squatted on the sands of the Negev and watched him pry into the sands of their forgotten history. They were timid and mistrustful, those Bedouin, but they hadn't run from him. He walked back without pause, refusing to look again at the stripped automobiles, the recreation area with its pool-sized midden, the burned out barracks and the attending wildflowers—refusing to look at any of it, not wanting to see anything more of the world that had been or the new one discovered today. He walked with the taste of wormwood in his mouth.

Elwood Station was an enclosed world, a fenced and fright-inducing world standing like an island of dogged isolation amid the survivors of that violent civil war. There *were* survivors. They were out there on the outside and they had fled from him—on the inside. Their fears centered on the station: *here* was the devil they knew. *He* was the devil they'd glimpsed.

But the station had a resident—not a visitor, not a raider from beyond the fence who plundered the stores in the wintertime, but a permanent resident. A resident devil who had repaired the fence and hung out the talismen to keep the survivors away, a resident christian who had dug a grave and erected a cross above it.

Chaney stood in the middle of the parking lot.

Before him: the impenetrable walls of the laboratory stood out like a great gray temple in a field of weeds. Before him: a mound of yellow clay heaped beside the Nabataean cistern stood out like an anachronistic thumb, with a single grave hard by. Before him: a two-wheeled cart made of reclaimed lumber and borrowed wheels.

Somewhere behind him: a pair of eyes watching.

SIXTEEN

Brian Chaney took the keys from his pocket and unlocked the operations door. Two lanterns rested on the top step, but no bells rang below as the door swung. A rush of clammy air fell through the doorway to be lost in the crisp, cleaner air outside. The sun rode high —near the zenith—but the day stayed chilly with little promise of becoming warmer. Chaney was thankful for the heavy coat he wore.

Quiet sun, clean sky, unseasonably cold weather: he could report that to Gilbert Seabrooke.

He propped the heavy door open by shoving the cart against it, and then went below for the first armload of rations. The rifle was left beside the cart, all but forgotten. Carton after carton of foodstuffs was hauled up the stairs and piled in the cart, until his arms were weary of carrying and his legs of climbing; but medicines and matches were forgotten and he made another trip. A few tools for himself were included as a tardy afterthought. Chaney very nearly overestimated himself: the cart was so heavily loaded after the last trip that he had difficulty moving it from the doorway, and so a few of the heavier boxes had to be left behind.

He left the parking lot, pushing the cart.

It cost him more than three hours and most of his

determination to reach the northwest corner of the fence the second time that day. The load moved fairly well as long as paved streets served him but when he left the end of the street and struck off through the high grass on his own back trail, progress was miserable. The cart was only slightly easier to pull than push. Chaney didn't remember seeing a machete in the stores, but he wished for a dozen of them—and a dozen bearers to work in front of him hacking a trail through the weedy jungle. The load was back-breaking.

When at last he reached the fence he fell down and gasped for breath. The sun was long past noon.

The fence was assaulted with a crowbar. The task seemed easier where the fencing had been patched over the remains of the truck; it was not as stout there, not as resistant to the bar as the undamaged sections, and he concentrated on that place. He ripped away the barbed wire and pulled it free of the truck shell, then pried out the ends of the original fencing and rolled it back out of the way. When it was done his hands were bleeding again from many cuts and scratches, but he had forced an opening large enough to roll the cart through beside the truck. The wall was breached.

The heavy cart got away from him on the downward slope.

He ran with it, struggling to halt the plunge down the hillside and shouting at it with an exhausted temper but the cart ignored his imprecations and shot down through tall grass that was no barrier at all—now—until at last it reached the plain below and flipped end for end, spilling its load in the weeds. Chaney roared his anger: the Aramaic term so well liked by Arthur Saltus, and then another phrase reserved for asses and tax collectors. The cart—like the ass, but unlike the collector—did not respond.

Laboriously he righted the cart, gathered up the spill, and trudged across the field to the railroad.

The dropped walking stick was a marker.

His small treasure was left there for finding, laid out along the railroad right-of-way for the frightened family or any other traveler who might pass that way. He put the matches and the medicines atop the largest carton and then covered them with his overcoat to protect them from the weather. Chaney spent only a little while scanning the distances along the tracks for sight of a man—he was certain his shouting and his cursing would have frightened away anyone in the area. As before, he was alone in an empty world. From somewhere in the timber he heard a bird calling, and he would have to be content with that.

In the late afternoon hours when the thin heat of the sun was beginning to fade he pulled the empty cart up the hill and through the gaping hole in the fence for a last time, stopping only to retrieve the crowbar. Chaney didn't dare look back. He was afraid of what he might find—or not find. To suddenly turn and look, to discover someone already at the boxes would be his undoing—he knew he would behave as before and again frighten the man away. But to turn and see the same untenanted world again would only deepen his depression. He would not look back.

Chaney followed his own trail through the verdant grass, seeking the beginning of the paved road. Some small animal darted away at his approach.

He stood at the edge of the parking lot, looking at

the abandoned garden and thinking of Kathryn van Hise. But for her, he would be loafing on the beach and thinking of going back to work in the tank—but only thinking of it; perhaps in another week or so he'd get up off his duff and look up train schedules and connections to Indianapolis, if they still existed in an age of dying rails. The only weight on his mind would be the reviewers who read books too hastily and leaped to fantastic conclusions. But for her, he would have never heard of Seabrooke, Moresby, Saltus—unless their names happened to be on a document coming into the tank. He wouldn't have jumped into Joliet two years ahead of his time and found a wall; he wouldn't have jumped into *this* dismal future, whatever year *this* might be, and found a catastrophe. He would have plodded along in his own slow, myopic way until the hard future slammed into him—or he into it.

He thought he was done here: done with the aborted survey and done with the very quiet and nearly deserted world of 2000-something. He could do no more than tell Katrina, tell Seabrooke, and perhaps listen while they relayed the word to Washington. The next move would be up to the politicians and the bureaucrats—let them change the future if they could, if they possessed the power.

His role was completed. He could tape a report and label it *Eschatos*.

The mound of yellow clay claimed his attention and he followed the gutter through the grass to the cistern, wanting to photograph it. He still marveled at finding a Nabataean artifact thrust forward into the twenty-first century, and he suspected Arthur Saltus was responsible: it had been copied from the book he'd lent Saltus, from the pages of *Pax Abrahamitica.* With luck, it would trap and hold water for another century or so, and if he could measure the capacity he would probably find the volume to be near ten *cor*. Saltus had done well for an amateur.

Chaney turned to the grave.

He would not photograph that, for the picture would raise questions he didn't care to answer. Seabrooke would ask if there'd been an inscription on the crossarm, and why hadn't he photographed the inscription? Katrina would sit by with pencil poised to record his verbal reading.

A ditat Deus K

Down there: Arthur or Katrina?

How could he tell Katrina that he'd found her grave? Or her husband's grave? Why couldn't *this* have been the final resting place of Major Moresby?

A bird cried again in some far off place, pulling his gaze up to the distant trees and the sky beyond.

The trees were in new leaf, telling the early summer; the grass was soft tender green, not yet wiry from the droughts of midsummer: a fresh world. Gauzy clouds were gathering about the descending sun, creating a mirage of reddish-gold fleece. Eastward, the sky was wondrously blue and clean—a newly scrubbed sky, disinfected and sterilized. At night the stars must appear as enormous polished diamonds.

Arthur or Katrina?

Brian Chaney knelt briefly to touch the sod above the grave, and mentally prepared himself to go home. His depression was deep.

A voice said: "Please . . . Mr. Chaney?"

The shock immobilized him. He was afraid that if he turned quickly or leaped to his feet, a nervous finger would jerk the trigger and he would join Moresby in the soil of the station. He held himself rigidly still, aware that his own rifle had been left in the cart. Oversight; carelessness; stupidity. One hand rested on the grave; his gaze remained on the small cross.

"Mr. Chaney?"

After the longest time—a disquieting eternity—he turned only his head to look back along the path.

Two strangers: two *almost* strangers, two people who mirrored his own uncertainty and apprehension.

The nearer of the two wore a heavy coat and a pair of boots taken from the stores; his head and hands were bare and the only weapon he carried was a pair of binoculars also borrowed from the stores. He was tall, thin, lanky—only a few inches less than Chaney's height, but he lacked the sandy hair and muscular body of his father; he lacked the bronzed skin and the silver filling in his teeth, he lacked the squint of eye that would suggest a seafarer peering into the sun. He lacked the buoyant youthfulness. If the man had possessed those characteristics instead of lacking them, Chaney would say he was looking at Arthur Saltus.

"How do you know my name?"

"You are the only one unaccounted for, sir."

"And you had my description?"

Softly: "Yes, sir."

Chaney turned on his knees to face the strangers. He realized they were as much afraid of him as he was of them. When had they last seen another man here?

"Your name is Saltus?"

A nod. "Arthur Saltus."

Chaney shifted his gaze to the woman who stood well behind the man. She stared at *him* with a curious mixture of fascination and fright, poised for instant flight. When had she last seen another man here?

Chaney asked: "Kathryn?"

She didn't respond, but the man said: "My sister."

The daughter was like the mother in nearly every respect, lacking only the summer tan and the delta pants. She was bundled in a great coat against the chill and wore the common boots that were much too large for her feet. A pair of binoculars hung around her neck: *he* felt closely observed. Her head was bare, revealing Katrina's great avalanche of fine brown hair; her eyes were the same soft—now frightened—delightful shade. She was a small woman, no more than a hundred pounds when free of the bulky boots and coat, and gave every appearance of being quick and alert. She also gave the appearance of being older than Katrina.

Chaney looked from one to the other: the two of them, brother and sister, were years beyond the people he had left in the past, years beyond their parents.

He said at last: "Do you know the date?"

"No, sir."

Hesitation, then: "I think you were waiting for me."

Arthur Saltus nodded, and there was the barest hint of affirmation from the woman.

"My father said you would be here—sometime. He was certain you would come; you were the last of the three."

Surprise: "No one else, after us?"

"No one."

Chaney touched the grave a last time, and their eyes

followed his hand. He had one more question to ask before he would risk getting to his feet.

"Who lies here?"

Arthur Saltus said: "My father."

Chaney wanted to cry out: how? when? why? but embarrassment held his tongue, embarrassment and pain and depression; he bitterly regretted the day he'd accepted Katrina's offer and stepped into this unhappy position. He climbed to his feet, avoiding sudden moves that could be misinterpreted, and was thankful he hadn't taken a picture of the grave—thankful he wouldn't have to tell Katrina, or Saltus, or Seabrooke, what he'd found here. He would make no mention of the grave at all.

Standing, Chaney searched the area carefully, looking over their heads at the weedy garden, the parking lot, the company street beyond the lot and all of the station open to his eye. He saw no one else.

Sharp question: "Are you two alone here?"

The woman had jumped at his tone and seemed about to flee, but her brother held his ground.

"No, sir."

A pause, and then: "Where is Katrina?"

"She is waiting in the place, Mr. Chaney."

"Does she know I am here?"

"Yes, sir."

"She knew I would ask about her?"

"Yes, sir. She thought you would."

Chaney said: "I'm going to break a rule."

"She thought you would do that, too."

"But she didn't object?"

"She gave us instructions, sir. If you asked, we were to say that she *told* you where she would wait."

Chany nodded his wonder. "Yes—she did that. She did that twice." He moved back along the path by way of the cistern and they carefully retreated before him, still uncertain of him. "Did you do this?"

"My father and I dug it, Mr. Chaney. We had your book. The descriptions were very clear."

"I'd tell Haakon, if I dared."

Arthur Saltus stepped aside when they reached the parking lot and allowed Chaney to go ahead of him. The woman had darted off to one side and now kept a prudent distance. She continued to stare at him, a stare that might have been rude under other circumstances, and Chaney was very sure she'd seen no other man for too many years. He was equally certain she'd never seen a man like him inside the protective fence: that was her apprehension.

He ignored the rifle resting in the cart.

Brian Chaney fitted the keys into the twin locks and swung the heavy door. His two lanterns rested on the top step, and as before a rush of musty air fell out into the waning afternoon sunlight. Chaney paused awkwardly on the doorsill wondering what to say—wondering *how* to say goodbye to these people. Only a damned fool would say something flippant or vacuous or inane; only a damned fool would utter one of the meaningless cliches of *his* age; but only a stupid fool would simply walk away from them without saying anything.

He glanced again at the sky and at the golden fleece about the sun, at the new grass and leaves and then at the aging mound of yellow clay. At length his gaze swung back to the man and woman who waited on him.

He said: "Thank you for trusting me."

Saltus nodded. "They said you could be trusted."

Chaney studied Arthur Saltus and almost saw again the unruly sandy hair and the peculiar set to his eyes—the eyes of a man long accustomed to peering against the sun-bright sea. He looked long at Kathryn Saltus but could *not* see the transparent blouse or the delta pants: on her those garments would be obscene. Those garments belonged to a world long gone. He searched her face for a moment too long, and was falling head over heels when reality brought him up short.

Harsh reality: she lived *here* but he belonged back there. It was folly to entertain even dreams about a woman living a hundred years ahead of him. Hurtful reality.

His conscience hurt when he closed the door because he had no more to say to them. Chaney turned away and went down the steps, putting behind him the quiet sun, the chill world of 2000-plus, the unknown survivors beyond the fence who had fled in terror at sight and sound of him, and the half-familiar survivors within the fence who were sharp reminders of his own loss. His conscience hurt, but he didn't turn back.

The time was near sunset on an unknown day.

It was the longest day of his life.

SEVENTEEN

THE BRIEFING ROOM was subtly different from that one he'd first entered weeks or years or centuries ago.

He remembered the military policeman who'd escorted him from the gate and then opened the door for him; he remembered his first glance into the room —his lukewarm reception, his tardy entrance. He'd found Kathryn van Hise critically eyeing him, assessing him, wondering if he would measure up to some task ahead; he'd found Major Moresby and Arthur Saltus playing cards, bored, impatiently awaiting his arrival; he'd found the long steel table positioned under lights in the center of the room—all waiting on him.

He had given his name and started an apology for his tardiness when the first hurtful sound stopped him, chopped him off in mid-sentence and hammered his ears. He had seen them turn together to watch the clock: sixty-one seconds. All that only a week or two ago—a century or two ago—before the bulky envelopes were opened and a hundred flights of fancy loosed. The long journey from the Florida beach had brought him twice to this room, but *this* time the lantern poorly illuminated the place.

Katrina was there.

The aged woman was sitting in her accustomed chair

to one side of the oversized steel table–sitting quietly in the darkness beneath the extinct ceiling lights. As always, her clasped hands rested on the tabletop in repose. Chaney put the lantern on the table between them and the poor light fell on her face.

Katrina.

Her eyes were bright and alive, as sharply alert as he remembered them, but time had not been lenient with her. He read lines of pain, of unknown troubles and grief; the lines of a tenacious woman who had endured much, had suffered much, but had never surrendered her courage. The skin was drawn tight over her cheekbones, pulled tight around her mouth and chin and appeared sallow in lantern light. The lustrous, lovely hair was entirely gray. Hard years, unhappy years, lean years.

Despite all that he knew a familiar spark within him: she was as beautiful in age as in youth. He was pleased to find that loveliness so enduring.

Chaney pulled out his own chair and slid down, never taking his eye off her. The old woman sat without moving, without speaking, watching him intently and waiting for the first word.

He thought: she might have been sitting there for centuries while the dust and the darkness grew around her; waiting patiently for him to come forward to the target, waiting for him to explore the station, fulfill his last mission, end the survey, and *then* come opening doors to find the answers to questions raised above ground. Chaney would not have been too surprised to find her waiting in ancient Jericho if he'd gone back ten thousand years. She would have been there, placidly waiting in some temple or hovel, waiting in a place where he would find her when he began opening doors.

The dusty briefing room was as chill as the cellar had been, as chill as the air outside, and she was bundled in one of the heavy coats. Her hands were encased in a pair of large mittens intended for a man—and if he bent to look, he would find the oversize boots. She appeared bent over, small in the chair and terribly tired.

Katrina waited on him.

Chaney struggled for something to say, something that wouldn't sound foolish or melodramatic or carry a ring of false heartiness. She would despise him for that. Here again was the struggle of the outer door, and here again he was fearful of losing the struggle. He had left her here in this room only hours ago, left her with that sense of dry apprehension as he prepared himself for the third—now final—probe into the future. She had been sitting in the same chair in the same attitude of repose.

Chaney said: "I'm *still* in love with you, Katrina."

He watched her eyes, and thought they were quickly filled with humor and a pleasurable laughter.

"Thank you, Brian."

Her voice had aged as well: it sounded more husky than he remembered and it reflected her weariness.

"I found patches of wild strawberries at the old barracks, Katrina. When do strawberries ripen in Illinois?"

There *was* laughter in her eyes. "In May or June. The summers have been quite cold, but May or June."

"Do you know the year? The number?"

A minute movement of her head. "The power went out many years ago. I'm sorry, Brian, but I have lost the count."

"I don't suppose it really matters—not now, not with what we've already learned. I agree with Pindar."

She looked her question.

He said: "Pindar lived about twenty-five hundred years ago but he was wiser than a lot of men alive to-day. He warned man of peering too far into the future, he warned of not liking what would be found." An apologetic gesture; a grin. "Bartlett again: my vice. The Commander was always teasing me about my affair with Bartlett."

"Arthur waited long to see you. He hoped you would come early, that he might see you again."

"I would have liked— Didn't anyone *know?*"

"No."

"But why not? That gyroscope was tracking me."

"No one knew your arrival date; no one would guess. The gyroscope device could not measure your progress after the power failed *here.* We knew only the date of failure, when the TDV suddenly stopped transmitting signals to the computer *there.* You were wholly lost to us, Brian."

"Sheeg! Those goddam infallible engineers and their goddam infallible inventions!" He caught himself and was embarrassed at the outburst. "Excuse me, Katrina." Chaney reached across the table and closed his hands over hers. "I found the Commander's grave outside—I wish I *had* been on time. And I had already decided not to tell you about that grave when I went back, when I turned in my report." He peered at her. "I *didn't* tell anyone, did I?"

"No, you reported nothing."

A satisfied nod. "Good for me—I'm still keeping my mouth shut. The Commander made me promise not to tell you about your future marriage, a week or so ago when we returned from the Joliet trials. But you tried to pry the secret out of me, remember?"

She smiled at his words. "A week or so ago."

Chaney mentally kicked himself. "I have this bad habit of putting my foot in my mouth."

A little movement of her head to placate him. "But I guessed at your secret, Brian. Between your manner and Arthur's deportment, I guessed it. You put yourself away from me."

"I think you had already made up your mind. The little signs were beginning to show, Katrina." He had a vivid memory of the victory party the night of their return.

She said: "I had almost decided at that time, and I *did* decide a short while afterward; I *did* decide when he came back hurt from his survey. He was so helpless, so near death when you and the doctor took him from the vehicle I decided on the spot." She glanced at his enfolding hands and then raised her eyes. "But I was aware of your own intentions. I knew you would be hurt."

He squeezed her fingers with encouragement. "Long ago and far away, Katrina. I'm getting over it."

She made no reply, knowing it to be a half-truth.

"I met the children—" He stopped, aware of the awkwardness. "Children they are *not*—they're older than I am! I met Arthur and Kathryn out there but they were afraid of me."

Katrina nodded and again her gaze slid away from him to rest on his enveloping hands.

"Arthur is ten years older than you, I think, but Kathryn should be about the same age. I am sorry I can't be more precise than that; I am sorry I can't tell you how long my husband has been dead. We no longer know time here, Brian; we only live from one summer to the next. It is not the happiest existence." After a while her hands moved inside his, and she glanced up again. "They were afraid of you because they've known no other man since the station was overrun, since the military personnel left here and we stayed within the fence for safety. For a year or two we dared not even leave this building."

Bitterly: "The people out there were afraid of me, too. They ran away from me."

She was quickly astonished, and betrayed alarm.

"Which people? Where?"

"The family I found outside the fence—down there by the railroad tracks."

"There is no one alive out there."

"Katrina, there *is*—I saw them, called to them, begged them to come back, but they ran away in fear."

"How many? Were there many of them?"

"Three. A family of three: father, mother, and a little boy. I found them walking along the railroad track out there beyond the northwest corner. The little fellow was picking up something—pieces of coal, perhaps—and putting them in a bag his mother carried; they seemed to be making a game of it. They were walking in peace, in contentment until I called to them."

Tersely: "Why did you do that? Why did you call attention to yourself?"

"Because I was lonely! Because I was sick and hurt at sight of an empty world! I yelled out because those people were the only living things I'd found here, other than a frightened rabbit. I wanted their company, I wanted their news! I would have given them everything

I owned for only an hour of their time. Katrina, I wanted to *know* if people were still living in this world." He stopped and took tighter rein on his emotions. More quietly: "I wanted to talk to them, to ask questions, but they were afraid of me—scared witless, shocked by sight of me. They ran like that frightened rabbit and I never saw them again. I can't tell you how much that hurt me."

She pulled her hands from his and dropped them into her lap.

"Katrina—"

She wouldn't look up at once, but steadfastly kept her gaze on the tabletop. The movement of her hands had left small trails in the dust. He thought the tiny bundle of her seemed more wilted and withdrawn than before: the taut skin on her face appeared to have aged in the last few minutes—or perhaps that age had been claiming her all the while they talked.

"Katrina, please."

After a long while she said: "I am sorry, Brian. I will apologize for my children, and for that family. They dared not trust you, none of them, and the poor family felt they had good reason to fear you." Her head came up and he felt shock. "Everyone fears you; no one will trust you since the rebellion. I am the only one here who does not fear a black man."

He was hurt again, not by her words but because she was crying. It was painful to watch her cry.

Brian Chaney came into the briefing room a second time. He was carrying another lantern, two plastic cups, and a container of water from the stores. He would have brought along a bottle of whiskey if that had been available, but it was likely that the Commander had long ago consumed the whiskey on his successive birthdays.

The old woman had wiped her eyes dry.

Chaney filled both cups and set the first one on the table before her. "Drink up—we'll drink a toast."

"To what, Brian?"

"To what? Do we need an excuse?" He swung his arm in an expansive gesture which took in the room. "To that damned clock up there: knocking off sixty-one seconds while my ears suffered. To that red telephone: I never used it to call the President and tell him he was a dunce. To us: a demographer from the Indiana Corporation, and a research supervisor from the Bureau of Standards—the last two misfits sitting at the end of the world. We're out of place and out of time, Katrina: they don't need demographers and researchers here—they don't have corporations and bureaus here. Drink to us."

"Brian, you are a clown."

"Oh, yes." He sat down and looked at her closely in the lantern light. "Yes, I am that. And I think you are *almost* smiling again. Please smile for me."

Katrina smiled: pale shadow of an old smile.

Chaney said: "Now *that* is why I still love you!" He lifted his cup. "To the most beautiful researcher in the world—and you may drink to the most frustrated demographer in the world. Bottoms up!" Chaney emptied the cup, and thought the water tasted flat—stale.

She nodded over the rim of her cup and sipped.

Chaney stared at the long table, the darkened lights overhead, the stopped clock, the dead telephones. "I'm supposed to be working—making a survey."

"It doesn't matter."

"Have to keep Seabrooke happy. I can report a family out there: at least *one* family alive and living in peace. I suppose there are more—there has to be more. Do you know of anyone else? Anyone at all?"

Patiently: "There were a few at first, those many years ago; we managed to keep in touch with some survivors by radio before the power failure. Arthur located a small group in Virginia, a military group living underground in an Army command post; and later he contacted a family in Maine. Sometimes we would make brief contact with one or two individuals in the west, in the mountain states, but it was always poor news. Each of them survived for the same reasons: by a series of lucky circumstances, or by their skills and their wits, or because they were unusually well protected as we were. Their numbers were always small and it was always discouraging news."

"But *some* survived. That's important, Katrina. How long have you been alone on the station?"

"Since the rebellion, since the Major's year."

Chaney gestured. "That could be—" He peered at her, guessing at her age. "That could be thirty years ago."

"Perhaps."

"But what happened to the other people here?"

She said: "Almost all the military personnel were withdrawn at the beginning; they were posted to overseas duty. The few who remained did not survive the attack when the rebels overran the station. A very few civilian technicians stayed with us for a time, but then left to rejoin their families—or search for their families. The laboratory was already empty in Arthur's year. We had been ordered underground for the duration."

"The duration. How long was that?"

The sharp old eyes studied him. "I would think it is ending just now, Brian. Your description of the family outside the fence suggests it is ending now."

Bitterly: "And nobody around but you and me to sign the peace treaty and pose for the cameras. Seabrooke?"

"Mr. Seabrooke was relieved of his post, dismissed, shortly after the three launches. I believe he returned to the Dakotas. The President had blamed *him* for the failure of the survey, and he was made the scapegoat."

Chaney struck the table with a fist.

"I *said* that man was a dunce—just one more in a long line of idiots and dunces inhabiting the White House! Katrina, I don't understand how this country has managed to survive with so many incompetent fools at the top."

Softly-spoken reminder: "It hasn't, Brian."

He muttered under his breath and glared at the dust on the table. Aloud: "Excuse me."

She nodded easily but said nothing.

A memory prodded him. "What happened to the JCS, to those men who tried to take Camp David?"

She closed her eyes for a moment, as if to close off the past. Her expression was bitter. "The Joint Chiefs of Staff were executed before a firing squad, a public spectacle. The President had declared a business moratorium on the day of the execution; government offices closed and the children were let out of school, all to witness the spectacle on the networks. He was determined to give the country a warning. It was ghastly, depressing, and I hated him for it."

Chaney stared at her. "And I have to go back and tell him what he's going to do. What a hell of a chore *this* survey is!" He hurled the drinking cup across the room, unable to stifle the angry impulse. "Katrina, I wish you had never found me on the beach. I wish I had walked away from you, or thrown you into the sea, or kidnapped you and ran away to Israel—anything."

She smiled again, perhaps at the memory of the beach. "But that would have accomplished nothing, Brian. The Arab Federation overran Israel and drove the people into the sea. We wouldn't have escaped anything."

He uttered a single word and then had to apologize again, although the woman didn't understand the epithet. "The Major certainly jumped into the beginning of hell."

She corrected him. "The Major jumped into the end of it; the wars had been underway for nearly twenty years and the nation was on the brink of disaster. Major Moresby came forward only in time to witness the end for us, for the United States. After him, the government ceased to be. After twenty years we were wholly exhausted, used up, and could not defend ourselves against anyone."

The old woman spoke with a dry weariness, a long fatigue, and he could listen to her voice and her spirit running down as she talked.

The wars began just after the Presidential election of 1980, just after the field trials into Joliet. Arthur Saltus had told her of the two Chinese railroad towns blown off the map, and suddenly one day in December the Chinese bombed Darwin, Australia, in long-delayed retaliation. The whole of northern Australia was made uninhabitable by radiation. The public was never told of the first strike against the railroad towns but only of the second: it was painted an act of brutal savagery against an innocent populace. Radioactivity spread across the Arafura Sea to the islands to the north, and drifted toward the Phillipines. Great Britain appealed to the United States for aid.

The re-elected President and his Congress declared war on the Chinese Peoples' Republic in the week following his inauguration, after having waged an undeclared war since 1954. The Pentagon had privately assured him the matter could be terminated and the enemy subdued in three weeks. Some months later the President committed massive numbers of troops to the Asian Theater: now involving eleven nations from the Phillipine Republic westward to Pakistan, and to the defense of Australia. He was then compelled to send troops to Korea, to counteract renewed hostilities there, but lost them all when the Chinese and the Mongolians overran the peninsula and ended foreign occupation.

She said tiredly: "The President was re-elected in 1980, and again for a third term in 1984. After Arthur brought back the terrible news from Joliet, the man seemed unable to control himself and unable to do anything right. The third-term prohibition was repealed at his urging, and some time during that third term the Constitution was suspended altogether 'for the duration of the emergency.' The emergency never ended. Brian, that man was the last elected President the country ever had. After him there was nothing."

Chaney said bitterly: "The meek, the terrible meek. I hope he is still alive to see this!"

"He isn't, he wasn't. He was assassinated and his body thrown into the burning White House. They burned Washington to destroy a symbol of oppression."

"Burned it! Wait until I tell him *that.*"

She made a little gesture to hush him or contradict him. "All that and more, much more. Those twenty years were a frightful ordeal; the last few years were numbing. Life appeared to stop, to give way to savagery. We missed the little things at first: passenger trains and airliners were forbidden to civilian traffic, mail deliveries were cut back to twice a week and then halted altogether, the news telecasts were restricted to only one a day and then as the war worsened, further restricted to only local news not of a military nature. We were isolated from the world and nearly isolated from Washington.

"Our trucks were taken away for use elsewhere; food was not brought in, nor medicines, nor clothing, nor fuel, and we fell back on the supplies stored on station. The military personnel were transferred to other posts or to points overseas, leaving only a token crew to guard this installation.

"Brian, that guard was compelled to fire on nearby townspeople attempting to raid our stores: the rumor had been spread that enormous stockpiles of food were here, and they were desperately hungry."

Katrina looked down at her hands and swallowed painfully. "The twenty years finally ended for *us* in a shocking civil war."

Chaney said: "Ramjets."

"They were called that, once they came into the open, once their statement of intent was publicized: Revolution And Morality. Sometimes we would see banners bearing the word RAM, but the name soon became something dirty—something akin to that other name they were called for centuries: it was a very bitter time and you would have suffered if you had remained on station.

"Brian, people everywhere were starving, dying of disease, rotting in neglect and misery, but those people possessed a leadership we now lacked. Ramjets had efficient leadership. Their leaders used them against us and it was our turn to suffer. There *was* revolution but little or no morality; whatever morality they may have possessed was quickly lost in the rebellion and we all suffered. The country was caught up in a senseless savagery."

"That's when Moresby came up?"

A weary nod.

Major Moresby witnessed the beginning of the civil war when he emerged on his target date. *They* had chosen the same date for the outbreak of the rebellion—they had selected the Fourth of July as *their* target in a bid for independence from white America and the bombing of Chicago was intended to be the signal. Ramjet liaison agents in Peiping had arranged that: Chicago—not Atlanta or Memphis or Birmingham—was the object of their greatest hatred after the wall. But the plan went awry.

The rebellion broke out almost a week earlier—quite by accident—when triggered by a riot in the little river town of Cairo, Illinois. A traffic arrest there, followed by a street shooting and then a wholesale jail delivery of black prisoners, upset the schedule: the revolt was quickly out of control. The state militia and the police were helpless, depleted in number, their reserve manpower long since spent overseas; there was no regular army left standing in the United States except for token troops at various posts and stations, and even the ceremonial guards at national monuments had been removed and assigned to foreign duty. There was no remaining force to prevent the rebellion. Major Moresby climbed out of the vehicle and into the middle of the holocaust.

The agony went on for almost seventeen months.

The President was assassinated, Congress fled—or died while trying to flee—and Washington burned. They burned many of the cities where they were numerically strong. In their passion they burned themselves out of their homes and destroyed the fields and crops which had fed them.

The few remaining lines of transportation which were open up to that moment ceased entirely. Trucks were intercepted, looted and burned, their drivers shot. Buses were stopped on interstate highways and white passengers killed. Railroad trains were abandoned wherever they stopped, or wherever the tracks were torn up, engineers and crews were murdered wherever they were caught. Desperate hunger soon followed the stoppage of traffic.

Katrina said: "Everyone here expected the Chinese to intervene, to invade, and we knew we could not stop them. Brian, our country had lost or abandoned twenty million men overseas; we were helpless before any invader. But they did not come. I thank God they did not come. They were prevented from coming when the Soviet turned on them in a holy war in the name of Communism: that long, long border dispute burst into open warfare and the Russians drove on Lop Nor." She made a little gesture of futility. "We never learned what happened; we never learned the outcome of anything in Europe. Perhaps they are still fighting, if anyone is left alive to fight. Our contact with the Continent was lost, and has never been restored to our knowledge.

We lost contact with that military group in Virginia when the electricity failed. We were alone."

He said in wonder: "Israel, Egypt, Australia, Britain, Russia, China—all of them: the world."

"All of them," she repeated with a dull fatigue. "And our troops were wasted in nearly every one of them, thrown away by a man with a monumental ego. Not more than a handful of those troops ever returned. We were done."

Chaney said: "I guess the Commander came up at the end—seventeen months later."

"Arthur emerged from the TDV on his target date, just past the end of it: the beginning of the second winter after the rebellion. We think the rebellion *had* ended, spent and exhausted on its own fury. We think the men who assaulted him at the gatehouse were stragglers, survivors who had managed through the first winter. He said those men were as surprised by his appearance, as he was by theirs; they might have fled if he had not cornered them." Katrina laced her fingers on the tabletop in familiar gesture and looked at him. "We saw a few armed bands roaming the countryside that second winter. We repaired the fence, stood guard, but were not again molested: Arthur put out warnings he had found in the book you gave him. By the following spring, the bands of men had dwindled to a few scavengers prowling the fields for game—but after that we saw no one. Until you came, we saw no one."

He said: "So ends the bloody business of the day."

EIGHTEEN

KATRINA PEERED across the table and sought to break the unhappy silence between them.

"A family, you said? Father, mother, and child? A healthy child? How old was he?"

"I don't know: three, maybe four. The kid was having himself a fine time—playing, hollering, picking up things—until I scared off his parents." Chaney still felt bitter about that encounter. "They all looked healthy enough. They *ran* healthy."

Katrina nodded her satisfaction. "It gives one hope for the future, doesn't it?"

"I suppose so."

She reprimanded him: "You *know* so. If those people were healthy, they were eating well and living in some degree of safety. If the man carried no weapon, he thought none was needed. If they had a child and were together, family life has been re-established. And if that child survived his birth and was thriving, it suggests a quiet normalcy has returned to the world, a measure of sanity. All that gives me hope for the future."

"A quiet normalcy," he repeated. "The sun in that sky was quiet. It was cold out there."

The dark eyes peered at him. "Have you ever admitted to yourself that you could be wrong, Brian? Have you even thought of your translations today? You were a stubborn man; you came close to mocking Major Moresby."

Chaney failed to answer: it was not easy to reassess the *Eschatos* scroll in a day. A piece of his mind insisted that ancient Hebrew fiction was only fiction.

They sat in the heavy silence of the briefing room, looking at each other in the lantern light and knowing this was coming to an end. Chaney was uneasy. There had been a hundred—a thousand—questions he'd wanted to ask when he first walked into the room, when he first discovered her, but now he could think of little to say. Here was Katrina, the once youthful, radiant Katrina of the swimming pool—and outside was Katrina's family waiting for him to leave.

He wanted desperately to ask one more question but at the same time he was afraid to ask: what happened to *him* after his return, after the completion of the probe? What had happened to *him?* He wanted to know where he had gone, what he had done, how he had survived the perilous years—he wanted to know *if* he had survived those years. Chaney was long convinced that he was not on station in 1980, not there at the time of the field trials, but where was he then? She might have some knowledge of him after he'd finished the mission and left; she might have kept in touch. He was afraid to ask. Pindar's advice stopped his tongue.

He got up suddenly from his chair. "Katrina, will you walk downstairs with me?"

She gave him a strange look, an almost frightened look, but said: "Yes, sir."

Katrina left her chair and came around the table to him. Age had slowed her graceful walk and he was acutely distressed to see her move with difficulty. Chaney picked up a lantern, and offered her his free arm. He felt a flush of excitement as she neared him, touched him.

They descended the stairs without speaking. Chaney slowed his pace to accommodate her and they went down slowly, one cautious step at a time. Kathryn van Hise held on to the rail and moved with the hesitant pace of the aged.

They stopped at the opened door to the operations room. Chaney held the lantern high to inspect the vehicle: the hatch was open and the hull of the craft covered by dust; the concrete cradle seemed dirty with age.

He asked suddenly: "How much did I report, Katrina? Did I tell them about you? Your family? Did I tell them about that family on the railroad tracks? What did I say?"

"Nothing." She wouldn't look up at him.

"What?"

"You reported nothing."

He thought her voice was strained. "I had to say something. Gilbert Seabrooke will demand *something*."

"Brian—" She stopped, swallowed hard, and then began again. "You reported nothing, Mr. Chaney. You did not return from your probe. We knew you were lost to us when the vehicle failed to return at sixty-one seconds: you were wholly lost to us."

Brian Chaney very carefully put the lantern down and then turned her around and pulled her head up. He wanted to see her face, wanted to see why she was lying. Her eyes were wet with threatened tears but there was no lie there.

Stiffly: "Why not, Katrina?"

"We have no power, Mr. Chaney. The vehicle is helpless, immobile."

Chaney swung his head to stare at the TDV and as quickly swung back to the woman. He wasn't aware that he was holding her in a painful grip.

"The engineers can pull me back."

"No. They can do nothing for you: they lost you when that device stopped tracking, when the computer went silent, when the power failed here and you overshot the failure date. They *lost* you; they lost the vehicle." She pulled away from his hard grasp, and her wavering gaze fell. "You didn't come back to the laboratory, Mr. Chaney. No one saw you again after the launch; no one saw you again until you appeared here, today."

Almost shouting: "Stop calling me Mr. Chaney!"

"I am . . . I am terribly sorry. You were as lost to us as Major Moresby. We thought . . ."

He turned his back on the woman and deliberately walked into the operations room. Brian Chaney climbed up on the polywater tank and thrust a leg through the open hatch of the TDV. He didn't bother to undress or remove the heavy boots. Wriggling downward through the hatch, he slammed it shut over his head and looked for the blinking green light. There was none. Chaney stretched out full length on the web sling and thrust his heels against the kickbar at the bottom. No red light answered him.

He knew panic.

He fought against that and waited for his nerves to rest, waited for a stolid placidity to return. The memory of his first test came back: he'd thought then the vehicle was like a cramped tomb, and he thought so now. Lying on the webbed sling for the first time—and waiting for something spectacular to happen—he had felt an ache in his legs and had stretched them out to relieve the ache. His feet had struck the kickbar, sending him back to the beginning before the engineers were ready; they had been angry with him. And an hour later, in the lecture room, everyone heard and saw the results of his act: the vehicle kicked backward as he thrust out his feet, the sound struck his eardrums and the lights dimmed. The astonished engineers left the room on the run, and Gilbert Seabrooke proposed a new study program to be submitted to Indic. The TDV sucked power from its present, not its past.

Chaney reached up to snug the hatch. It was snug. The light that should have been blinking green stayed dark. Chaney put the heavy boots against the bar and pushed. The red light stayed dark. He pushed again, then kicked at the bar. After a moment he twisted around to peer through the plastic bubble into the room. It was dimly lit by the lantern resting on the floor.

He shouted: "Goddammit, go!" And kicked again.

The room was dimly lit by lantern light.

He walked slowly along the corridor in the feeble light of the lantern, walked woodenly in shock tinged with fear. The failure of the vehicle to move under his prodding had stunned him. He wished desperately for Katrina, wished she was standing by with a word or a gesture he might seize for a crutch, but she wasn't visible in the corridor. She had left him while he struggled with the vehicle, perhaps to return to the briefing room, perhaps to go outside, perhaps to retire to whatever sort of shelter she shared with her son and daughter. He was alone, fighting panic. The door to the engineering laboratory was standing open, as was the door to the storeroom, but she wasn't waiting for him in either place. Chaney listened for her but heard nothing, and went on after the smallest pause. The dusty corridor ended and a flight of stairs led upward to the operations exit.

He thought the sign on the door was a bitter mockery—one of the many visited on him since he'd sailed for Israel a century or two ago. He regretted the day he had read and translated those scrolls—but at the same time he wished desperately he knew the identity of that scribe who had amused himself and his fellows by creating the *Eschatos* document. A single name would be enough: an Amos or a Malachi or an Ibycus.

He would hoist a glass of water from the Nabataean cistern and salute the unknown genius for his wit and wisdom, for his mockery. He would shout to the freshly scrubbed sky: "Here, damn your eyes, Ibycus! Here, for the long-dead dragons and the ruptured fence and the ice on the rivers. Here, for my head of gold, my breast of silver, my legs of iron and my feet of clay. My feet of clay, Ibycus!" And he would hurl the glass at the lifeless TDV.

Chaney turned the keys in the locks and pushed out into the chill night air. The darkness surprised him; he hadn't realized he'd spent so many bittersweet hours inside with Katrina. The parking lot was empty but for the cart and his discarded rifle. Katrina's children hadn't waited for him, and he was aware of a small hurt.

He stepped away from the building and then turned back to look at it: a massive white concrete temple in the moonlight. The barbaric legions had failed to bring *it* down, despite the damage caused elsewhere on the station.

The sky was the second surprise: he had seen it by day and marveled, but at night it was shockingly beautiful. The stars *were* bright and hard as carefully polished gems, and there were a hundred or a thousand more than he'd ever seen before; he had never known a sky like that in his lifetime. The entire eastern rim of the heavens was lighted by a rising moon of remarkable brilliance.

Chaney stood alone in the center of the parking lot searching the face of the moon, searching out the Sea of Vapors and the pit known as Bode's Crater. The pulsating laser there caught his eye and held it. That one thing had not changed—that one monument not destroyed. The brilliant mote still flashed on the rim of Bode's Crater, marking the place where two astronauts had fallen in the Seventies, marking their grave and their memorial. One of them had been black. Brian Chaney thought himself lucky: he had air to breathe but those men had none.

He said aloud: "You weren't so damned clever, Ibycus! You missed *that* one—your prophets didn't show you the *new* sign in the sky."

Chaney sat down in the tilted cart and stretched out his legs for balance. The rifle was an unpleasant lump under his spine and he threw it aside to be rid of it. In a little while he leaned backward and rested against the bed of the cart. The whole of the southeast sky was before him. Chaney thought he should go looking for Katrina, for Arthur and Kathryn, and a place to sleep. Perhaps he would do that after a while, but not now, not now.

The stray thought came that the engineers had been right about one thing: the polywater tank hadn't leaked.

Elwood Station was at peace.

Don't miss these

ACE SCIENCE FICTION SPECIALS

A distinctive new series of quality science fiction

88600 — 60¢
WHY CALL THEM BACK FROM HEAVEN?
by Clifford D. Simak

89850 — 75¢
THE WITCHES OF KARRES by James H. Schmitz

65300 — 60¢
PAST MASTER by R. A. Lafferty

71860 — 60¢
THE REVOLVING BOY by Gertrude Friedberg

66200 — 60¢
PICNIC ON PARADISE by Joanna Russ

83550 — 60¢
THE TWO-TIMERS by Bob Shaw

79450 — 60¢
SYNTHAJOY by D. G. Compton

72600 — 75¢
THE RING by Piers Anthony & Robert E. Margroff

81780 — 75¢
A TORRENT OF FACES by James Blish & Norman L. Knight

14245 — 60¢
THE DEMON BREED by James H. Schmitz

37465 — 60¢
ISLE OF THE DEAD by Roger Zelazny

38120 — 95¢
THE JAGGED ORBIT by John Brunner

47800 — 95¢
THE LEFT HAND OF DARKNESS by Ursula K. LeGuin

Ask your newsdealer, or order directly from Ace Books (Dept. MM), 1120 Avenue of the Americas, New York, N.Y. 10036. Please send price indicated, plus 10¢ handling fee for each copy.